# Trusting
## Blake

# Trusting Blake

## ESTELLE MASKAME

INK ROAD

First published in 2021 by Ink Road
INK ROAD is an imprint and trademark of
Black & White Publishing Ltd
Nautical House, 104 Commercial Street
Edinburgh, EH6 6NF

1 3 5 7 9 10 8 6 4 2        21 22 23 24

ISBN: 978 1 78530 363 0

Typeset by Iolaire Typesetting, Newtonmore
Printed and bound by Clays Ltd, Elcograf S.p.A.

MIX
Paper from
responsible sources
FSC® C018072

*To all my readers who have followed my journey from the beginning and are still here now, thank you!*

# 1

There isn't enough adrenaline in this world to power my legs much farther. No amount of rage can fill my lungs with breath. No amount of pain can fuel my body to take another step.

The concrete beneath my feet sprawls out before me, but the streets are a blur through my burning tears, the passing cars nothing more than smudges of color, and the lack of clear vision has my head throbbing as though a million and one needles are jabbing into my skull.

Wheezing, I collapse against the nearest mailbox. My throat burns as I fight for air, but my chest heaves so violently it's near impossible. Sweat pours down my face and neck, as the sun shines relentless above.

I don't know how far I've run. I don't know if I've even gone in the right direction.

My knees buckle and I sink to the scorching sidewalk. I don't know where in Fairview I am, and I definitely don't know how far the Harding Estate is from here. And even if I did, I have already exhausted my cardio capacity. My heartbeat must surely be at its absolute maximum right now – one beat faster and it may just explode.

Sobbing, panting, I grab my phone from my pocket. A swarm of notifications fills my screen, but I swipe them away and navigate straight to my contacts, blinking fast and drawing my phone up close in an attempt to find Sheri's name. I call the number, pressing the phone to my ear, my other hand clasped over my face in an effort to hide from the world. I can tell that I'm on a residential street, and I don't imagine these folks are all that used to peering out their windows to find a sobbing teenager slumped against the post of a mailbox. I am too hurt right now to even begin to process any feeling of embarrassment.

"Mila—" Sheri answers.

"Do you know?" I splutter, gripping my phone harder. "Have you seen the headlines?"

Sheri doesn't respond. There's a long pause, and if it weren't for her shallow breaths, I'd think she'd hung up. Finally, in a low voice, she asks, "Where are you?"

There's no surprise or confusion. No *What headlines?*, so there's my question answered: Sheri *has* seen the news.

"I don't – don't know," I sniff, surveying my surroundings once more in hope of some clarity, but my eyes sting too much to do anything more than flutter. "Can you come get me? Please?"

"Of course, Mila. Send me a pin of your location. I'm

grabbing the van keys right this second, okay, honey?" Sheri says. I hear the clang of keys and the sound of a door falling shut. "I'll be right there. I'm coming."

I hastily end the call and ping Sheri my current location, praying that she drives fast. I don't want to be alone right now, but I don't want to be with anyone else other than family who understands the gravity of the situation. Mostly, I want my mom.

*Oh, Mom ...*

I close my eyes and try to picture the scene back home in Thousand Oaks right now. Has Mom only found out the truth at the same time as the rest of the world? Is my parents' marriage unraveling in our home right now while Ruben strings together an emergency contingency plan to twist this story into something less damning?

Is this story even *real*?

I suck in a deep breath and think.

The tabloids do nothing *but* turn innocent photos and videos into something they're not. That's where they get their views from, their revenue – from big, shocking stories that create waves of scandal and delighted outrage. That photograph ... the one of Dad and Laurel Peyton locking lips in that restaurant ... it can't be real. It must be a mistake, a misunderstanding. Dad wouldn't hurt Mom like this. He wouldn't hurt *me*.

But he hurt LeAnne Avery before, and as she said ...

*Once a cheater, always a cheater.*

I'm going to throw up.

This time, I really wish it *was* because of too much

3

expensive champagne and not from the shattering of everything I knew about my father.

"Are you alright, sweetheart?" a concerned voice calls from across the street.

The distraction suppresses the bile rising in my throat and my watery gaze locates the sound: an elderly woman watching me from her lawn with her rosy cheeks pinched together with worry.

"NO!" I yell back. "My dad is a liar! Everett Harding is a fraud!"

I'm not thinking straight. I *can't* think straight.

And will my phone just stop vibrating for *one damn second*?

"You're Everett Harding's daughter?" the woman asks, and despite the fuzziness in my head, I know that I shouldn't have screamed out my emotions like that.

"No," I lie like a total lunatic, then scramble to my feet, wipe my tear-soaked cheeks, and trek a little down the street until I'm out of sight from her.

Okay. *Deep breaths. Calm down. Think clearly.*

In Hollywood, an affair between two A-listers is huge. I have seen it happen to others in the industry so many times before. It completely takes over the entertainment press. Dad's and Laurel Peyton's careers are going to be ruthlessly torn to shreds, and everyone around them is going to be dragged into the drama. That means Mom and me.

I cannot, despite my fury and my heartache, make things worse.

I can't say anything. To anyone. I can't discuss my

feelings with anyone but family. And I certainly shouldn't be yelling crap about Dad to strangers in his hometown.

All I can do right now is get back to the ranch, pack my bags, and book the first flight back to LA. There is no time for goodbyes, not for Savannah and Tori, not for Blake. I need to go home, because this is one family secret I can't be left out of.

And when Sheri's van skids to an erratic halt five minutes later, my chest heaves.

"Oh, Mila ..." Sheri whispers as I throw open the door and climb into the passenger seat.

Sheri looks older somehow. There are lines of frustration etched around her eyes, a paleness to her skin, and disappointment in the heartbroken look she gives me. Still, she is a thousand times more composed than I am.

"How could he do this?" I rasp, staring numbly ahead at the windshield. "*Again.*"

"I don't ... I don't understand him," Sheri says with an intense exhale of air. "I'm so sorry, Mila. I don't know what to say."

I don't know what to say either.

We head back to the ranch in silence. Even the radio is switched off, and the burning beam of sunlight hitting my face makes me ... angry. My mind feels like storm clouds and rolling thunder.

The Harding Estate's luxurious security gate and stone walls loom like a fortress in the distance as we weave down the winding back road, and the closer we get, the deeper the splices of my heart cut.

I hate this life.

I hate Hollywood. I hate the media and the paparazzi. I hate the production companies, the fans, the security guards. I hate Dad's management crew, I especially hate Ruben fucking Fisher, and I hate the thousands of mindless rules forced upon me. I hate the feeling of the world watching me.

And I hate these stupid security gates and everything they represent.

But mostly, right now ... I hate Dad.

I hate what he has done to our family.

To me, to Mom, to Popeye, to Sheri.

Before I realize what I'm doing, I've slammed my fist straight into the dashboard of Sheri's van. I scream. Really, really scream. My throat hurts, but still I scream so loud I'm sure I can be heard from miles away, and I pound my hands uncontrollably against the car in a fit of rage.

"Mila!" Sheri yells, slamming the brakes. She grasps my wrists and fights against me to keep my balled-up fists steady, but I thrash against her until I finally admit defeat and burst into tears.

"I HATE HIM!" I scream between sobs.

"I know, I know," Sheri says soothingly, pulling me in tight to her chest. She strokes my hair, her chin resting against the crown of my head, and she holds me for what feels like forever.

It's the sound of a phone ringing that breaks us apart.

It's not mine. I turned mine off already and have no plans to turn it back on anytime soon, but Sheri grabs hers from the center console and frowns at the screen.

"It's your mom," she says.

"My mom?" I snatch the phone from Sheri's hand and accept the call, pressing it to my ear.

For a fleeting second, Sheri almost tries to grab the device back, but then thinks better of fighting with me in my current irrational state.

"Mom, it's me. I'm coming home," I burst out, my words rapid-fire.

"Mila …" Mom breathes across the line. Her voice is cracked, dry, like she has shed a million more tears than I have. "You aren't coming home."

"Yes! I am!"

"No, you're not," she says firmly, then, with a sniff, she adds, "I'm coming to you."

"What?"

"I'll be with you tomorrow. I promise, Mila. Please, I need to speak with Sheri."

Mom is coming to Fairview? That makes sense, I guess. LA with Dad is probably the last place she wants to be right now. The farther away from the chaos we both are, the better.

"Mom?" I whisper.

"Yes?"

"Are you okay?"

She is silent for a while, then finally she replies, "Are you?"

That answers my question.

I bite down hard on my lip and wipe tears away from my damp face as I listen to her shallow breathing.

"Stay at the ranch. Don't leave, don't talk to anyone,

and please stay off the internet and avoid TV," she orders. Then, her voice breaks as she says, "I'm so sorry, Mila. I love you. We both do."

I don't know about that anymore.

I hand the phone to Sheri and then get out of the van. The gate is just up ahead, and I drag my feet past the towering stone walls and let myself in via the electric remote I've learned to keep on me at all times. Tracking my way up the dirt road, I spot Popeye stomping around with an ax slung over his shoulder.

My grandfather may be aging, and he may be sick, but that doesn't stop him from finding a release for his anger. I watch as he manages, albeit a little awkwardly, to toss split logs into a growing pile of wood. Furiously, he slams that ax through the logs over and over, and then he staggers out from beneath the tree into the blistering sun, sinks down onto the grass, and buries his head in his hands.

Popeye wasn't a huge fan of Dad's life choices even before this.

The sight of him breaks my heart all over again, but I have to turn my back on him and slip unseen into the house. I have my own rage to deal with, and if I don't retreat to my room for some privacy, I'm worried I'll not only do my best to smash up Sheri's van, but that I'll start destroying the house too.

In the safety of my bedroom, I slam the door and throw my phone across the floor. I don't bother to check if I've smashed the screen; instead, I draw my blinds, crawl fully clothed into my bed, and bury myself under my comforter.

# 2

At first, when I peel open my eyes the next morning, I'm convinced it was only a nightmare. A really, really intense nightmare that I seem to remember every detail of. And why do my eyes and throat feel so dry and painful?

Rolling over, I spot my phone on the floor all the way across the room. *Huh.* I always leave my phone charging on the bedside table overnight ... I stretch out my legs – why do my shins throb? – and get out of bed to retrieve my phone. When I turn it over in my hand, I see the smashed screen. The thick cracks, the missing pieces of glass.

I shiver as my body goes cold.

I really did throw my phone last night.

It wasn't a bad dream – all of it really happened. The headline ... Running from Blake's house ... Crying on the streets of Fairview ... Yelling at old ladies ...

*The affair.*

Just as my head fills with the horror of it all, there's a soft knock on my door. "Mila?"

"Come in," I mumble, staring blankly at my damaged phone. I have to remind myself to keep breathing.

Aunt Sheri warily pushes open my bedroom door, like she's afraid of what she'll find on the other side. An emotional wreck of a teenager, that's what. "I think you'll need some caffeine today," she says, presenting me with a steaming mug of fresh coffee.

"I don't like hot coffee. Only iced. You know that."

"Mila, I think you'll *really* need this today," she repeats with a slight twitch of a sad smile, forcing the mug into my hand. "Oh. Your phone. When did you do that?"

"Yesterday." My tone is devoid of any emotion. I can't meet her gaze, but I don't think she's trying to look me in the eyes either. "What time is it?"

My phone has been turned off since yesterday, so I can't tell if it's entirely broken or if it's only the screen that's damaged, but I'm not ready yet to switch it back on to check. Ruben, Dad's manager, is still controlling my social media accounts, so I don't have access to them even if I wanted to. Right now, that's probably for the best. That fuzzy image of Dad and his co-star, Laurel Peyton, will be circulating all over Instagram. Their names will be trending on Twitter. Their fan pages on Facebook will be chaotic.

"Just after nine. You've been out cold since yesterday afternoon," Sheri says. She sits down on the edge of my bed and awkwardly straightens out my comforter. "And I suppose that broken phone of yours explains why a very persistent boy has been blowing up the landline for the past hour."

I perk up in surprise, giving her all my attention. "Blake?"

"Yes. Blake," she says, and I only now notice how tired

she looks. Unlike me, I don't think Sheri has had much sleep at all. "He's worried about you. He thinks you're leaving town."

"Did you tell him I'm not?"

"I didn't tell him anything, other than that if you want to talk, you'll call him back."

I exhale a sigh of relief. "Thanks. I don't know if I'm ready to talk about things yet."

"That's probably a good idea right now," Sheri agrees, and I think she, too, knows to keep her mouth shut over the next few days. We Hardings really do need to maintain a low profile more than ever. "Your mom will be here soon. She's on the first flight out, and your grandfather and I have agreed that it's best if both of you stay here for a while."

"You don't mind?" I ask, surprised. Mom has never visited without Dad before, and considering the relationship Sheri and Popeye have with Dad, I'm not sure what that means for Mom.

"We're not letting you stay in hotels. We have room enough here," Sheri explains with a kind smile. "Besides, it's not your mom I have issues with. It's your asshole of a father—" Mortified, she quickly stops herself. "Sorry, Mila. I shouldn't talk about him like that in front of you."

"But you're right," I say. "He *is* an asshole."

"Hmm." Sheri rises from my bed and tucks a loose strand of curly hair behind her ear. "You must be hungry. Grab yourself some breakfast, and then how about we order takeout for lunch?"

"That sounds nice."

There is a very big elephant in the room, one that we are tiptoeing around the edges of, but what can we possibly say? Until more details emerge of Dad's alleged affair, there is no point discussing it. Right now, there are too many questions that need answers, and neither of us can provide them.

Sheri gives me a brief hug. "We're downstairs if you would like some company," she says, then leaves me to be by myself again.

Moving over to the window, I set down the mug of coffee Sheri gave me and gaze out over the ranch's well-maintained fields that sit beneath a clear blue sky and a blazing ball of sunshine. Another beautiful day, *of course.* Beyond the stone walls, I wonder what exactly the world thinks of Dad right now.

What are Savannah and Tori saying about such a Hollywood scandal that revolves around my parents? What about all the local Fairview High students I've interacted with over the past month? What about Blake?

I feel nauseous at the thought of my dad's name being on everyone's lips.

And maybe it's my twisted curiosity, or just the need to believe it for myself, but I take a deep breath and, elbows propped up on the windowsill, switch my phone on. The screen may be lined with thick cracks, but the device still works. It boots up while I wait with bated breath, and then, all at once, a thousand different alerts sound out as the smashed screen fills with notifications. Missed calls, unopened text messages.

There are missed calls from Mom, from Sheri, from Ruben, from my closest friends back home in LA, from Savannah, and even from distant relatives I haven't spoken to in forever. There are none from Dad, but thirty-seven from Blake Avery. They range from yesterday afternoon up until early this morning, when I guess he decided to give up trying my cell in favor of the Harding Estate landline instead.

He thinks I'm leaving. I thought I was going to leave too. What exactly I would have done once I got home, I don't quite know. I just don't want to be kept in the dark about anything more than I already have. I want to be there. I want to comfort my mom. I want to confront my dad. I'm old enough now to be told the truth.

But I don't need to go home anymore, because Mom is coming here, to Fairview, to the Harding Estate where the towering walls will shield her. I am staying exactly where I am ... and I want Blake to know that.

I hesitantly return one of his thirty-seven missed calls. I perch myself on my windowsill and draw my knees in tight to my chest, my lip caught between my teeth in trepidation. I don't really want to talk to anyone right now, and I'm not quite sure what to say, but Blake at least deserves some reassurance that I am, in fact, not going anywhere after all.

He answers on the second ring, as though his phone is already in his hand, expecting my call.

"Mila, *finally*," he says with deep relief in that gorgeous accent of his. He exhales loudly, and I picture him running his hand through his hair. "Are you okay?"

"No," I say flatly.

"Of course – sorry, that was a stupid question,"he groans, and then, nervously, he asks, "Have you left Fairview yet?"

The obvious concern in his voice makes me feel, surprisingly, a little better. While the world is focused on Everett Harding, at least Blake is only worried about me. "I'm not going home," I tell him. "I'm staying here for now."

"Wait. You are?"

"Yeah. My mom is on her way."

"Ohh," he says, but the change in his tone is unmistakable. No more panicking that I'm heading out of town. "I feel so fucking bad, Mila," he mumbles after a moment of silence. "I didn't mean for you to hear the news from me ... and especially not from my mom."

"I'm not mad at you, or even your mom, Blake," I say gently, because I know exactly who the real villain is in this situation. "I'm mad at my dad."

"Is there anything I can do to make this easier for you? Let me keep your mind occupied. Let's take Bailey to the dog park, or let's head into the city and try out some new honky tonks, or ...I don't know. Anything."

"That sounds nice, but ... I don't know if I can right now." I can't bear the thought of leaving this ranch and heading out to do anything *normal* when my entire world has fallen apart, but I like that Blake has given me the option. It's comforting to know that despite the mess my life is in, he's still looking out for me.

"Yeah, yeah, for sure. I get that. But maybe it would help. Get away from all the drama, you know?"

I shake my head. "I'm sorry."

He's quiet for a while, then, "Mila," he says solemnly.

"Yeah?"

His voice is low and full of doubt. "We're okay, right? You and me?"

"Of course we are," I whisper. "I just can't think straight right now, but thank you for checking up on me."

"No problem. I'm always here if you need me."

"Thanks." Then, because I need to be clear with him, I add, "But please don't call the ranch landline again."

He laughs, the sound hollow. "Yeah, sorry. I was worried about you, Mila."

"That's nice, but don't be. I'll be fine," I reassure him, though there is nothing convincing about my words. There's nothing to suggest that I'll be fine. "Talk later. Bye, Blake."

Without giving him the chance to say anything more, I hang up. It's the most I can offer him right now – short, blunt answers – but at least he knows now that I'm not leaving. We can see each other again once I figure out what the hell has happened to my family.

Speaking of family ... I still haven't spoken to Popeye. There's a lot of anger in the air, but we can't simply ignore one another. The next few days, weeks, months ... they are going to be hard. There will be some really difficult conversations. Things might *not* turn out okay. But I have to face reality.

Having reassured Blake, I now need to check in with Popeye. Grabbing the coffee Sheri made for me, I take a sip that scalds my mouth and then head downstairs, feigning confidence and strength with each step. I need to be brave. What good is sobbing going to do? What will endless crying achieve?

There's no sound. No TV, no radio, no voices. Popeye and Sheri aren't downstairs, so I step into a pair of Sheri's boots by the door and head out into the fresh air, still dressed in yesterday's clothes. My shirt smells musky, I feel like I haven't brushed my teeth in forever, and I'm pretty sure I have a severe case of matted hair that is going to be painful to fix. But there are worse things in the world right now and I just don't *care*.

Over at the stables, I spot them. Popeye has pulled up a lawn chair at the stable entrance where he sits with his gaze locked on the horizon over the rolling fields that stretch out around us. I hear Sheri shuffling around inside the stables with the horses.

"Hey, Popeye," I say softly as I approach. The beating sun feels a hundred times worse than usual against my already sticky, sweaty skin.

Popeye cranes his neck to look at me, and he immediately frowns. "Wow, don't you look …"

"Ravishing?" I joke.

"Like trash," he deadpans. "We do have showers in this place, and you are more than welcome to use them, you know." A second later, he cracks a smile and I at least manage to roll my eyes. Like with Sheri, it is easier to tiptoe around the real conversation we should be having, but then Popeye's smile grows sad as he sits up. "Come here, sweet Mila."

*Ugh. So much for no more crying.*

I lean down into Popeye, and he pulls me in close for a shaky hug. There is no way to contain your emotions when your grandfather embraces you like this. It's like when you're teetering on the brink of a breakdown, and someone decides to ask if you're okay – instant blubbering mess.

"It'll be okay," he whispers into my ear, squeezing me tighter. "Your parents love you, no matter what."

I nod against his shoulder and then pull back, wiping my cheeks. God, I've cried so much that it straight-up *burns* to shed a tear now. "But how are *you* feeling, Popeye?"

"Angry. Disappointed," he grumbles. "The one thing I'm not, however, is confused. Your father has always made choices that don't make sense to me. We will just have to see how he explains this one."

"Do you think he'll call?"

Popeye scoffs and leans back against the lawn chair, but he still appears rigid and uncomfortable. "It'll be a miracle if he does. You, however," he says sternly, wagging a finger at me, "have nothing to worry about. He will talk to you, I'm sure. You and your mother need answers more than the rest of us."

"Mila?" Sheri calls from inside the stables.

I frown, brush my hand over Popeye's, then follow the sound of Sheri's voice. She is grooming one of her horses – the same one, I believe, that took off with Tori a few weeks ago – and stops mid-brush to shoot me a funny look.

"Are those my boots?" she asks.

"Yeah."

"You're such a style icon," she says, and I fold my arms in protest. She returns to brushing, watching me out of the corner of her eye. "Now that you're alive, would you like to help out? Maisy over there needs a good brush-down. And so do you from the looks of it." She tilts her eyes to where the horse-grooming kit is. "Don't trap yourself up in that room all day. It's better to pass the time being productive."

To my left, a horse lets out an attention-seeking neigh. It's Fredo, my favorite. He's the only one I trust not to throw me off the saddle.

"Hey, Fredo," I say, turning to greet him. He nuzzles my chest, and I rest my head against him, stroking beneath his chin. I wonder if he senses all our sadness. "Aunt Sheri, can I take him for a ride? Fresh air and all."

Sheri casts me a doubtful look. "But you haven't been out on your own yet."

"Yeah, but between you and Savannah, I've learned everything I need to know. Look, I can even saddle him up on my own now!" I start toward the block of saddles lined up on the far wall, but Sheri steps out in front of me, blocking me with her arm. She smiles.

"First Maisy needs that brush-down, and then Fredo says to take a shower."

# 3

The buzzer for the gate sounds just after six that evening.

Popeye, Sheri, and I sit in silence in the living room, stuffed after polishing off the leftovers from the Thai takeout we ordered earlier for lunch, and the abrupt sound makes us start all at once. I scoot forward on the couch, eyes wide and hands interlocked.

"I'll get it," Sheri says, crossing over to the kitchen to check out the live footage from the security camera outside the ranch gate.

The buzzer has gone off several times today – the driver delivering our food, one of the nosy neighbors from farther down the road fishing for gossip, and a few local reporters hoping to be the first to hear Everett Harding's family's thoughts on his shocking affair. Through the gate's speakerphone, Sheri told them politely, precisely, "No comment," but I'm sure what she really meant was, "Just let me tell you exactly where to shove your notepads."

"Is it another one?" I call across the living room, exchanging a wary look with Popeye, who is as disgruntled as ever at strangers showing up at his ranch.

"No," Sheri says, and she turns around to meet my eyes. I see the apprehension in her face. "It's your mom."

"Finally!" I gasp, springing to my feet.

"NO, Mila," Sheri warns, her voice so sharp and unfamiliar that it stops me in my tracks. I stare questioningly at her. "There is some press lingering out there already," she explains. "It's better for your sake if you don't let them see you. Stay here, and I'll go help your mom."

And with that, Sheri turns and rushes out the front door.

"I *hate* this freaking life," I mutter under my breath as I move back to the living room window instead.

I watch, feeling useless, as Sheri grants access and the electronic gate begins to swing open. It's kind of a blur, how fast it happens.

In the distance, I lay eyes on Mom. As soon as the gate has cracked open wide enough for her to squeeze through, she is inside the safety of the walls, an oversized pair of sunglasses shielding her eyes. She pulls her luggage behind her, and before the gate can even finish opening, Sheri is closing it again. There is still enough time to catch a brief glimpse of the crowd of paparazzi that has already assembled and that annoying flash of camera shutters that I haven't witnessed in weeks. It will forever amaze me how quickly they travel to chase the news. The LA press will have followed Mom to the airport back home, I bet, and then tipped off their Nashville outlets.

The gate clangs shut, keeping the paps at bay. They won't leave, though. They'll camp out there all night. We are used to the chaos that these guys seem able to create at will, but I have a horrible feeling that things are about to get ... wild.

I can see Mom's relief by the way her shoulders fall and the hug she gives Sheri. Now that prying eyes can't spot me, I abandon my post by the window and burst outside, nearly tripping down the porch steps.

"Mom!" I yell, running down the dirt road.

*I want to hug her, I want to hug her, I want to hug her.*

I need her to tell me everything will be okay. I need to hear it from *her*.

"Shhh!" Sheri hisses, pointing over her shoulder. We may be out of sight, but that doesn't mean those outside the gate can't hear us.

"*Mila*," Mom whispers as I reach them, and she pushes her sunglasses up. There are tears in her eyes at the sight of me, but she looks ... ashamed, guilty, broken. "I'm so sorry."

"Don't you dare!" I practically growl at her, then almost put her in a chokehold as I throw myself into her arms and squeeze her the tightest I ever have in my entire life. I haven't seen her in a month, and this wasn't how I imagined it would be when I saw her again. Hugs? Sure. Tears? No. "You have nothing to be sorry about, Mom. This is Dad's fault!"

"I'll take your luggage inside, Marnie," Sheri says and takes off back up the road toward the house with Mom's suitcase rolling behind her.

"This is a *mess!*" Mom groans as we reluctantly let go of

one another. She steps back and places her hands on my shoulders.

For once, she isn't the glamorous wife of a movie star. She is bare-faced without a single smidge of makeup, though her lash extensions are still prominent. I seem to have forgotten how hazel her eyes actually are. Her dark hair is down, but it's lying flat and lifeless against her high cheekbones, unstyled. She's wearing jeans and a tank top – an outfit usually reserved for inside our home – and I can tell just by how unfamiliar she seems that Mom is deeply hurt and struggling to function.

"You look… different," I say. "You look like you." Younger, natural, *normal*. But I don't say that.

"And you have all these freckles!" Mom pinches my cheek, and I don't even try to stop her – I'm just so relieved that she is here.

"Oh, Mom." I pull her back in for another hug. "I can't believe this is really happening."

"I know, honey." Mom sighs, stroking my hair, and I don't quite know whether she's doing it to comfort me or herself. "But we'll figure this out."

"Marnie!" Popeye's deep, gravelly voice calls from the porch, interrupting our hug. He waves his hand, beckoning us to join him and Sheri inside.

Mom takes my hand in hers and together we make our way toward the house. I know how nervous she is from how tightly she's grasping my fingers. This will be immensely uncomfortable for her, I imagine, staying here at Dad's family home. She last visited years ago, and these are hardly ideal circumstances for her return.

"Good afternoon, Wesley," she greets as she slowly drags herself up the porch steps. It's unlike Mom to carry herself without style and elegance, but right now, she doesn't need to be perfect. She's safe here.

"That arrogant, selfish jerk," Popeye grumbles, fiercely shaking his head and unable to keep his thoughts to himself for a second longer. "He's never happy, is he? How are you doing?"

"I'm wrapping my head around it," Mom admits, then gives a pointed glance in my direction. "But remember this is Mila's father we're talking about, so maybe let's keep the name-calling to a minimum."

"Oh, Marnie, the poor girl isn't blind!" Popeye huffs, and I stare at him in amazement, wondering where my sweet-tea-drinking, sunset-gazing grandfather has disappeared to. He is always so ... gentle ... around me. But with Sheri? And Mom? He's just full of anger and aggravation with no filter.

Mom turns to me. "Mila, I am so glad to see you, sweetheart, but can you give us a minute to talk?"

"You don't need to keep me out of the family discussions anymore," I say firmly, locking my eyes on hers. "I'm sixteen. I can handle it."

"Oh," says Mom. She studies the unflinching expression on my face for what feels like forever, perhaps wondering just how much I've grown up over this past month.

Back in California, I didn't question anything. I did whatever Ruben insisted, I followed the rules, I believed our family was happy. But after a month in Tennessee uncovering secrets, I'm not oblivious anymore, and Mom appears disarmed at this thought.

"Marnie, would you like me to show you upstairs?" Sheri asks as she appears behind Popeye, returning from delivering Mom's luggage up to her room. There are plenty spare bedrooms in this place, and Sheri and I already established that Mom should stay in the room next door to me.

"Actually," Mom says, "I think I'd rather sit down and talk first. Let's get the worst part out of the way, right?" She attempts a chuckle, but it only sounds like the saddest, most anxious sigh in the world.

"Good plan," says Popeye. "I have questions."

This isn't going to be easy; I know that. Mom is already holding up as best she can, and I'm amazed she's managing to be this composed to begin with. I try to catch her eye as we all move indoors, but she won't look my way. She barely even checks out the house, just keeps her head down, gaze trained on the wooden floor.

In the living room, Popeye takes up residence in his worn armchair. Sheri doesn't sit down; instead, she fiddles around with the random knick-knacks on the coffee table, pretending to tidy but only making things worse, and then excuses herself to the kitchen to fetch water for us all. Mom and I sit down together on the couch opposite Popeye, and I wring my hands together, idly wondering who will speak first.

"First of all," Mom begins, "thank you for letting me stay

here. I know things are – complicated. I do really appreciate this. It's so much better for Mila." She glances sideways at me, her expression guilt-stricken, then touches my hand. "Things were already getting pretty crazy back home."

"You are welcome, naturally," Popeye murmurs as he rubs hard at his thick brows, then his tone turns louder and gruffer. "But what the heck has been going on over there? Because yet again it appears that Everett has only thought of himself and not what his actions will mean to the people around him. How many times is he going to make the same mistake?"

"Dad!" Sheri gives him a stern look as she returns with a pitcher of water and some tumblers. "A little sympathy, maybe?"

"It's okay," Mom says, holding a hand up to Sheri. "I understand how you feel about him right now, Wes, but Mila is in the room."

"Didn't we already establish that Mila is old enough to be here?" Popeye counters.

"Yes," I jump in quickly, squeezing Mom's hand and giving her a nod. I'm not a kid who needs to be protected. I don't want to be banished upstairs to my room, pressing my ear to the door, trying my best to eavesdrop. I want to be part of this conversation. I deserve to hear the truth for myself, not some watered-down, sugar-coated version. And, like Popeye, I have questions of my own. "How did you find out, Mom?"

Mom sighs, realizes there's no point tiptoeing around the subject in front of me, and answers, "From Ruben."

"Ruben?" I say, scrunching my face up, confused. I assumed Mom would have been confronted by the tabloids like the rest of the world ... I certainly didn't think she'd find out from Ruben.

Mom nods, takes a deep breath. "He'd been given the heads-up that some photos had been leaked ...So, he broke the news to me a few hours before it hit the press, but only because he was desperate to strategize a damage-limitation plan of action. I'm afraid I told him where he could stick his *strategizing*, and I walked straight out of there."

"But did you get the chance to talk with Everett before you left?" Sheri asks, finally sitting down on the opposite couch, bolt upright and as clearly uncomfortable as the rest of us.

I'm glad Sheri asked, because I'm wondering the same. Has Mom even heard Dad's side of the story, or did she immediately flee?

"Yes," Mom says in a tiny voice.

"And?" Popeye prompts. "What was his excuse *this* time? He clearly hasn't changed a damn thing over the years."

Sheri looks as though she wants to shrivel up and disappear. Popeye's constant references to Dad's previous affair – the one he had *with* Mom – are excruciatingly uncomfortable, to say the least. Mom ignores the remarks, but I can tell they are grating on her.

"Look, I ... I had my suspicions." She takes a gulp of water and I notice her hand tremble on the glass. "I just can't believe they've turned out to be true."

"I suppose you know the signs to look out for," I hear

Popeye mutter under his breath. The words are barely audible, so I convince myself I heard him wrong.

"*Suspicions?*" I ask Mom, taken aback. What did she suspect, exactly? How can I not have noticed anything at all? I know I'm their kid, but still ... I feel like all the air is knocked out of me.

"I'm sorry, Mila," Mom says, her bottom lip quivering as she scoots closer to me. "I tried to explain it away, but I just ... I wish I had dealt with this properly long before now. Maybe then you wouldn't have had to find out the way you did. Maybe then we wouldn't all be in such an awful situation."

Popeye clears his throat, and his voice comes out harsher than I've ever heard it. "A situation that you yourself once were happy to put LeAnne Avery in."

"Dad! We're not here to dredge up the past," Sheri gasps, her hand flying to her mouth, stunned. She gapes at Mom. "I'm so sorry."

Mom is silent. She stares across at Popeye, a flash of hurt in her eyes, but her expression strangely brazen. "Wesley, please. That's ancient history now, water under the bridge, so, for Mila's sake, can we be civil? You don't have to feel sorry for me, but please have some consideration for Mila."

Sheri has her hand pressed over her eyes now, unable to look, as if anticipating an actual bomb to explode, but all I can think is: *So Popeye really doesn't like Mom?*

It's amazing all the details you miss when you're young. Four years ago when we all visited for Thanksgiving, there was no tension, no drama. Just smiles and happy laughter around a sumptuous dining table. But that's because I wasn't reading between the lines back then. I didn't know that I had to. Now, however, I'm horribly aware of the suffocating strain in the atmosphere.

Popeye stubbornly gets to his feet, and as he shuffles past a mortified Sheri, he looks at me. "Mila, I wouldn't change you for the world," he says, "but it's a real crying shame that your parents are so selfish."

# 4

It's the longest, most unbearable night of my life.

Popeye and Mom won't talk to each other. Sheri says things just got overheated and they'll be better once the dust settles, but I have my doubts. It seems that Popeye is too stubborn to do anything but voice his opinions, and what is Mom supposed to do? Tread carefully around the Harding Estate until somehow, one way or another, she finds resolution with Dad? And how can she do that when he's thousands of miles away? Does Mom even *want* to resolve this? What if she wants a divorce?

Maybe I would stand a chance of finding out if she hadn't shut herself away in her room. It might be right next to mine, but she won't talk to me either, stating she needs the evening to gather her thoughts before we sit down in the morning, just the two of us, for a real conversation.

So, unlike last night when I was dead to the world for hours and hours, tonight I'm wide awake. It's after midnight, the house is silent, and moonlight streams in through my window. I'm in my PJs – my favorite Victoria's Secret set, matching satin shorts and a cami – sitting cross-legged on the floor, staring at the wall, lost in my thoughts. I am too wired to even attempt to sleep, but still, the sound of my phone buzzing makes me jump out of my skin.

Considering the time, I figure it must be one of my friends from back home calling to check in on me, having *clearly* forgotten the time difference, because obviously it's too late for any normal person to call.

I crawl over to reach for my phone on my bedside table, and smile at the name on my screen.

"Blake," I answer, keeping my voice low. Mom is only in the room next door, maybe also unable to sleep. "Do you know the time?"

"Yup. Twelve thirty-nine," he says cheerfully. "Good thing you're awake. Can you do something for me?"

This has one of Blake's impromptu ideas written all over it. Last time he called me in such a spontaneous playful mood, we ended up at a honky tonk in Nashville together. What could he possibly have in mind *now*?

"*Riiiiight*. What exactly do I need to do, Blake?" I reluctantly ask, pinching the bridge of my nose between my thumb and forefinger, waiting for the impending headache.

"I need you to go downstairs."

"Why?"

"Mila, trust me," he says with a sigh, as though he expected nothing less than such resistance from me. "Go downstairs to the front door."

Only because I can't sleep anyway do I get up and creep out into the hallway, keeping my footsteps light. I pause every few steps, listening, but I hear no movement from Mom's room, so I continue downstairs.

"Okay, I'm at the door. Now what?"

"Walk outside," Blake says. "Are those stables a few hundred feet away from the house?"

"Um, yeah," I whisper, my phone wedged between my shoulder and my ear as I slide on a pair of shoes that I left by the door. I should really run back upstairs for a sweater, but I figure it can't be that cold outside. It's the middle of summer in Tennessee, after all.

"Okay. Head toward the stables, and then turn right and walk diagonally toward the rear of the ranch. Just direct yourself toward the corner of the walls," Blake instructs in a calm, collected voice as though it's totally normal to send me off on an adventure across the ranch at midnight.

"Blake, seriously. Why am I doing this?"

"Are you walking yet?"

I sigh and quietly slip through the door, down the porch steps, and make for the stables. "Yeah, but it's dark out here and all I can hear are crickets." Although I know I am safe and protected by the ranch's security features, I still glance over my shoulder repeatedly as I walk, leaving the house behind. Across the ranch, the fields aren't even visible, and I can't make out anything in the distance. I don't particularly like this. "Okay, no. You're freaking me out. I'm turning back."

"Mila, c'mon. Keep walking. You're not scared of some *crickets*, are you?" Blake teases, and his friendly laughter makes this whole thing slightly less creepy.

"*Fine*," I huff, trekking through the long grass as it tickles my bare legs. "I'm past the stables. Walking diagonal now."

"Okay," Blake says, and then to my complete and utter disbelief, he hangs up the call.

I stop dead in my tracks and stare at my phone in anger. Does he think this is funny? Playing pranks on me in the dead of night. Is this an attempt to cheer me up?

But then I hear it – his voice.

Not through my cellphone, but right here at the ranch.

"*Mila!*" he whisper-yells from somewhere up ahead. "Mila, keep walking!"

Am I dreaming? To be honest, this seems like the sort of weird dream I usually have.

Confused, I follow the sound of his voice, continuing diagonal like he told me until finally through the darkness, the rear walls of the ranch come into focus. And there's someone there, way up high, their silhouette cradling the wall.

"Well, howdy, Mila!" a voice calls out. "What are the chances of meeting you here on this damn fine wall at midnight? And while you're wearing such an elegant outfit!"

"Blake!" I gasp, running forward and pressing my hands flat against the wall, tilting my head right back to stare up at him in alarm. What the *hell* is he doing? "How are you? How did you get up there?"

"So, funny story," Blake says nonchalantly. Without an ounce of fear, at the top of the eight-foot wall, he gets to his feet and paces effortlessly back and forth on what must be a very, very narrow ledge. He stretches out his hand to gesture into the distance, to the opposite end of the ranch. "Did you know there's a crowd of press guys outside the gate? Like, with cameras? Even at this hour."

"Yeah. They'll camp out there overnight."

"Well, I figured if I wanted to see you, I had to get creative," he says, quitting his pacing to stare down at me. Under the moonlight, I see the glisten of his dark eyes and the smugness of his smile. "I didn't stop by the gate. Didn't even slow down. Just kept on driving ... and then I decided to take a detour."

"Blake," I murmur anxiously, gulping at how close to the edge of the wall his foot is. At least there's not even a hint of a breeze. "Sit down, please. How did you get here? To the back of the ranch? There aren't any ... roads."

"So? There's grass, and I have a truck," says Blake. He lowers himself back down, dangling his legs, pursing his lips at me. "Don't give me that look, Mila."

"You went off-road, and then what? How did you climb the wall?"

"Again, I have a truck." He points over his shoulder. "It's not that hard to park against the wall, climb on the roof, and then ... Well, I'm a superb athlete, as you know. So, ta-da! Here I am."

"But why?"

Again, he doesn't seem surprised by my lack of response to what he thinks is his five-star humor. He crosses his arms over his chest as if to remind me of his buffness. "Why what?"

"Why did you come here?"

"Why do you think, Miss Mila? To see you, of course!" he says with a sincere, gentle smile. "I wanted to see for myself that you're okay, and also because I want you to know that if you ever need to get out of here to do something fun and *normal*, I have your escape route all figured out."

I cock my head to the side and smirk. "You think I'm agile enough to scale an eight-foot wall?"

"With how good you dance, nothing would surprise me," Blake teases, and I don't know how it's even possible with how *awful* I feel, but my stomach lurches with nervous excitement. "But no. I have the truck on this side to get you down, but you need to figure out what you can use on your side to help you climb up. There must be some old ladders lying around this place, right?"

I'm not so thrilled at the prospect of scaling this wall even with a ladder, but that twist of excitement inside me urges me on. "I can have a look around tomorrow."

"And I bet your aunt and grandfather don't venture to the very back corners of the ranch?"

"No."

"See, foolproof!" he exclaims, fist-bumping the air.

I hug my arms around my chest, feeling a shiver run down my spine. Goosebumps cover my skin, and I feel like a complete idiot standing here in satin PJs and old sneakers at nearly one in the morning, talking to Blake from eight feet below him.

"Mila," he says, and I lock my eyes on his. "Take this."

He pulls his hoodie up over his head, his T-shirt catching

to reveal his tanned, defined stomach. I don't even bother tearing my eyes away as he smooths his shirt back down, then throws me his hoodie. It's way too big for me, but I pull it on regardless and keep my hands tucked up warm inside the long sleeves.

"Thank you," I manage to say, because honestly? I don't know how he has the power to make me blush at a time like this. "Not just for this," I continue with a small laugh, holding up the oversized, baggy sleeves of his hoodie. "But for coming out here to see me."

"Uh, Mila," he says after a minute, getting back up to his feet and staring off at something behind me. "Is the gate supposed to be opening?"

"What?" I squint far, far across the ranch to where the house looks tiny and the gate beyond it even smaller, and Blake isn't imagining things – the gate really is moving.

With bated breath, I watch in open-mouthed confusion, racking my brain for a possible explanation. I thought everyone was asleep, and even if they weren't, I doubt anyone would leave the ranch this late, especially with the reporters camping out, waiting like a pack of hungry dogs.

But it very quickly becomes apparent that no one is leaving the ranch.

Someone is arriving.

I make out the dark shape of an SUV pulling in, the flashing of cameras reflecting off the paintwork, and then the gate begins to close again, shutting out what seems to be a way bigger crowd than was there earlier. The SUV's headlights shine ahead as it moves slowly, smoothly up the dirt road, and I get the most sickening feeling of realization, a heavy thud that falls straight to my stomach.

"Oh my God," I murmur. "I think—"

"What, Mila?" Blake whispers, his eyes following the SUV as its beams illuminate the house.

"I think," I say, "that my dad has come home."

# 5

"Your dad?" Blake says, his features creased in surprise. "What the hell?"

"I don't know," I stutter. My focus is still locked on the SUV as it draws to a stop directly in front of the porch, and my feet begin moving on their own accord. "I'm sorry, Blake. I have to go." And then I throw a look over my shoulder with an apologetic grimace, "Again," because it feels like all I do is run away from him lately. I'm glad he hasn't given up on me – I could do with a shoulder to lean on, and he seems to know this.

"Remember I'm here if you need to escape!" I hear him whisper-call after me, and I turn to wave. He gives me a sympathetic smile of reassurance, which makes my heart swell, then he disappears over the other side of the wall where – I hope – he lands safely in the back of his truck.

As I run back across the ranch and through the fields at lightning speed, my thoughts shift from Blake to Dad. It can't be. It can't be him. I know it was once his family home, but ... I can't believe Dad is here in Fairview. Has he followed Mom all the way out here? Does he want to fix the damage he's caused?

When I reach the stables, I flatten myself against the building and take a closer look at the Harding Estate's newest arrivals. The driver opens the door and a lanky figure steps out, stretching his slim legs. He rests a hand on the door, analyzing the house before him with an assessing tilt of his head. Unmistakably Ruben.

The passenger door swings open next and my breath catches as I'm filled with an overwhelming sense of dread. Broad shoulders, dark hair, sunglasses shielding his eyes as always even though it's after midnight and pitch dark ... Dad. I guess it makes sense that he's here, but this soon? I don't know if I'm ready to face him yet.

He gets out of the SUV and swipes the sunglasses from his face, tossing them back into the vehicle and pushing the door shut. Unlike Mom, Dad doesn't appear all that different. Even in the shadowy dark, I can tell his outfit is perfectly pieced together and fashion-shoot ready, and his dark hair is gelled in its signature style. He does, however, rub at his eyes as if to wipe away signs of stress or fatigue.

When I last saw Dad a month ago, I was angry at him for sending me to Tennessee. Now that I see his face again, I am *livid*. He looks indifferent, impassive. Detached. He doesn't feel like the father I once knew.

"Hmm. Spacious, but in the middle of goddamn nowhere," Ruben remarks, rubbing his chin as he grimaces at the house, and the arrogance in his voice is like nails against a chalkboard to me. "Can't say I'm surprised you wanted to get out of here."

"Don't start," Dad warns him. But when he, too, turns to face the house, hands on his hips, he releases a sigh that's audible from all the way over here.

Cautiously, I take a step forward. And then another. And another.

Ruben is the first to spot me approaching. "Oh, good evening, Mila!"

Dad twists around, his expression panicked now, his surprised eyes locking on mine. I'm only a few feet away from him, but it feels like a million miles. All closeness between us is gone. I can feel the distance in an almost tangible way that I can't explain, a trust that has been broken.

"Dad ..."

"Mila," he says, blinking fast, caught off guard by my sudden appearance. "What are you doing out here?"

"What are *you* doing here?" I fire back, sensing heat raging through my body. "Do you think you can just show up and everything will be fine?"

Dad's features flood with guilt and he stares fixedly at the ground. "I'm sorry, Mila," he says in a low, quiet voice.

"Mila, you haven't seen your dad in a month," Ruben says. "How about you give him a break and let him actually arrive before you get all dramatic?"

I shift my glare and stare at Ruben in pure disgust. "Are you kidding me?"

Ruben sighs exasperatedly, shaking his head as if life's

too short for these kinds of things. "Everett, I told you your daughter has developed a bit of an attitude problem over the summer."

*Seriously?*

Then, like a bullet straight to Dad's chest, I say, "I'm allowed to *develop* an attitude if I've just found out my dad's been having an affair."

"Quiet!" a voice hisses from the porch.

The three of us turn at once to where Sheri stands by the open front door, a robe drawn tightly around her, her usually gentle face like stone.

"All of you, inside," she orders, gesturing to the gate. "We have company, remember? Let's keep a semblance of dignity, shall we?"

"Ah, you must be Sheri!" Ruben exclaims, striding toward the porch. "How very nice to finally meet Everett's sister!"

With as much disdain toward Ruben as I have, Sheri glowers at him with zero patience and holds up her hand as if to halt him in his tracks. "No introductions required, Ruben. This is not exactly a social occasion."

Ruben falters slightly from the no-nonsense greeting. He is always the one who runs the show, and he definitely isn't pleased at being spoken to that way by a woman who he probably classes as one of Dad's inconsequential relatives from "the middle of nowhere." I am cheering her on, silently. Team Sheri all the way.

I'm the first to head inside. I storm past Dad, push past Ruben, and join Sheri by the door. From this vantage point, Dad and Ruben look like a pair of lost passersby, both afraid to be the first to make a move. They exchange an uncertain glance.

"Well, Everett, I don't know what the heck you were thinking." Sheri sighs. "But are you coming inside, or did you decide to show up without warning at one in the morning just for the fun of it?"

"Sheri," Dad says, and I glimpse the real hostility between them now. It has been years since they last saw one another, and in that time, more and more frustration has been building here at the Harding Estate. "Thank you for letting us in."

"Did I have a choice?" Sheri counters, pursing her lips at him and crossing her arms in true doorman style. "It looked like those piranhas out there were about to smash your windshield."

"Well, the rental company sure wouldn't like that," Ruben says sardonically, but no one laughs.

"Ruben, please shut the hell up," Dad snaps, squeezing his eyes tight. I've never heard him be so openly aggressive with his manager – plus, Dad usually makes a conscious effort not to curse when I'm around. Tensions are running at an ultimate high right now.

Ruben holds up his hands in surrender. "Jesus! I'm going for a smoke," he mutters, then stalks off into the field to light up a cigarette.

We stand, watching in silence as the flame flares in the darkness and the smell of nicotine drifts over in the still air.

Then both Sheri and I start at the sound of a voice rising behind us.

"Everett—" comes a gasp from over my shoulder. "What are you doing here?"

I turn and find Mom in a wide-eyed state of shock. She must have heard the commotion, but like me, did not expect Dad to turn up on the property at this hour. Her hair is piled messily into a bun, loose strands framing her bare cheeks, and she wipes her eyes as though she can't believe what she's seeing. Half asleep, she seems younger, somehow. More vulnerable.

"Marns," Dad pleads, and I'm shocked at the genuine shake in his voice. He takes the porch steps two at a time until he's standing right before us all. "I'm here to see *you*. We really need to talk."

Mom, Sheri, and I are like one big barrier of rage. Instinctively, I broaden my shoulders and straighten my posture, ensuring Mom is kept behind me. I feel this overwhelming urge to protect her.

"You opened the gate for him?" she asks Sheri.

"Trust me, I was severely tempted to leave him to be picked to pieces by those vultures out there, but I have to consider the neighbors," Sheri says, arms still folded over her chest, and when I steal a quick peek at her, I notice she hasn't taken her eyes off Dad yet. She is most un-Sheri-like – who knew she could be this bold?

"And you brought *Ruben*?" Mom adds, eyes narrowed, as she spots the plume of smoke emitting from the aloof figure in the distance.

"Marns, please hear me out," Dad begs, and I stare at him, wondering what has happened to my badass, confident movie star of a father. The dad who insists on performing his own stunts. The dad who has mastered the perfect Hollywood smile full of charm. The dad who always looks a million bucks. "You left without giving me a chance to explain."

Mom places a hand on my shoulder. "You sure do have a lot of explaining to do, Everett. *A lot*. And not just for me, but for everyone here. Mila, Sheri, your father. You've made a real mess – and you need to fix it."

"I know," Dad agrees, bowing his head.

"Marnie," Ruben says guardedly as he returns, tossing his glowing cigarette butt to the ground with complete disregard for the ranch. He steps in line next to Dad on the porch and puts a hand on his shoulder. "Don't you worry. He's here to talk things through. Right, Everett?"

Dad shrugs off Ruben's arm at the same time as Mom purses her lips in disbelief at Ruben's blasé attitude, like this is just another publicity slipup that he'll work his magic to resolve. But the weariness in Dad's features, in his whole being, makes it clear that even he knows that negative publicity is the least of his concerns right now.

The Harding family is in a total crisis.

"Please, everyone, just come in off the porch," Sheri urges again, running a hand over her fatigued face. "This isn't the time or the place."

Mom is the first to move. She turns around and disappears into the living room, and I copy Sheri when she stands back from the door to allow Dad and Ruben to enter. Dad's discomfort is palpable, and Sheri keeps pressing her lips together, as though to keep herself from making any remarks about Dad not having been in this house for years. Ruben, on the other hand, gazes coolly around the house as if it's a museum piece. Like, what? He's never seen floral drapes before?

As Sheri locks the front door, I start for the living room too, but she grasps my wrist.

"Mila," she whispers, staring intensely into my eyes, "you do realize the entire ranch is covered by security cameras, right? Not just the gate?"

Oh.

*Ohhhh.*

"You saw me?" I ask, feeling my chest tighten. Well, there goes my escape route out of this ranch. Sheri has me all figured out already.

"We have motion detection," she continues, releasing her grip on my arm. "The alerts woke me up. I thought somebody was trespassing and I was getting ready to call the cops, but then I spotted this highly suspicious young lady in short satin PJs sneaking around like Juliet herself." She cocks her head and raises a brow. "And as for her Romeo ..."

"I'm sorry," I say sheepishly, hugging my arms around my chest. "We were only talking. I won't do it again."

"Just tell Blake to be careful on those walls," she says.

"How'd you know it was Blake?"

Sheri scoffs, but it turns into one of her sweet smiles. "Who else would it be? That boy can't stay away from you. He spent the morning blowing up our landline, remember?"

44

Oh, yeah. Right. I forgot about that.

"Mila, I'm the only one who ever checks the cameras, okay? So if you ever ... miraculously disappear ... I'm the only one who will know how you did it."

I furrow my brows at her, then brighten.

"Does that mean—"

"*Shhh*," she mouths, pressing her index finger to her lips. "Now, let's endure the chaos and recriminations brewing over there."

Together in our PJs, we move toward the living room, but my head is spinning even faster. Sheri is so much cooler than I first gave her credit for. I feel united with her, like we are allies in this messed-up life. I reach out and give her hand a squeeze.

"Can Marnie and I talk?" Dad's voice asks. "Alone?"

And I'm brought straight back to the horrible scenario before me.

Mom sits rigid on the edge of the couch, staring blankly at the clock on the wall. It's after one now, and while the rest of the town sleeps peacefully, the Harding Estate is in turmoil. Ruben haughtily examines the knick-knacks on the mantelpiece like a dealer in vintage collectibles.

"No," I say loudly, finding my voice as I take a courageous step into the room. "I want to hear what you have to say."

"Mila, just let me talk to your mom," Dad replies. "We can talk, just us two, in the morning, okay? I promise."

I'm about to stand my ground, but when I exchange a look with Mom, she nods. She is tired and hurt, and Dad is guilty and desperate, and I think maybe it *is* best if my parents talk privately, at least tonight. There are so many mixed emotions and, despite how much I want to hear the truth, I know deep down that this conversation isn't meant for me.

"Okay," I concede, and Sheri, Ruben, and I leave the room together. We take ourselves off to the kitchen, where Sheri does a quick check of the security cameras. I should probably head back to my room, but I sit down at the table, afraid to miss out on anything at all.

"So, here we are," Ruben says, flexing his hands. "It looks like we're in for a long night. We just had an interminable flight, and I had to navigate these godawful roads all the way from the airport. What more does a guy have to do to get a drink around here?"

Sheri gives him the stink-eye over her shoulder. "I'm sure you were well catered to in first-class," she retorts, but then opens the refrigerator and pulls out a jug of sweet tea. She sets it down hard. "This is a self-service establishment. Glasses are in the drawer over there."

Ruben huffs, then reluctantly pulls out a chair next to me. "I was hoping for a nip or two of bourbon."

"Try the Hilton over in Nashville," Sheri deadpans. "I'm sure they have a fully stocked bar there."

"Actually," Ruben says, holding up a finger.

Sheri and I stare at him with worried expressions, already dreading his next words.

"Everett's plan was that we stay here." He has the good grace to look down at the table for a moment. "If you have the space, that is?"

"What?" I blurt. "You want to stay *here*?"

All of us cooped up together on this ranch is a recipe for disaster, or even all-out war. Sheri has been in Ruben's presence for approximately five minutes and already she can't bear his pompous attitude, and Mom came here to get *away* from Dad, not to end up trapped here with him. Not to mention Popeye, who seems to be sleeping through all the commotion, but will surely hit the roof when he finds out that Dad and Ruben are here. And they have the nerve to assume they can stay?

"Everett paid for the security around here, didn't he?" Ruben points out, snapping back into professional mode. "I think it's only fair he gets to make good use of it until things are resolved. Considering the nature of this excursion, I thought it best we kept things as low key as possible and left Everett's entourage at home. There's no need to make this unfortunate situation into more of a circus than necessary."

"Oh, sure," Sheri drawls. "Because we all must bend over backward to protect dear Everett from his own damn wrongdoings."

"Wow." Ruben snorts and turns to me. "I see where you've picked up your new attitude from."

"Sheri doesn't have an attitude," I say, staring him down. It feels like I have waited almost my whole life to stand up to Ruben. Usually, I would keep my mouth shut and nod along to his wishes. But not anymore. If Blake can stand up to his *mom*, I sure as hell can talk back to Ruben. "She's as sweet as can be … when she actually likes someone."

Sheri laughs out loud, then buries her head into a cupboard, pretending to look for something while Ruben and I pursue an intense stare-off. He's put out by my words, but I don't care. I've had enough of his over-the-top controlling Hollywood bullshit. Why can't he just be a normal human being? Why can't Dad? Why can't we all?

There's a creak from the staircase and the shuffle of footsteps. Then, a raspy voice asks, "What in the world is going on? What is *he* doing here?"

Sheri and I spin around in alarm. Popeye appears at the foot of the staircase, unstable from being newly awoken, and rubs his one good eye fiercely, as though he can't believe Ruben Fisher is really in his kitchen.

"Wesley. It's been a long time since we last met," Ruben says politely, and I wonder: *when* did Popeye ever meet Ruben? Ruben has never been to Fairview. "Apologies if our late-night arrival woke you."

Popeye blinks wildly, truly horrified at the fact that Ruben is, in fact, not an illusion. He checks the clock on the wall, then glowers at Sheri, then me, then Ruben, trying to figure out what is going on. How long until he works out that his son is in the next room?

Sheri moves across the kitchen to him. Placing her hand soothingly on his arm, she guides him toward the table. "Dad, I think you should sit down. Ruben isn't the only one who's here."

# 6

There's a knock on my bedroom door. It's after nine, so I'm already awake and showered, and have been avoiding heading downstairs for breakfast. Instead, I've satisfied my hunger by stealthily snacking on a packet of Sour Patch Kids while braiding my hair.

"Mila, it's me," Dad's voice sounds through the closed door. "Can I come in?"

So, he has kept his promise. He has come to talk to me. No Mom, no Ruben, just the two of us. My body tenses with nerves – I was already angry at Dad even before news of his affair leaked, and I have so much I need to settle with him. It can't wait forever. It's time I voice my thoughts, and time he treated me like an adult.

"Yes," I say.

The door creaks open to reveal him, one shoulder leaning against the frame, his hands stuffed into the pockets of a pair of board shorts. His hair is flat and damp from the shower. "Can we talk outside? It's too nice to be indoors."

"Okay."

In silence, I follow him downstairs. As we pass the

kitchen, I see Mom and Sheri at the table, and they promptly hush as they watch Dad and me walk by. God only knows where Ruben and Popeye are, but after last night, I suspect Popeye has locked himself away in a fit of rage. When Dad and Mom finally emerged from the living room after what felt like the longest talk ever – the rest of us still wide awake, tensions too high to sleep – Popeye exploded. His yelling was a blundering garble, but the gist was clear: how dare Dad show up here after what he's done and expect to be welcomed in with open arms?

And after much battling back and forth, Popeye eventually stormed back upstairs. But only because of Sheri's insistence that so much hostility isn't good for his health. By two in the morning, everyone ran out of steam and retreated to our individual rooms; Sheri begrudgingly allowing Dad and Ruben the privilege of staying here at the ranch. I still don't know how the conversation between my parents went down, but hopefully I'll find out from Dad right now.

I expect us to sit on the porch, but no. Dad leads me all the way outside and into the fields, then drops down to the ground and stretches out his legs. I join him, crossing my legs and fiddling with dry blades of grass to keep my hands busy.

"It's peaceful out here," Dad starts gently to break the ice, tilting his head back to the clear skies above. "Except if you focus too much. Then, above the sound of birdsong, you can hear what's going on outside the gate."

I listen hard, and he's right: if you put your mind to it,

you can hear the collective buzz of voices in the distance from the journalists and paparazzi that have been out there since yesterday. I don't doubt for a second that, by now, the throng has doubled in size as word has spread that Everett Harding is in town. It will only continue to grow the longer Dad stays inside the safety of the walls. The anticipation will build and build and build, as the hyenas circle, poised to snap the best shot of a shamed movie star trying to sneak away from this ranch.

"You brought them here," I point out. My tone is unforgiving.

"I know, and I'm sorry." Dad lowers his head and draws his knees up to his chest, hunching forward like a child in the long grass. The morning sun beams over us, and if Dad and I were basking in the warmth together under any other circumstances, I would love how nice this is. "Where should I start?"

"You can start with why you cheated on Mom."

Dad flinches at the bluntness of my words. There is no point tiptoeing around the real issue here, but I don't think Dad expects me to be this ... hard and composed. "Mila—"

"Why, Dad?" I push, ripping a handful of grass straight out of the ground. "Didn't you learn from your mistakes with LeAnne Avery?"

"LeAnne Avery has nothing to do with this," he warns, fixing me with a cautioning look that I only scowl at in return. "This is different."

"How is it different? Cheating is cheating."

Dad's dark eyes fixate on me, boring into me with

the strangest of looks, as though for a second he doesn't recognize me as his daughter. I would have never dared to talk to him this way a month ago, but I'm not so sure that I recognize him anymore either.

"Because I'm not in love with Laurel," he finally says. "We're just close friends, and there are things in our world that others don't understand. *You* wouldn't understand. Your mom wouldn't understand. But Laurel does, and we often vented to one another."

Mom mentioned yesterday that she'd had her suspicions about Dad and Laurel before now. Is this what she meant? Was Dad heading out to meet with Laurel outside of their work commitments?

"But Laurel is single. You're *married*. Why couldn't you vent to Mom?" I ask, my tone still cold. I refuse to feel sympathy for him. "What do you even have to complain about?"

"You're too young to get it, Mila."

"I'm not too young to know that you got caught kissing your co-star."

"Right." Dad scratches at the back of his neck, his cheeks flaring red. "It's inexcusable, I know. Believe me, I've made mistakes in my life, a whole damn lot of them, but taking things too far with Laurel has been the worst." There is a firmness to his words now and he solemnly looks me in the eye. "Ruben may have followed me out here, but please don't think for a second that I'm only here to save face. I don't care if I lose endorsement contracts. I don't care if I never land another role in my life. I don't care if the world turns against me. I'm here because I love your mom. I love you, Mila."

I study his gaze, expecting him to break the eye contact, but he holds it. As much as I have questioned Dad recently, I don't question whether or not he is lying to me at this exact moment. I want this to be the truth. It has to be the truth. I need to believe my dad.

Relaxing my shoulders only slightly, I ask, "Why *is* Ruben here then if this isn't just yet another publicity crisis?"

"Because he's Ruben," Dad answers. "He is surgically attached to my hip, and I know he may be a bit of an over-bearing nightmare, but he's here to do what he believes is best for me."

Silence falls between us. Dad stares off toward the gate again, most likely tuned into the sound of the waiting press, and I shred up more of the dry grass and pray that Popeye doesn't get mad at me for it. To be honest, I think a few small bald patches in his fields are the least of his concerns right now.

"Ruben sees you as a saint," I grumble. "I throw up on the sidewalk and I'm the worst daughter in the world. *You* have an affair with your co-star and he sees it as his job to corral the rest of us into playing happy family so that this will all be swept under the rug. But you're *not* a saint, so how can I ever trust you again?"

"I know this will take time. I know that. But I could lie to you, Mila. I could deny the accusations, but I'm not. I'm telling you the truth."

"Truth or not, this is about so much more than just Laurel," I say, my face set in a deep frown. "It's everything else. It's Popeye. It's LeAnne Avery."

Dad clenches his jaw at the sound of her name. He's already warned me not to mention her again, and now his gaze narrows. "LeAnne," he repeats, filling the word with contempt. "I never asked you how you found out. Did Sheri tell you?"

"No. LeAnne told me herself. Straight to my face," I spit, remembering that awful night after the bonfire when she drove me home and broke the news to me that she was once engaged to Dad. I didn't deserve to find out that way. It might have happened way before I was born, but surely my parents shouldn't have kept that a secret. Surely they realized information like that would find its way to me eventually. I would have much rather heard the truth from Mom and Dad than from a stranger, one who obviously holds a massive grudge against them still – and, by extension, me.

Dad stands up, furious. "How dare she! How the hell did the two of you even end up in conversation?"

"I met her at church," I say quickly, because I don't dare to mention Blake yet. I *did* meet LeAnne at church, so it's not a lie. The way Dad seethes even at the mention of her name makes it pretty clear that Sheri and Popeye were right – he will not be happy to find out that Blake and I are … something.

So, for now, I'm keeping a secret too. I learn from Dad, I guess.

"That woman is … She's out of her mind," Dad grumbles, angrily shaking his head. "She's got some nerve talking to you."

"But why shouldn't she talk to me? And she told me the truth, right? You *did* cheat on her with Mom," I say, still cross-legged on the grass and staring up at him as calmly as I possibly can right now.

Dad groans and places his hands on his hips, his stance wide. "That was twenty damn years ago, Mila. It's history."

"History that's repeating itself."

"Mila, please don't. It's not your place to throw things in my face."

Now I get up from the ground. I rise to my full height, dust myself down, and take a step closer to Dad. We are face to face, sun burning down over us, our tempers even hotter.

"You know what I think, Dad?" I growl. "I think you're a coward and a fraud. You sent me out here because you were scared that I might stir up bad publicity, but the only person ruining your image is *you*."

And because I don't think I can maintain my composure for a second longer, I spin around and storm away before I burst into tears in front of him.

I leave Dad in the long grass by himself and race back to the house, seething. A hot mess of tears and fury and confusion. Too much damage has been done, and I don't know what it will take for me to forgive him, let alone trust him, again. One conversation is nowhere near enough to fix things. There is a lot to sort out, and it's going to take time, and it's not always going to be civil.

As I head back inside, Mom and Sheri glance up from the dining table, apparently waiting to hear how my little talk with Dad went, but I barely even look at them. I head straight for the stairs and disappear into the safety of my room.

All of these difficult conversations, all of this suffocating tension, all of the family drama, not knowing which way to turn for the truth … it's as far from a carefree summer as possible.

I don't want to be here. I want to escape.

And thanks to Blake, I know exactly how.

Grabbing my phone, I pull up his number and call him. As the dial tone sounds, I dash around my room, shoving my wallet, my remote for the gate (for backup), and some lip balm into my shoulder bag.

"Good morning, Mila," Blake answers cheerfully, evidently pleased to hear from me so soon after our late-night talk in the moonlight.

"I need out of this ranch," I say without missing a beat. "Please meet me at the wall."

# 7

I've got splinters in my fingers and can feel myself sweating with exertion as I drag an old wooden ladder through the fields toward the far corner of the ranch.

Blake should be here soon. He promised to leave the minute he hung up, and it doesn't take too long to drive over here.

When I reach the spot where Blake and I spoke last night, I set the ladder up against the wall and wipe the dirt from my hands.

A few minutes later, I hear the purr of an engine and the soft roll of tires through the grass pulling up on the other side of the wall. I can't see anything, so I'm praying it's who I want it to be – not one of those vultures at the gate. The engine dies and a car door opens.

"Mila, are you there?" Blake calls over the wall.

"I'm here," I say, my chest relaxing with relief. I'm actually getting out of here, and most importantly, getting out of here *undetected*. At least by the press. My parents and Ruben, on the other hand? Yeah, I expect trouble from them when they discover I'm nowhere to be found within the ranch boundaries.

"I'm glad you called," he tells me, just as I hear the thud of what sounds like him leaping into the truck bed. "Did you find a ladder, by any chance?"

"I did! It's right here."

"Okay. Hang on."

There's some more scuffling, and then Blake's thick dark hair appears at the top of the wall, partly hidden beneath a baseball cap. He places his hands flat on the wall's edge and effortlessly pulls himself up from his truck, balancing precariously at full height.

"Didn't take you long to want to get out of here, huh?" he teases, arching a brow.

"Please just get me out of here before anyone notices," I urge.

"Come on up."

My shoulder bag swinging at my side, I grab hold of the ladder and climb the few steps toward Blake. When I can't get much farther, balanced on the final rung and my hands gripping the top of the wall, Blake crouches down and smiles at me from inches away.

"Do you need assistance, Miss Mila?"

I give him a heavy look, unimpressed, and stick my hand out to him. With a breathy laugh, Blake slips his hand into mine and squeezes tight. I can feel the callouses on his fingertips from too much guitar strumming, but his skin is warm, and his grip is strong as he hauls me from the ladder onto the wall next to him. He keeps his hand locked around mine.

"Thanks," I say softly, gazing at our hands.

Blake skims his thumb over the back of my hand and lands a quick kiss in my hair. "Now let's go have some fun."

On the other side of the wall, his truck is parked as close as possible, his passenger-side mirror practically touching the stone. It makes it easier to slip down onto the truck's roof. Blake nonchalantly leaps off the wall and onto the roof as though he's some sort of parkour kid who does this all the time, then looks back up at me.

"Sit down," he instructs.

I do as he says, sitting on the stone wall and dangling my legs over the edge. Freedom awaits. And right now, I don't care about any punishment.

I'm glancing back over my shoulder one last time, but my gaze is drawn back to Blake when, out of nowhere, he clasps his hands around my waist. My mouth forms a surprised "O", and as though I'm weightless, Blake guides me down off the wall and onto the roof next to him. We are pressed close to one another, his hands resting on my hips, and I realize I'm holding my damn breath.

And clearly Blake notices, because he smirks. "Still nervous, huh?"

I gently whack his arm and push him back from me. He just *loves* the effect he has on me, the smug little ego-head. But I can't deny that I enjoy it, too.

I climb down onto the truck bed, then swing over the tailgate and down onto the trodden, overgrown grass of the field on the other side of the wall. I'm pretty certain this land once belonged to Popeye, but I have no idea who currently owns it, only that the land here is unused. Moving around to the driver's side of the truck, I jolt at the sudden flash of golden fur from inside.

"You brought Bailey!" I gasp excitedly, throwing open the door and sticking my head inside, only to be smothered in slobbery kisses. I rake my hands through his soft puppy coat, burying my face into his furry neck and giggling at how ticklish it feels when he licks my ears.

"Of course I did," Blake says from behind me, nudging me forward eagerly. "If a puppy can't cheer you up, then what the hell can? Now get in!"

"Aww, c'mon, Bailey!" I coo in the shrillest baby-talk voice ever. I wrestle with him to shove him farther back into the truck so that I can clamber in and over the center console into the passenger seat, and before I know it, Blake is buckled in next to me and Bailey sits joyfully on my lap with his tongue lolling out of his mouth.

Blake rolls down my window for Bailey to stick his head out. "So, I hope you don't mind, but I have a plan."

"Oh?" I say, my tone piqued with curiosity.

"We're swinging down the street to pick up Savannah and Myles," he explains, his attention laser-focused over Bailey to the side mirror as he maneuvers the truck away from the wall. "And Tori spent the night there last night, so she's coming too. They're all worried about you, and we all want to do something fun to keep your mind off things. I thought you'd like to have them around too, but if you're not ready to see them yet, just tell me and I'll call them right now and cancel, okay?"

My heart flutters a little. For as much as I believed Blake to be a complete pompous jerk when I met him at the tailgate party when I first arrived in Tennessee, he has proven me so wrong. He can be so sweet and considerate sometimes, and already I feel like a weight has been lifted from me just being around him.

"No, that's a great idea," I reassure him, and I untangle my hand from Bailey's fur and place it over Blake's instead where it rests on the gear selector. "Thank you."

Blake visibly relaxes and drives one-handed, keeping his other beneath mine, and the truck bumps and weaves its way across the uneven ground. We head through the field, back toward the road, and I realize we'll need to drive by the Harding Estate's entrance to get to the Willowbank ranch down the street where Savannah and Myles live. While I have heard the voices from over the walls, I haven't actually seen the commotion with my own eyes.

"Is it bad?" I ask, biting down hard on my lower lip. "Outside the gate."

"Worse than yesterday," says Blake. "You'll see in a second."

And as we pull out of the field and turn the corner of the ranch's walls onto the road, I feel nauseous at the sight of all the abandoned vehicles dumped up on the edge of the road. Poor Popeye, having his ranch surrounded like this ... And the neighbors. God, they won't be happy at such disruption to their usual peaceful solitude. The closer we get to the gate, the more it sinks in just how crazy a life Dad lives – and expects us, his family, to live too.

The gate is surrounded. Tents are set up, filming equipment from the local news stations lines the edge of the road, and paparazzi mingle around in small huddles, cameras slung over their shoulders, waiting for the precise moment the gate opens. There's plenty going on, but it's all very calm right now. Individuals engaging in small talk, reporters keying vigorously into cellphones ... But the second they hear the buzz of that gate opening, all hell will break loose. They'll be fighting for the prime spot, shoving each other out of the way to snap the most sensational photos, yelling inappropriate questions, banging on car windows.

And at the sound of Blake's truck approaching, a few of the paparazzi glance up and move to clear the road. Blake gives me a sideways glance. "Should you hide?"

"Yes."

There's a pair of sunglasses in the center console that I make a lunge for, slipping them over my eyes, and then I glance at Blake and promptly swipe his baseball cap straight off his head. I shove it over mine, pull the bill down low, and bury my face in close to Bailey.

We crawl past crazy slowly, but it's only because the road is so packed with people, equipment, and vehicles that Blake has to be careful not to hit anything. I peek around Bailey, examining the scene up close, and I think there's no way these are all local paparazzi from Nashville. It's obvious some of these reporters have followed Dad all the way out here from LA. His presence here is definitely big news.

Suddenly, Bailey is overcome with excitement at all this activity and such commotion. He shoves his nose out the open window and releases a series of gruff barks that grabs the attention of half the crowd. Heads begin to turn.

"Bailey, no!" I hiss, wrapping my arms around him and yanking him back into my lap.

Blake races to roll up the window and steps on the gas a little, and in a frenzy of panicked seconds, we clear our way through the thick of the crowd. There is a clear road ahead, straight to the Willowbank ranch. Bailey ceases his barking and licks my forehead. I can't stay mad at him.

"That was less than ideal," Blake says. "Do they know you're in town?"

"I don't know," I reply, pulling off his cap. I think I'll stick with the shades for now. "No one saw me arrive with my mom or my dad, so I think they might assume I'm still back home." Leaning toward him, I position his cap back on his head for him.

"Hmm," Blake murmurs, as though he's thinking hard. "Maybe what you need is ... a baseball cap of your own."

A few minutes later, we arrive at the Willowbank ranch and wind our way up the dirt track toward the house. Up on the porch, my friends are already waiting. Savannah and Tori race down the steps and sprint over to the truck, while Myles casually saunters behind them. I didn't realize how nice it would feel to see familiar, welcoming faces, rather than the tense expressions etched onto the faces of my family members. This is exactly what I need to cheer me up. No drama allowed.

"Mila!" Savannah squeals, breathless, as she dives into the backseat of Blake's truck. Her strawberry blond hair is in a high ponytail that swings wildly around her shoulders in rhythm with her manic head movements, and as always, she's wearing a pair of very odd, very unique earrings. Today, they are ... mini hot dogs. "Are you okay? I'm so glad you got out of there! The past few days must have been so hard, but we're all here now. We're going to do something fun! What do you want to do? Please tell us and we'll do it. Anything! Right, Blake? If Mila wants to visit ... I don't know – Disney World, for example – you'll drive us there, right? *Right?*"

Even though it's only been a couple of days, I realize how much I've missed Savannah's sweet and fabulous babbling. It's exactly what I need right now. And I also forgot how totally cool and upfront Tori is.

"Savannah, shut *up!*" Tori says with a lighthearted groan, shoving Savannah farther into the backseat so that she can climb in after her. The neon pink streaks in her dark hair shine under the sunlight. "Mila doesn't want to take a ten-hour drive to see sweaty humans in absurd costumes and drink overpriced cokes."

"But the fireworks! And Space Mountain!"

"*No,*" Tori rebukes. "People have *died* on that ride. Did you know that? Anyway!" She settles into the middle seat and fixes her gaze on me, right as Bailey scrambles from my lap into the backseat to smother the two of them with wet kisses. "Hi, Mila. Are you okay?"

"I think so," I say with a smile.

"She has her escape route out of that ranch sorted," Blake comments, "but now she needs to figure out how to get around town incognito. We nearly just had a run-in with the paparazzi back there."

"Tori, you're hogging the backseat," Myles mutters as he finally reaches the truck. "Move over so that Bailey's favorite human can squeeze in. Hey, dude! It's me!"

Tori rolls her eyes and scoots closer against Savannah so that Myles can join the two of them, Bailey spread out over the three of them, tail wagging, paws all over the place. Thank God I'm riding shotgun. I stretch out my legs to take advantage of the privileged space I have around me, and Blake eyeballs his cousins and Tori in the backseat.

"Myles, you're sitting on my hand!" Tori whines at the same exact moment she receives a whack across the face from Bailey's tail.

Myles smirks and says, "You mean your hand is touching my ass."

"You guys!" Savannah pleads, gesturing for them both to be quiet. She grabs the back of my chair and leans forward, sticking her face near mine. "So, Mila. What would you like to do today? What will cheer you up?"

"Honestly?" I say as my lips curve into the only real smile I've had in days. "Just being with you guys is enough. But Blake does have a point." I glance over at him, and he raises a brow. My smile only widens. "I need a new identity."

# 8

The drive to Nashville feels a million times more exhilarating when you're breaking the rules.

I should be tucked up at the Harding Estate, utterly isolated from the outside world, but yet I'm here in Blake's truck with the windows down, my hair dancing in the breeze, country music at full volume as we speed down the highway toward the city. In the rearview mirror, I watch Bailey shove his head out the back window behind me, the wind ruffling his fur while Savannah retains a tight grip on his collar. Beside me, Blake drives with one hand on the wheel and one arm propped up on the door, and he's singing along to the music, which is something he hasn't done around me before. Usually, he just hums, but today he is in full performance mode, his voice a melodic undertone to the radio, but then there's Tori in the backseat, who is trying to outdo him by singing even louder, except she can't sing whatsoever, and Myles keeps begging her to shut up. She only sings louder, eyes closed and all, and I try hard to smother my laughter.

We have collectively decided that the best place for me to switch up my identity is none other than the mall, and Savannah is adamant that Opry Mills is the best one in the city, so under her strict instruction, that's where we're heading. We head through downtown while Bailey barks at random passersby on the streets, cross over the river, and then continue on the highway until I spot the looming mall ahead with what looks like a hundred football fields' worth of parking lot space. Luckily, I have spent pretty much zilch over the past month despite constantly asking Sheri for more cash at my parents' expense, so I have a nice stash of accumulated allowance that I can now run wild with even though my parents took away my credit card before I left for Fairview. When was the last time I was even in a clothing store? It worries me that I can't remember.

"What about Bailey?" I ask as Blake turns into a parking spot in one perfect swing.

"Uncle Myles will take him," Myles offers. "We'll go for a walk and I'll get him an ice cream cone, because there's no way I'm going *shopping*. Oh, and I'm starving, so I need to find myself a McMuffin or two."

"You already ate an entire stack of pancakes for breakfast," Savannah interjects.

"I'm on a *bulk*, Savannah. How do you expect me to make gains like Blake if I don't carb load?"

"You may want to give working out a shot, buddy," says Blake as he closes all the truck windows and kills the engine.

Myles raises an eyebrow. "Do you want me to dog-sit or not?"

"CAN EVERYONE PLEASE JUST GET OUT OF THE TRUCK BEFORE I DIE FROM BEING SUFFOCATED BETWEEN THE BENNETTS AND A GOLDEN RETRIEVER?" Tori screeches.

Myles huffs and pushes open the truck door with his foot, and Tori shoves him the rest of the way out. Savannah climbs out the other side with Bailey, and for a brief moment after they close the doors behind them, Blake and I find privacy.

"They're idiots, right?" he says, shaking his head as though he's the wiser, more mature adult who's responsible for them and is mortified by their behavior. But I think Blake forgets that he once sloppily rammed a quesadilla down his throat on purpose in front of me.

"Yeah," I agree, then grin as I open my door. "In the best possible way."

Outside the truck and in the blazing heat radiating from the concrete, Tori is already calling shotgun for the drive back home, and Blake tosses a leash and a bottle of water over to Myles.

"Give him some water and keep him on shaded grass, if you can," Blake instructs. "And don't let him greet any other dogs because he *really* has a thing for the females right now."

"Sounds like him and Myles are perfectly matched then," chimes Savannah, much to the amusement of Tori, who cackles with laughter.

Myles ignores his sister and clips the leash to Bailey's

collar. "Call me when y'all are finished in there. Mila, good luck designing your undercover identity. Maybe try a Batman cape."

Tori coughs. "Bat*woman*."

"Thanks, Myles," I say. "Bye, Bailey!"

Without even acknowledging his separation from Blake, Bailey turns and trots off happily with Myles.

"Well, let's go shopping!" Savannah cheers, already on the move, making a beeline for the mall's closest entrance. Tori chases after her, and I make to follow them both, but Blake reaches out for my wrist.

"Wait," he says. "You might need this."

Moving his body closer to mine, he whips off his baseball cap and places it on my head. His fingertips drop from the bill of the cap down to my cheekbones, his hands brushing against my sun-warmed skin, and he delicately tucks loose strands of my hair behind my ears.

"Shame to hide those cute freckles, but—" His dimples deepen as he smiles and adds, "Just in case."

"Hurry *up!*" Tori yells back at us.

Blake and I break apart and take fast strides to catch up with her and Savannah. What I really want to do is grab hold of his arm and find a quiet corner where I can feel his lips against mine again. It seems like forever since I last kissed him. Before I know it, though, we arrive at the entrance and my chance is gone. Blake holds the door open for me, and into the heaving mall the four of us go.

It's Saturday, and I forgot how chaotic a mall like this can be. Back home, Mom and I tend to shop down on

Melrose Avenue or over in Malibu, and Dad prefers the grander style of Rodeo Drive, where stores will close to the public just so he can buy a shirt in peace. That's when he actually decides to shop for himself rather than Ruben parading personal shoppers around the house with racks full of the latest fashion.

But an indoor outlet mall like this is fun in its own right. So many stores, so many people, so many scents coming from the food court. Music plays softly throughout, barely audible over the clashing of a thousand voices.

Tori spins around and looks me up and down with great intensity, one hand angled on her hip. "I think you need—"

"Earrings," Savannah suggests.

Tori glares at her. "*No,*" she says, then focuses back on me. She taps her index finger against her cherry-painted lips. "I think you need a new hairstyle."

My gaze drops to the ends of my hair. I'm a natural blond, though these caramel highlights are maintained with regular appointments with my hairstylist. I have never been brave enough to ask for anything different, except the one time I got a mere three inches trimmed off. I like the warm look and my current length. But a new style? That sounds like exactly what the new Mila Harding needs.

"You're right," I agree with a nod. "I do."

"You do?" Blake repeats in surprise.

"Yes! Are there hair salons in this place?" I ask the girls, and I think how horrified Mom would be right now if she knew I was about to let a random hairstylist at an outlet mall touch my hair. Mom is very down-to-earth about most things, but hair and makeup are not one of them. Too bad I make my own rules now.

"This way!" Savannah says. She heads off, darting around other shoppers while her earrings swing wildly, until she abruptly stops and waves a pair of jazz hands at the storefront before her. "Ta-da!"

Wedged between a pretzel store and a brow bar is a hair salon. Inside, stylists are hard at work, brandishing hair dryers, combs, and scissors. They look way too busy to accept a random walk-in who has yet to decide what she actually wants to do to her hair.

Tori, bold as ever, struts straight inside, breezes past the shelves of styling products, and approaches the one stylist who appears to be without a client and is checking his schedule at the front desk. I keep my head bowed in embarrassment as we follow her.

"Hello there," she says in a deep, solemn voice. "We need an emergency appointment to transform our friend's hair. Super important. Can't explain. Can you help? *Love* the quiff, by the way."

The stylist subconsciously touches his perfect hair, gentle enough not to flatten it, and his curious gaze moves around each of us individually. "Which friend? You?"

Blake, upon noticing the stylist's eyes focused on him, shakes his head and retreats. "No!" he almost yelps, then gestures to me. "Her."

"Ah, *you*," the stylist says, jabbing a finger at me. "Take off the hat and let me see what I'm dealing with."

Sheepishly, I do as he asks and shake out my hair. The

confusion that crosses the stylist's face only makes me blush, because we both know there is nothing wrong with my hair. Amazed, he reaches out to run his fingers through the ends, examining the strands with an expert eye.

"You don't even have any split ends," he accuses as though we're wasting his time. "Barely any root growth, and zero dryness. Feel how soft this is! What's the issue?"

"I want something new. Something that isn't so ..." I shrug and shield myself back under Blake's hat. "*Me.*"

"Please help her," Savannah pleads, pressing her palms together and blinking at the stylist, her eyes deliberately wide, childlike.

"Okay! Take a seat," he says, snatching a gown from the rack behind him and marching through the salon to an empty station in the far corner. We all scramble after him. "Oh, the whole *squad* is staying?"

"For moral support," explains Tori.

I sink down into the padded salon chair and the stylist whips the cape around me, then removes the baseball cap from my head. As he runs his hands through my hair again, I stare at my reflection in the mirror. Nerves are running high, because I *never* do spontaneous stuff like this, but this is what normal teenagers do – they rebel; they make impulsive decisions; they discover who they are. And I don't want to just be everyday sunshine and typical honey highlights. I want to be bold like Tori, kind like Savannah, funny like Myles, passionate like Blake.

I see their faces now, mirrored back at me from where they're bunched up together on a couch. Savannah and

Tori are riddled with adrenaline-fueled excitement on my behalf, waiting to see what the outcome of this impromptu hair switch-up will be, and Blake watches me closely with a soft gaze. Our eyes meet in the mirror, and he smiles in the most intimate way, like he's ... proud. It wasn't that long ago when we kissed on the tailgate of his truck and I told him I was afraid I'd never be anything more than Everett Harding's daughter. Who knew that my life would turn into a complete whirlwind since then?

"Well," the stylist says, head tilted. "Do you have any ideas in mind?"

"Tori," I call, spinning the chair around to look at her. The salon's fluorescent lightning catches the vibrant pink of her hair, making the color shine bright. "Do you mind if I use you for inspiration?"

Three hours, a hairstyle makeover, and an utterly ridiculous shopping haul later, the four of us break through the exit doors and into the fresh air. I'm laden with bags full of new sunglasses, baseball caps, earrings selected by Savannah, and clothes picked out by Tori (which I would never personally choose for myself). Lots of distressed denim and bright, clashing colors.

"At long last, they appear!" Myles exclaims.

He's lying on a picnic bench beneath a parasol with Bailey sprawled out by his feet, the leash knotted around the bench leg. A row of Gatorade bottles is lined up on the table next to a party size bag of chips. Bailey lifts his head at the sound of Myles' voice, then leaps to his feet at the sight of Blake approaching. His tail repeatedly whacks the bench with uncontrollable glee, and he attempts to lunge forward, but restricted by his leash, he whimpers instead.

"Hey, Bails!" Blake calls, quickening his steps to reach him. He crouches low to let Bailey jump all over him while he scratches his furry ears in return. "Were you a good boy?"

"Do you even know how many times we have walked around the entire outskirts of the mall?" Myles asks as he stands and dramatically stretches his legs. He unties Bailey's leash and hands back control to Blake. "Nine. *Nine times!* I passed the same panhandler nine times and each time he demanded a dollar. So I spent nine bucks walking your dog while you guys took your sweet time browsing sale racks, and don't even get me started on—" The words die in Myles's throat when his gaze finds me. His mouth falls open. "Whoa, Mila! *Damn!*"

"Cool it," Blake mock-growls. He pats Bailey on the head then straightens back up, glancing over his shoulder at me. He smirks as he tells Myles, "That girl is mine."

I blush hard and touch my new hair. The luscious scent of shampoo is overpowering, all floral and sweet, and the texture of my hair is even softer than it already was. It feels strange at first, reaching out for the ends that are no longer past my bust, and instead having to readjust to my new length just below my shoulders. I've never, ever worn my hair this short before, but my neck feels so much *cooler* in the sun without the extra weight of five inches of hair. Inspired by the few pink streaks in Tori's hair, I decided to take it a step further – goodbye honey highlights, hello pastel pink. All of my natural blond is segmented with pale pink highlights, creating an overall rose-gold look that is emphasized by the beach waves the stylist finished off with. I don't quite look like myself anymore, but I feel like a new Mila, and that's exactly what I wanted. Tori and Savannah will not stop gushing over how much they love the look and are adamant that when I pair my new hair with my shopping haul, I'll be a total badass.

"Tori, how does it feel to be outdone on the pink hair trend?" Myles teases, flashing her a wink.

"This pink? This pink is *neon*. In-your-face pink. Punk-band pink," Tori says defensively, pointing to her head. "Mila's shade is sweeter, like summer and pink lemonade. But you're right, Myles. She rocks it *way* better than me."

"Thanks," I say, suddenly shy, my cheeks matching my hair, and then I laugh. "I don't think my parents will like it as much as you guys do, though."

"Myles!" a voice yells.

We all turn, and crossing through the parking lot toward us is Myles's … girlfriend? Booty call? FWB? Whatever. They were all over each other at the tailgate party and the bonfire, and I'm *pretty* sure there was some fumbling around in the dark at the movie theater when we all went to see Dad's latest movie. It's Cindy, but she's not alone. Her best friend Lacey is by her side.

Lacey, who apparently has a monumental crush on Blake.

"Hey, Cindy!" Myles greets her, then grabs Bailey's leash

back from Blake. "Bet you can't resist a man with a puppy by his side, huh?"

"*Man?*" Savannah snorts, exchanging a humorous look with Tori. "I'll believe that when he finally sprouts a wisp of facial hair."

Despite the confident high I've been riding with my new style, the sight of Lacey sends me plummeting into the depths of self-consciousness. My skin prickles under the heat of the sun and I wish I could swipe Blake's hat from his head one last time to shield myself, but I doubt it would make a difference.

Cindy advances toward Myles – who has not-so-subtly puffed out his chest – and Lacey hovers a few feet away from us girls and Blake. Her long brunette hair is pulled back into a perfect ponytail, the red streaks splashed throughout still visible.

"Hi, Blake," she greets. "Hey, Tori. Savannah." She looks at me and her immaculate brows pinch together, seemingly unsure of who I am, and then she realizes. "Mila? You went ... pink."

"Only two hours ago," I say, attempting a breezy laugh.

I have only been around Lacey a couple times and we have never really spoken to each other, but somehow she puts me on edge. It's weird. I have never felt intimidated by other girls before, because I have always only ever viewed them as friends rather than competition, but Lacey ... I just have this strange certainty that she is someone to watch out for, a gut feeling that I have trouble on my hands. "It suits you," Lacey states with a smile that, bizarrely, seems sincere. She averts her gaze back to Blake, which is clearly no hardship for her. "Are you guys leaving?"

"Yeah, we're done here," Blake replies amiably. "Myles has been left on dog duty for too long."

"Ha – he's on Cindy duty now," Lacey jokes in a low voice, giving Cindy and Myles a pointed glance.

I take a very conscious step closer to Blake and nudge my hand against the back of his. "Hey, where are we headed next? Lunch?"

"Oh, and Mila," Lacey jumps in quickly before Blake can reply. It's so minuscule, I almost miss the way she narrows her eyes at my hand near Blake's. "How are you doing, by the way? You know ... with everything going on?" Her tone is convincing enough, but the pursing of her lips gives away her faux sympathy.

"Hey, give me the keys to the truck so I can get out of this heat and crank up some AC," Tori interrupts, stepping between Lacey and me. She holds her hand out to Blake, and while he passes her his keys without objection, she shoots me a concerned look as though she's worried that I'm upset. My expression tells her otherwise. I'm okay, really. "C'mon, Savannah. You don't wanna get heatstroke *again*," she insists, spinning around and grabbing Savannah's arm. "Bye, Lacey. See ya, Cindy."

"Anyway," Blake says as Tori and Savannah trek off across the parking lot in search of his truck. "We're off to grab some food, but just to warn you, it's *packed* in there." He points over his shoulder to the mall's entrance. "Enjoy your weekend, Lace."

"Wait, Blake," she says, then runs her fingertips through her ponytail. "Your mom mentioned getting together for dinner soon. We haven't done it in a while!"

I keep my expression blank, but inside I am seething because I know exactly what she's doing right now. But Blake, clearly buying her innocent family-friend performance, is totally oblivious. What if Lacey has dinner with him and LeAnne all the time? How long will it take to make herself a permanent fixture in his life the minute I leave town?

"Yeah, sounds good," he responds casually.

He moves away to retrieve Bailey from Myles, who's busy flirting with Cindy, but in the few seconds that I am alone with Lacey, I don't even look at her. Instead, I shove my hand into one of my shopping bags and fish around for a pair of new sunglasses, breaking off the tag before placing them over my eyes and tilting my face to the sun. Neither Lacey nor I say another word, but I sense her watching me.

"Let's go, Mila," Blake says as he steps back by my side with Bailey in tow. "C'mon, Myles!"

Reluctantly, Myles mutters his goodbyes to Cindy while shooting Blake daggers out of the corner of his eye. However, Lacey can't resist having the last word before we all leave.

"Isn't it the July tailgate next weekend?" she asks Blake. "I missed last month's, but I promise I won't miss this one. You were great at the bonfire, by the way, Blake. You should sing at the tailgates too."

"Yup, a week today," Blake confirms, then shyly looks away. "Thanks."

Together, Lacey and Cindy head into the mall, and I follow Blake and Myles through the parking lot. Bailey pads along beside us, but I can't even admire how cute his fluffy tail is wagging in the sun right now.

In a quiet voice, I ask, "You call her Lace?"

Blake glances at me. "Huh?"

"Lace," I repeat, keeping my voice low as Myles strides on ahead of us. "You call her by a nickname?"

"I've called her that since grade school," he says with a laugh, then playfully digs his elbow into my ribs as though it's not a big deal.

But it is when he's the only person I've heard call her that.

# 9

The sky is growing dark by the time Blake and I head back to the ranch. We have dropped off the others, and Bailey is splayed out asleep on the backseat. When we drive past the ranch's main entrance, the crowd from this morning is still there, and I keep my head down and pretend to rifle through the glove box until we safely pass. Off-road we continue through the field along the edge of the stone walls of the ranch, and Blake parks the passenger side of the truck as close to the wall as he can get, leaving no space for me to open my door.

"So," he starts, putting the truck in park. He lowers the volume of his music until it's only a quiet hum in the background. "How much trouble do you reckon you're in?"

"A lot," I admit. "But it's been worth it."

From the collective sing-along in the truck, to transforming my hair at the mall, to dancing all afternoon at Honky Tonk Central, to eating dinner on an outdoor patio under the dipping sun at a barbecue joint. Today has been exactly what I needed to feel sane again. And now, returning home, I am too happy to care about the consequences that await me on the other side of these walls.

"Good," Blake says. "I'm glad you had fun."

I place my hand over his and maintain eye contact with him. "Thanks to you," I tell him, then laugh. "But you can't keep me here all night. I can't open the door, genius."

"Climb over."

"What?"

Blake smirks and flips our hands over, interlocking his fingers tightly around mine. "Climb over, Mila."

It gets very, very quiet in the truck all of a sudden. Bailey's soft snores fade away and I can no longer hear the beat of a country song. My breathing intensifying, I release my seatbelt and carefully move my body over the center console, over Blake.

He clasps my hips and pulls me up hard against him, and I gasp.

My body is wedged between the steering wheel and Blake's chest, straddling him. He angles his jaw up toward mine and the scent of spearmint lingers between us. Our mouths are so close, barely inches apart. Am I breathing? I don't think so. No, seriously, I'm definitely not breathing.

"I didn't say it earlier," Blake murmurs in a husky tone as his dark eyes travel down my body and back up, "but you look *so* damn hot." He runs his hand from my hip up to my hair, tucking a section behind my ear.

"You like the pink?" I ask, my voice a squeak.

"I like you."

And then our lips clash like an exploding firework, all

magical and deafening, all bright colors and pretty skies. That's how kissing Blake makes me feel. I cup his jaw in my hands and lean into him, my skin tingling where his fingers grip the curve of my hip harder. It is the perfect end to a day that I desperately needed, my mouth against Blake's. Desire pumps through my veins at the feeling of my body this closely pressed to his, and it feels so sexy, straddling him like this when we are completely alone out here. Nothing but a sprawling, overgrown field and a dark sky above us with specks of stars, and that soft tinkle of a perfect country song.

Breathing hard, we pull apart. I keep Blake's face steady between my hands as I gaze into his eyes, and the dimples in his cheeks pop like never before when he smiles at me.

"I have to go," I whisper, but leaving this truck is the last thing I want to do right now. I want to stay here with Blake all night and forget about everything that awaits me at the Harding Estate.

Blake presses his forehead to mine, nodding against me.

We both know that I have to go. I kiss him lightly again, stroke my fingers over his brows, then quickly destroy the intimacy of the moment as I attempt to scramble off him. It's not exactly attractive, the way I struggle to kick open the truck door and haul myself over Blake, but his soft, breathy laughs only make me laugh too. Even Bailey lifts his head from the backseat, curious to see what the ruckus is.

"Bye, Bailey," I say, giving him a little wave. "Goodnight, Blake."

I turn away from the door and move to the rear of the truck, preparing myself for scaling the wall.

"Mila," Blake whispers. I glance back and find that he's stepped out of the truck too, one arm resting over the open door with the sweetest smile I've ever seen him wear. "How would you feel about maybe officially being my girlfriend?"

I do a double-take – I had so not expected this. "Your girlfriend?"

"Yeah," he says, then looks down at the ground as he kicks at the dirt. "You think I'm good enough to date Everett Harding's daughter?"

"You think *I'm* good enough to date the Mayor of Nashville's son?" I fire back teasingly.

"I think," Blake murmurs, meeting my gaze, "that Mila Harding and Blake Avery are good for each other."

There's no point even *trying* to hide it – the beaming grin that takes over my face, my cheeks stretched wide, and the fizz of electricity that radiates all through my body. My feet begin moving and I run back to Blake, leaping into his arms and wrapping my legs around him.

"Yes, yes, yes!"

Blake stumbles, knocked a little off balance by the impact of me throwing myself at him. He steadies us and locks his arms around me, fitting his hands around my butt. "Yes, *what*?"

"Yes, of course I'll be your girlfriend!"

And now I'm the bold one, high on giddy excitement, landing a thousand kisses on every inch of his gorgeous face. I think I even plant a kiss on his *actual* eyeball, but I don't care, and neither does he by the hearty sound of his smothered laughter.

*Mila Harding has a boyfriend. A boyfriend who plays acoustic guitar and sings country songs. A boyfriend who takes her dancing at honky tonks. A boyfriend who rescues her in his truck from her family ranch. Mila Harding has a boyfriend and that boyfriend is the unbelievably gorgeous Blake Avery.*

"Hey, Miss Mila, what has happened to you?" he jokes as he sets me back down.

My cheeks blazing – *that* hasn't changed – and my heart thundering, I try to relax the smile on my face so that I don't appear so frenzied, but it's impossible. "I'm sorry – I don't know why I just did that."

"It's cute. I like the confident Mila," Blake reassures me, then he winks. "But I like the nervous one too."

"Okay, I'm leaving now," I tell him, embarrassed, and walk away before I have another lapse in self-control. I heave myself over the truck's tailgate, climb onto the roof, and hoist myself up onto the wall. Blake watches me in admiration, as though he expected me to need his help again, but I'm riding a total high right now. "Bye, boyfriend!" I call and blow him a final playful kiss.

Blake blows me one back, then rolls his eyes at our shared cheesiness. "Goodnight, Mila."

On the other side of the wall, the ladder from earlier is still there, thankfully. I lower myself down, the ragged stone scraping my hands, and find my footing on the highest rung. And then I descend into the darkness of the

Harding Estate as a girl with new memories, new hair, and a new boyfriend.

I should be more worried than I am, but as I tramp through the field toward the house, I'm practically skipping. I can't wipe the grin from my face. Any punishment be damned. What are my parents going to do this time? Ship me halfway across the country in a different direction? Ha.

The motion-sensing security cameras must have detected me already, because the front door bursts open before I've even reached the porch. I freeze mid-step and draw my shoulders in tight, peering through half-closed eyes at the fuzzy sight of Mom and Dad while I await the tirade of yelling.

But they can't raise their voices out here, not with all those paps outside the gate.

"*Mila Harding,*" Mom snaps in the sternest voice I have *ever* heard her use with me. It's potent enough to make my stomach drop.

Dad stomps out onto the porch and leans over the wooden railing, pointing his thumb behind him to the door where Mom waits. "Inside," he orders. "I mean it, Mila."

Keeping my head down, I slink up the steps, past Dad, and through the front door. Dad promptly shuts it behind us all, and that's when I spot Sheri hovering a few feet away. It's also now, under the bright light, that my parents notice something different about me.

"What have you—" Mom gasps as she leans forward

to take a section of my hair in her hand and weaves the strands through her fingers. "What have you *done?*"

"Just a bit of a refresh." I shrug. "Don't you like it?"

"I do," Sheri comments with an impressed nod, and Dad fires her a look that could incinerate her on the spot.

"Never mind your hair. Where the hell have you been?" he demands furiously, stepping into line next to Mom, who is still blinking at my new look in a dazed sort of way. It's the wrong time to think it, but I don't mind being yelled at by my parents if they're doing it together. This feels nicer than having the two of them discuss whether or not Dad's sordid little affair will ruin our family forever.

"I went out with my friends," I answer with another nonchalant shrug.

"Which friends? I'll need their names," I hear Ruben snap from the entry to the kitchen, and I turn to look at him the way I always do – with sheer disdain that his voice has found its way into the conversation.

"You aren't supposed to go out with anyone!" Dad yells, but I know that his high levels of frustration are a buildup of everything else going on right now; those deep lines of stress in his forehead aren't just from worrying about me. "Did you talk to anyone at the gate? Did you say *anything?*"

"I didn't go near the gate."

Dad steps back. "What?"

"Well," Sheri says, carefully tiptoeing her way into the conversation. "There *are* other ways to get out of here if someone really wants to. And I'm sure Mila was discreet about it. Right, Mila?"

"Right," I agree with a confident nod. Thank God I have Sheri – I don't know what I would do around here without her on my side.

"She took off!" Dad cries, narrowing his eyes at Sheri. "I don't care how she did it. The point is that she *did*."

Mom finally absorbs the shock of my new hairdo and comes back to life. "You couldn't have answered your phone? You couldn't have at least let us know *where* you were?"

"It's been turned off," I say, calm as ever. Inside, I suppress the desire to do a little happy dance right here in the hall. I wonder how Blake is feeling right now as he drives home. Is he singing along to his music a little louder than usual? Is he smiling even when stuck at a red light?

"New rule," Ruben cuts in. "Your phone does not get turned off from now on."

I roll my eyes, much to the anger of my father.

"Mila," he snaps. "This is serious. You can't just disappear on your own in a city you don't know at a time like this. What if you'd been spotted?"

Mom flicks a barely concealed hostile glance at Dad before her eyes dip to the floor and her expression dulls. For a second, she looks far away, like she'd love to be any place but here. I wonder what I've missed while I've been gone – what conversations have been had, what apologies have been made, what forgiveness, if any, has been given. By the look on Mom's face at Dad's reminder of the family crisis at hand, I get the sense that not much progress has been made. The air is still thick with friction, but at least they can seemingly still work together when it comes to being parents. Even if they're both nothing more than equally exasperated with me.

"Well, that's why I changed my hair," I say with a half-hearted laugh, twirling pink strands around my index finger. I thrust my shopping bags toward Dad. "And look! Lots of new sunglasses to hide behind!"

"Mila!" Dad's nostrils are flaring now thanks to my clear lack of care for the severity of the situation. It's not that I don't understand – I do, perfectly – it's just that I really *don't* care. I'm so over all of this. "It's not safe! They'll hound you out there. You'll be followed and harassed."

I shake my head slowly. "You're the celebrity, Dad. Not me," I remind him. And maybe it's because I can feel Ruben's infuriated gaze on me, but my steely calm erupts into bitter anger. "I'm not putting my life on pause just because *you* monumentally messed up."

Mom glances at Dad impassively. "Well, I can't say she's wrong there, Everett," she says icily.

Dad recoils and his shamefaced expression gives me a pang of regret. So maybe that was a little harsh, but it *is* the truth. And, apparently, an uncomfortable truth at that, because Dad turns and walks away, disappearing upstairs. Ruben tuts at me and follows after him, like Everett Harding's own faithful disciple.

"What a day." Mom wearily runs her hands over her face. "I'm just glad you're safe, Mila."

"I'm sorry I was gone for so long."

"We were worried. But Sheri had a feeling you were out with a friend and that you'd eventually show up."

"*Oh*," I say in a high-pitched tone, turning my back on Mom and facing Sheri instead. I smirk at her. Sheri didn't have a "feeling" – she has access to the security cameras and probably watched Blake haul me up onto the wall this morning with her very own eyes.

Sheri refrains from smiling. "Just a hunch," she says, her tone neutral.

"I'm taking a shower." Mom sighs, scraping her hair back and twisting it into a low ponytail before heading upstairs, her steps sluggish.

Sheri and I watch her until she's out of sight, then we exchange a look. Sheri is the first to crack, rushing over to me with a beaming smile.

"Oh, honey, you have *no* idea how much they've all been flipping out today," she tells me in a hushed voice. "Be glad you missed all that commotion. It was like being in a soap opera."

Though I'm not sure I really want to know, I can't help myself. "What happened?"

Sheri looks at me for a moment, seemingly debating whether she should involve me in this mayhem, then clearly makes up her mind. "Well, it was all very civil at first with your parents, but then suddenly the whole damn house was shaking from their yelling. It sounded like your mom had a few choice words she needed to get off her chest, but I can't say that your dad took it lying down. Popeye got so fed up he retreated to the shed." She shakes her head with a smile that's somewhere between sadness and frustration. "Anyway, I guess it's good that they got things aired." Then, changing the subject, she can't help but examine my hair, running her fingers through its soft texture before stepping back to tell me, "I love this look on you."

"Thanks," I whisper, then because I'm bursting to share my news: "Can you keep a secret?"

"Of course!"

I reach out for Sheri's wrists and pull her close to me again, checking over her shoulder that my parents are definitely gone, then I meet her curious gaze. "Blake asked me to be his girlfriend." I twinkle my eyes at her. "I said yes. Obviously."

"Oh, Mila, Mila, Mila," Sheri gasps. "If only you weren't already in trouble, you definitely would be now."

# 10

I don't know how we manage to sit down for breakfast together.

Well, we're not exactly gathered around the kitchen table, but still, we're all in the same room and no one is yelling. That has to count for something.

I'm chewing my cereal as quietly as possible, careful not to disturb the awkward silence, while Mom pokes her knife into her poached eggs opposite me, a zoned-out look on her face. Sheri is frying bacon while Ruben leans against the counter next to her, unimpressed by the chipped Dumbo the Elephant mug he's chugging his instant coffee out of. Dad, on the other hand, has his hands pressed to the window frame and is totally still as he looks out over the ranch. And Popeye? Popeye stares at Dad, his rage bubbling just beneath the surface as he sucks on an endless number of Jolly Ranchers – his chosen method of stress-relief.

"Are you going to look at me?"

I stop mid-crunch. Sheri clatters the tongs against the frying pan. We all turn to Popeye, who has spoken for the first time this morning – everyone, that is, except the one person he has directed the question at.

Dad bows his head at the window, and I see his shoulders drop. Quietly, he says, "What, Dad?"

Popeye smacks his hand hard against the cabinet. "Look at me, son!"

I'm on pause, fearful that I'll choke on my breakfast if I don't breathe soon, but I'm wide-eyed and taken aback by Popeye's outburst. I know he and Dad talked the morning after Dad and Ruben arrived, but they have been dancing around each other since then. I'm not sure what they spoke about, but Dad is definitely still walking on eggshells.

The bacon sizzles unattended on the stove behind Sheri. Ruben's eyes are closed as he rubs at his temples. Mom glances rapidly between Dad and Popeye, a look of concern on her face.

Dad, after the longest pause in history, turns around. He locks eyes with Popeye and through stiff lips he says again, "*What*, Dad?"

"Was that so hard, Everett? To look at me?" Popeye remarks. "You're staying in *my* house. The least you could do is stop actively avoiding me, but maybe you're too ashamed of yourself."

"Hey, c'mon now, Wesley," Ruben says as he hastens over to Dad's side like the ultimate protector. I mean, how *dare* someone talk to the great Everett Harding like that?

Popeye snaps his head around. "It's Mr. Harding to you."

"*Mr. Harding*," Ruben reluctantly corrects, spreading his

hands wide. "Let's not raise our voices, huh? Let's just be calm and civilized."

Flabbergasted, Popeye can't even muster a reply. He stares agape at Ruben as though he is truly from another planet, and I don't blame him. Ruben, for as much as he's aided Dad over the years, can also be a bit of a bumbling idiot when it comes to reading the room.

"No," Dad says. He extends his arm in front of Ruben's chest, keeping him back, as he steps forward and fastens his weary gaze on Popeye. "Let him vent. C'mon, Dad. Tell me exactly what it is you wish to say to me. What you've wanted to say out loud for years."

"*Ooookay!*" Sheri turns the stove down and flaps a dishtowel over the bacon as she dashes over. "Everett, Dad, stop it."

But they don't stop.

Popeye moves forward too until he and Dad are in each other's faces. They are equal in height. It's the strongest I've seen Popeye all summer, with his shoulders broadened and his hands balled into fists by his side. They tremble, but still. Popeye kinda looks like a badass.

"I think," he snarls, "that you will never be happy. You can't just settle for a normal existence like the rest of us. You always want more, more, more. More glamor, more adulation. More attention. Nothing is ever good enough for you, is it? Not this ranch, not us – your family."

I flinch, but Dad seems to take it in his stride. "Here we go again!" he groans, like a bored kid. "*How dare I want more out of my life than the family ranch? How dare I not*

93

*want what you want for me?* That's what it's really all about, isn't it?" Dad scoffs. "I'm not sorry, Dad – not even a little – for living my own life."

"Everett," I hear Mom caution as she stands from the table.

"You know why I don't visit?" Dad continues, jaw clenched in fury now. "Because you look at me like dirt. You can't admit that I actually made it, that I provide better for my family than I ever could have if we'd stayed here living what you like to call a *normal* existence."

I finally swallow my mouthful of soggy cereal and clink my spoon down hard against the bowl. As Dad glares into Popeye's face, I notice something in his eyes, something other than rage. There is pain. Dad is hurt.

Over the past few weeks, I couldn't help but notice the way Popeye spoke badly of Dad and his choices in life. How flippantly he dismissed Dad's success and the tone of disapproval whenever he spoke of him. I tried not to overthink it, but I can't dismiss that Popeye, sweet but oh-so-old-fashioned Popeye, was never all that supportive of Dad's – to him, unfathomable – dreams. And until right now, I never considered what that would feel like for Dad, but that flicker of a lifetime of disappointment in his eyes makes me wonder. I thought Dad didn't visit because he was too busy living the high life to care about the small town he left behind. I didn't imagine for even a second that perhaps he didn't go home often because this small town makes him feel rejected.

Popeye shifts on his feet, narrowing his eyes at Dad.

"You think I want to be proud of a son who can't remain faithful? Who has no morals? Who will stop at nothing to get his own way? You traded in LeAnne Avery for Marnie when LeAnne was smart enough to suggest you pursue a sensible degree, because if anyone has the audacity to challenge you, you throw them out of your life!"

I am totally rooted to my chair, my body frozen. This is ... intense. Are there any boundaries that Popeye and Dad won't cross? How the *hell* did we ever survive Thanksgiving dinner together once upon a time? How much effort did my family have to put into maintaining a facade to protect me as a kid?

"How many times do we need to talk about LeAnne?" Dad snaps. "I already explained that to you – two decades ago! Why do you have to bring her up again *now*?"

"Enough." Mom's voice cuts through the strained atmosphere, and suddenly she is by Dad's side, pulling him back from Popeye. I'm finding it extremely confusing to watch – Mom, who's supposed to be furious at Dad, stepping in to remove him from the situation. Her hand tightens on his arm, tugging him away.

"I smell burning," Ruben says, sniffing the air, and for a moment I'm even more confused – can he smell flames leaping out from the massive episode of Harding drama being acted out in front of us?

"The bacon!" Sheri gasps at the exact same second the fire alarm goes off.

This is, officially, the biggest breakfast disaster of my life.

Mom pulls Dad from the kitchen, the two of them

disappearing in the midst of the ear-piercing *beeps*, while Ruben remains leaning against the counter. He wears a look of indifferent weariness as he watches Sheri grab the sizzling frying pan full of charcoaled bacon from the stove and a grumbling Popeye pull out a chair to stand on to turn off the fire alarm.

Chaos. There is no other word for it. Complete and utter chaos.

I make a swift exit from the kitchen in search of my parents, and I find them in the living room, face to face. Dad is seething. His shoulders rise and fall with his deep, angry breaths, and his nostrils flare. Mom offers her hands out to him, trying to calm him down. I watch from the doorway. What *is* this? It's not that I don't *want* my parents to stay together despite everything, it's just that it feels a bit too soon to find Mom being there for him like this.

I move into the room, my steps light. "Mom? Dad?"

Mom steps away from him, almost guiltily, and Dad turns his head. The sheer intensity of emotion I can read on his face would honestly have me believe that he was in the middle of rehearsing a scene for an upcoming movie. I've never seen Dad, in real life, look such a mess.

"I'm sorry, Mila. I know he's your grandfather, and I shouldn't talk to him like that in front of you, but I just ..." He exhales a long breath. "I need a minute."

He strides out of the room and his footsteps can be heard on the stairs. Mom looks at me, and I throw my hands up in that universal signature of "what the hell is going on?"

"Aren't you mad at him?" I ask.

"Of course I am," Mom says, then pushes her hair off her face with her manicured fingers. "But your dad and your grandpa ... It's a sensitive subject. I know how much it hurts him."

"Hurts who? Popeye?"

Mom gives me a strange look, as though I should know this. "No, Mila. Your dad."

I'm trying to make sense of her words when Ruben dashes into the room, Dumbo mug still in hand, bringing the smell of scorched bacon with him. "Where is he?"

Mom stares at him in despair, but eventually answers with a nod to indicate "upstairs." Ruben turns to leave, and I wonder if I should stop him. I doubt Dad will appreciate Ruben chasing him down when all he seems to want is a second to himself.

"Let's hurry up and get to church so I can pray that he sees sense one day," Popeye mumbles a moment later as he follows Sheri into the living room. She has broken out into a sweat and loose strands of hair wisp around her cheeks. Meanwhile, Popeye is still a ball of unfiltered anger.

"Church?" Ruben repeats as he sticks his head back around the doorway, having overheard Popeye. "I'm sorry, but unless that church is stationed right here on your ranch, Wesley, then I'm going to ask that you don't attend."

"*Mr. Harding!*" Popeye snaps, turning to point a finger at Ruben. At this point, I'm amazed Popeye hasn't kicked his LA ass out on the street for his consistent lack of respect.

Ruben holds up his hands apologetically, but it's

painfully clear that he doesn't actually care. "I was *saying*," he continues, "that it's best not to go to church today. We have lots of visitors outside, remember? And, Mr. Harding, they will follow you."

"Those lowdown scavengers! They won't stop me from living my life!"

"He has a point," I say, and Ruben fixes me with a death stare.

"Ruben, it's a Sunday and we will be attending church," Sheri decrees. No apologies. Good for her. They shouldn't be sorry for getting on with their normal lives, the same way I'm not sorry for disappearing yesterday with my friends and Blake.

Oh, excuse me. *My boyfriend.*

My boyfriend who will also be at church today.

"I'm going too," I say in a voice so chirpy it surprises even me. "We go every week."

"Maybe we should all go."

The sound of Dad's voice entering the conversation startles us all. He appears at the doorway, a little behind Ruben, and interlaces his fingers behind his head while taking a deep breath. In the minute that he's been gone, he seems to have pulled himself together and appears much more composed. But he could be acting, I guess.

"You don't go to church," Ruben huffs, shaking his head in astonishment.

"But maybe I should," Dad says steadily. "I used to go every Sunday when I was a kid."

Sheri glances nervously at Popeye, and Popeye cocks his

head at Dad. "You're seriously deluded if you think you're going to show up at *our* church just so you can look good to the media."

"No, no, no." Ruben begins to pace the room the way he always does when he's in a tailspin and trying not to panic. "This is such a bad idea, Everett. They are just *waiting* to pounce on you out there."

Dad ignores Ruben's attempt at reasoning – which, to his credit, is sensible – and keeps his eyes trained on Popeye with the occasional glance at Sheri.

"You think I want to get harassed?" Dad asks. He is much calmer than earlier, but there is still a distinct undertow of exasperation in his voice. "Just consider, for one damn second, that maybe I want to go to church because I think it will be good for us all to attend. As a family."

"In that case," Ruben adds, "I'll come with you."

"No, not this time," Dad tells him. "It's best that it's family only."

Ruben flinches as if physically wounded. Dad's his one and only client and they have worked together for years. It's very unlike Dad to go against what he recommends.

"Are you sure?" Mom asks, but only because I think *she's* unsure of the idea.

Dad nods, then looks at Popeye with an odd mixture of pleading and loathing in his eyes. This is hard for him, but he knows it must be done, however reluctantly. "Dad, this is an olive branch that I am offering you. Please accept it."

Popeye twists his hands, undecided.

"I think Everett is right," Sheri says in a quiet voice as

she casts a glance at Popeye, like she's afraid he'll accuse her of taking Dad's side over his. "Maybe it *will* be good for us."

But wait. Have they actually thought this through?

The spark of excitement I felt at realizing Blake will be at church is now matched by a lurch of serious apprehension.

If Blake's there, then his mom will be too …

Even if we get past the hordes at the gate unscathed, I have no idea how my parents will deal with LeAnne Avery.

Popeye clears his throat; he has made a decision. "Okay. This family is going to church."

# *11*

It's like bracing for impact in those nanoseconds of realization before your car collides with another. This sickening feeling of absolute doom while your stomach drops, and all you can do is cling to your seatbelt and brace, brace, brace.

That's how it feels to be facing the Harding Estate gate, waiting for it to swing open and for the car to be swarmed. It's inevitable, and it's something my parents and I are used to. Popeye and Sheri, on the other hand, are in for a shock. I don't think they realize just how crazy the next couple of minutes will be.

"Visors down," Dad orders.

I am wedged in the backseat between Dad and Mom, Popeye rides shotgun, and Sheri sits a bundle of shaky nerves behind the wheel of her minivan. She pulls down her sun visor, then reaches out to do the same for Popeye. It barely makes a difference, but anything that attempts to shield us a little more is worth trying.

"Can't even leave my own home without being attacked," Popeye grumbles, which is only slightly melodramatic. We aren't going to be *attacked*. The van, however …

Sheri grabs the remote from the center console and opens the gate.

We all sit rigid as the gate electronically sweeps open to reveal the throng outside. They grab their cameras and bunch together in one frantic, scrambling huddle, pulling forward into the open gap the gate has left. They know better than to take a single step onto the property, as they could then be arrested for trespassing, so they stay as close as possible to the boundary like a solid, defiant barrier.

"They're blocking the road!" Sheri says as the cameras begin to flash.

"Just drive forward," Dad directs. "They'll move."

Sheri looks like she may pass out at the thought of potentially ramming a crowd of paparazzi, but Dad's right. They always move. No picture of Everett Harding is worth the cost of a hospital visit.

The van creeps forward, and forward, and forward ...

Until we are in the midst of the crowd that circles every inch of the van. I hear the rumble of metal as bodies press against our vehicle and see blinding flashing as cameras are shoved up against the windows, mostly focused on the backseat to see if the elusive Everett Harding has finally emerged.

Next to me, Dad has his chin tucked down tight against his chest and his hands shield his face over a pair of sunglasses. On my other side, Mom hides beneath her big, woolen shawl. As for me and my not-so-subtle pink hair, I don't even try to hide. What's the point? It's obvious that we're all here together, so I just stare blankly straight ahead at some of the paps nearly throwing themselves onto the hood of the van.

Despite the windows being closed, there is no way to shut out the muffled voices. It is painful to listen to; there is nothing to do but ignore it. Popeye gets especially shifty in the passenger seat.

"EVERETT, WHERE IS LAUREL PEYTON NOW?"

"MARNIE, HAVE YOU FORGIVEN HIM?"

"EVERETT, OVER HERE! WHY WOULD YOU BETRAY YOUR FAMILY?"

Sheri revs the engine a little, and at last, the mass of bodies parts enough to let us break through. The open road lies ahead of us, and Sheri steps on the gas, but we aren't out of the woods yet. I look behind me and see cars ready to go, the paps and reporters racing toward their vehicles, flinging open doors and jumping in. They'll flag us all the way to church, where they'll continue to harass us, and I'm not sure how well that will go down with the Fairview community. Does Dad really believe this is a good idea?

The press is still hot on our heels as we tear into the parking lot. I've never seen Sheri drive so wildly before, and I can tell she is completely out of her comfort zone. Church is for contemplation and peace, not hordes of paparazzi chasing a shamed movie star, and it doesn't take a genius to know that the weekly Sunday congregation won't be too fond of such disruption.

We are a little late, so there are no churchgoers mingling outside in the morning sun. They are all inside and seated, and the service has most likely already begun, which I think is actually *worse*. Now we will become a complete spectacle when we try to slip inside.

"What will Pastor Lowes think of us?" Popeye asks Sheri as he tucks his bible beneath his arm. "Bringing all this ... unholy fuss."

"Shut off the engine and go!" Dad instructs from the backseat, anxiously watching out the rear window as a stream of vehicles rolls into the lot. It will take them no time to jump out with their cameras poised, so we need to act fast.

The van jolts to a stop, parked over two spots, and we all release our seatbelts at lightning speed and throw open the doors. I'm used to this, the feeling of always *rushing*. In the world of fame, there's no time to dither. It's always: *Quick! Get inside, keep your head down, run to the car.*

And because we are pros at this, my parents and I are already out of the van and speed-walking toward the church doors in perfect sync with one another. When we reach them, I breathe a sigh of relief, but Dad pauses and turns back around. Popeye can't walk this fast. His movements are slow, and despite Sheri tugging on his arm to hurry him up, the paparazzi are already all over them.

Without a word, Dad sprints back to take Popeye's other arm, and together with Sheri, they shepherd him toward the door.

"MR. HARDING, WHAT DO YOU THINK OF YOUR SON'S AFFAIR?" someone yells amid the clamor of what feels like hundreds of other questions.

For the tiniest of moments, Popeye searches for the voice among the crowd, and his lips move as though to form words, but then he thinks better of it. I get the sense that there's a lot Popeye would tell the world if he could, but it's a line I don't think he'd ever cross. He has his pride, and Dad is still his son, despite everything.

"They are dirtbags!" Sheri spits as she, Dad, and Popeye reach us inside and pull the doors firmly closed behind them. It shuts out the crowd, but their collective voices can still be heard.

"Shhh," Popeye hisses. He shrugs Dad's hand from his arm and points his bible in the direction of the main hall, then shuffles off ahead of us, clearly annoyed about being late and the undignified nature of our arrival, not to mention having intrusive questions thrown at him.

"I'm not sure about this," Mom whispers only to me. She is so unnaturally pale, she may as well be a ghost.

Our footsteps light, we follow Popeye to the main hall where the service has, indeed, begun. The preacher is introducing today's theme from behind his lectern: redemption. *How relevant.* As always, the pews are packed full, but we silently emerge from the back of the hall and into the empty last row. The sound of late arrivals stirs up some curiosity that causes heads to turn.

You can see it in their expressions as recognition dawns on them. That look of disbelief followed by a rise of the eyebrows as they turn to nudge the person next to them. More people tune out the preacher to crane their necks to see if it's true that Everett Harding has really turned up at their local church service. A quiet rustle of gossip rises steadily until the preacher silences it with a glare.

Dad sinks down in the pew and has yet to remove his sunglasses. He stares straight ahead at the preacher, but I know he senses all the eyes on him.

My gaze scans the audience, row by row, until I spot the Bennett family. Savannah has her eyes on us, and she's staring with her mouth hanging open in complete fangirl mode. I grimace at her to show my discomfort at this very public family outing, and then continue searching. Up near the front, as always, I find him.

Blake appears to be paying attention for once, but with all the commotion, he gives a quick flick of his head to see what's going on. The perfectly trimmed hair around the nape of his neck has me envisioning running my hands up through the tousled locks, but I shake off the tremor of desire. I'm in *church*. Next to my *parents*.

And Blake is next to his mom, obviously. I knew she would be here, and now there will likely be a very uncomfortable encounter between her and my parents after the service. It's a ticking time bomb. Through the entire service, I am wiping beads of panicked sweat from my brow. Maybe I should have texted Blake and warned him, but so far, LeAnne hasn't looked back over her shoulder. It's such a politician move, keeping her focus so deliberate despite everything unfolding around her.

When the service ends, people get up a lot quicker than they usually do and become a tidal wave of bodies heading for the rear of the hall. I expected us Hardings to have slipped out first, but Dad thinks we'll be able to throw the paparazzi for a loop if we all split up and head for the van individually. So that's exactly what we do, except for Popeye and Sheri, who stick together. I weave myself deep into the thick of the churchgoers heading for the door, until someone grabs my arm.

"I know we're in church, but ..." Savannah blinks, starstruck, as she whispers, "*Oh my God!*" She points through the crowd to Dad's head, even more distinguishable because he's the only fool wearing sunglasses indoors. "He's right there! Like, in the flesh! That last pew? I've sat there before! I've sat on the same pew as him!"

"Savannah." I take her hand between both of mine and squeeze hard to snap her out of her obsessed rambling. "He's my dad, and I'm beyond angry at him right now, remember?"

"Oh! Of course," she says, biting a nail in embarrassment. "Such an *asshole*," she whispers, and I give her a little smile of approval. She's right, but I wouldn't have expected Savannah to swear at church.

"Better," I reply. "I gotta go. Warning: It's crazy out there."

Outside, no one makes a speedy getaway today. People are lingering and milling about, trying to pretend nothing is out of the ordinary, but there is far too much to talk about – the bizarre presence of paparazzi here in Fairview and the fact that Dad is somewhere in the crowd. The paps lined up on the edge of the lot ferociously scan the crowd for his face – and those of the rest of us Hardings,

I guess. A few people approach Dad, some to shake his hand, others clearly to try to engage him in conversation. I skim the crowd quickly.

Sheri's van is not far now. I squeeze my way through bodies toward it—

"Mila! You guys are stealing the show today, aren't you?"

"Blake," I gasp.

His hand touches my hip as he closes in on me. Of course, I knew he was here, and despite how badly I would love to hang around and mingle with him like our previous Sundays, I need to slip away unnoticed. I need to get to the van, like, *now*. But Blake's dazzling smile shines and all I can think is how *hot* he looks in his dress pants and shirt with a loose tie. I wish more than anything that I could just grab hold of him and escape somewhere just the two of us – no paps, no family drama, just me and him together.

"What's up with all the cameras?" he asks with a pointed nod over my shoulder. "Did they follow you here?"

"Sort of," I say, ducking down slightly. I'm not tall enough to be noticeable over the heads of everyone else, but this pink hair of mine isn't exactly subtle. "I need to leave. I'll call you—"

A firm hand latches onto my shoulder. "Mila, come on!"

The sound of Dad's voice directly behind me has me praying that a sinkhole will swallow me up right here and now. I clench my teeth and shut my eyes, horrified, and Blake retracts his hand from my hip.

"Oh. Hey, Mr. Harding," he says in a low, nervous voice. I peek through half-closed eyes and see him gawking at

Dad, unsure how to react at bumping into my celebrity father.

But Dad barely notices him. He grips my shoulder harder, steering me around, and I can sense panic radiating through his fingertips. He wants to get back into the relative safety of the van, and at this point, so do I. This is absolutely not the time to introduce my dad to Blake.

Just as Dad is guiding me away, another familiar voice, one that grates on me immensely, calls, "Blake!"

Everything suddenly feels like it's moving a million miles an hour, so many people and a hubbub of gossip and camera flashes and paparazzi lurking across the lot, and then LeAnne Avery comes into perfect focus.

She yanks Blake by his elbow, and I can't help but notice that there is something different about her. Her dark hair is as pin straight as always, her attire is immaculately formal, and her features are sharply intense. But not in the normal composed, strong way. No, for once, LeAnne has an edge of worry to her, her posture tense and anxious. "Let's go. Now," she orders.

Dad's hand goes slack on my shoulder. He turns around. "LeAnne?"

All the color drains from LeAnne's face as she almost flinches in response to her name. "Everett," she breathes, as if in defeat.

Blake looks at me. I look at Blake. We are wide-eyed, waiting.

If I had to guess how Dad and LeAnne would react to bumping into each other, I would have guessed there'd be aggressive yelling and resentful glares, given the way they have both spoken about each other, but really, they both look like they're facing the ghosts of their past.

"You need to leave," LeAnne hisses after staring for a second, her voice finding its strength. But I can hear that she's not angry – she's concerned. "You shouldn't be here."

"You and I," Dad says, gesturing at her, "need to talk." The shock of seeing LeAnne has quickly faded, and I'm guessing that these are his true feelings rising to the surface. With his eyes still shielded behind his sunglasses, he edges toward her and keeps his voice as low as possible to avoid being overheard. It's nearly a whisper, but the threat is clear: "But don't you *dare* talk to my daughter again."

"*Excuse me?*" LeAnne's entire demeanor shifts as she transforms back into the controlling, intimidating woman I know her as. She purses her lips, her sharp gaze full of spite. "How about *you* keep your daughter away from my son."

Dad tilts his head to look at me, his curiosity piqued. Then he glimpses Blake, landing where LeAnne's hand is still grabbing his elbow, and I become increasingly aware that the circle of churchgoers around us is tuned into this encounter. I imagine most Fairview locals know all about the history between their town's two most-famous alumni.

"Hey," Blake says, trying desperately to ease the thick wall of tension and doing his best to appear nonchalant, offering his hand to Dad with a pleasant smile that is nothing like his signature smirk. It's very … polite, and very fake. We might be in the midst of a deeply bizarre situation but, hey, first impressions matter. "I'm Blake."

LeAnne slaps his hand down and flashes him a look of betrayal. At this exact moment, a break in the crowd offers the paparazzi a direct line of sight to our awkward tableau.

"MAYOR AVERY, WHAT IS YOUR CONNECTION TO EVERETT HARDING?" is the one question that rings out above all others.

LeAnne, horrified, stares back at the jostling cameras as they click, click, click, snapping pictures of Dad and her in the same frame. She shields her face behind her hand, grabs Blake by his shirt sleeve, and immediately drags him away in the opposite direction. Her instincts are so fast that Blake and I don't even have the chance to catch each other's eye one last time to telepathically wish the other good luck for the shitstorm we're about to be swept up in. Again, I think how what I'd like more than anything right now would be to take off in Blake's truck with the music blasting to tune out everything but him and me.

Dad ducks his head low, places his hands on my shoulders from behind, and barrels me through the churchgoers toward Sheri's van at supersonic speed, while more pushy demands from the paps echo in our ears. Sheri, Popeye, and Mom have somehow made it back to the safety of a locked vehicle, but a door unlocks as we arrive and Dad throws it open and practically *lifts* me into the backseat.

He shoves me along into the middle and Mom urges Sheri to "Drive, drive, drive!" She thumps her hand against the back of the headrest as if to spur her on.

"Okay, okay, I'm not a horse!" Sheri grumbles as she floors the gas. The crowd of churchgoers jumps back, pretending not to gawk at us as Popeye clings to his seatbelt, his bible on his lap, and I get crushed between my parents. We all duck, instinctively – even Popeye – as the paparazzi sprint into position to snap some final pictures before we disappear out of sight.

But before I've had chance to let out a sigh of relief ...

"Mila," Dad snaps, whipping his sunglasses off. "Who the hell is Blake?"

The atmosphere changes immediately. The focus is no longer on the ongoing crackle of tension between Dad and Popeye; it has completely shifted to me. Dad glares at me with an expectant look, and Mom turns to me, her perfect brows pinched together questioningly. Sheri catches my eye in the rearview mirror and there's sympathy in her soft gaze – she was willing to keep my situation with Blake on the down low, but there's not much she can do to save me now.

"Blake is LeAnne's son." Popeye clears his throat and twists around in the passenger seat to look directly at Dad. He doesn't care to hide his disgruntled expression and I'm sure everyone at church will have noticed just how pissed he is at his family. "You remember she had a son, *right?* Before Mila came along."

Dad doesn't reply. His dark, tired eyes are burning straight through me. "Why did LeAnne ask me to keep you away from her son?"

"Wait. You spoke to LeAnne?" Mom asks in a sharp

voice, leaning forward to look past me to Dad. "Back there at church?"

"She attends every week," Popeye comments with unmistakable smugness in his voice now. "She stopped being a member of that other church down the street years ago. She and her boy have been coming to ours for a long time."

Mom's pale cheeks erupt into color, a vivid red. "And you didn't think to mention that to us, Wesley? Sheri? *Mila?*" She presses her lips firmly together and aims her attention at me, as though I'm the one who has betrayed her, like I purposely ambushed her and Dad with an apparition from their past. Why am I in the firing line here! Did she forget it was Dad who insisted we all go to church in the first place?

Yet again I am crushed between the two of them, and I tuck my shoulders in tight, my hands laced in my lap. I'm thinking of an answer that makes sense, but I don't have one. Luckily, Dad doesn't care, because all he wants is an answer to his own question: "Mila, are you friends with her son?"

Popeye and Sheri exchange a look of concern on my behalf. They know I've been hanging around with Blake for the summer, they warned me weeks ago that my parents wouldn't like it, and what have I done? Only gone and become Blake's girlfriend, that's what. But Popeye doesn't know that part. I glance forward at Sheri; she's chewing her lower lip as she drives, as though anticipating that our innocent little secret is about to be exposed.

I knew I'd have to tell my parents about Blake. I just didn't imagine I'd be doing it while trapped between them in the backseat of a speeding minivan weaving its way to the ranch.

"Umm," I say, twiddling my thumbs, "yes."

"Well, friendship cancelled," Mom declares, and I can't help but be surprised at the edge in her voice as I sense her body pull very subtly away from me. Over the past few days, she has been subdued and emotional, but now her expression is tough and unfamiliar. "You can't be friends with *LeAnne's son*."

"Why?" I angle toward her, crossing my arms in defiance. "Because you and Dad had an affair behind her back that neither of you were ever going to tell me about?" I challenge. "You expect me to stay away from Blake simply because you screwed up a long time ago."

I sense Mom and Dad flinch at my ruthless words, but Popeye shifts in his seat to glance back at me. "Good for you, Mila," he says. Maybe he didn't expect me to defend myself against my parents, but Mom and Dad have made so many of their own mistakes that it's, quite frankly, laughable that they believe they can reprimand me for my actions.

"Also," I add, emboldened by Popeye's approval, "we're more than *friends*. In fact, Blake is my boyfriend."

Dad actually laughs. A hard, cold laugh that slices through the stifling air in the van. "No," he says, vehemently shaking his head. "*No way*, Mila."

"She's sixteen, Everett," Sheri speaks up from the front.

She must be driving faster on the way home, because we're already barreling down the quiet country road toward the Harding Estate, outrunning the paps once more. "I don't think you can tell her who she can and can't date."

*Oh, Sheri. My favorite aunt in the whole entire world.*

"When you have kids of your own," Dad snaps back at her, "*then* you can tell me how to raise my daughter."

"Hey!" Popeye snarls. "Watch your step."

Dad immediately looks contrite and holds up his hands in apology, his tone softening. "Sorry, Sheri. That was out of line." I glance sideways at him. He sounds like he means it.

"Forget it," Sheri says in a resigned voice. "You're always out of line."

We pull up at the gate where a handful of reporters are still waiting, and all of us know it won't be long before the rest follow us back from church. Sheri floors it through the opening gate and all the way up the dirt track toward the house. She yanks her keys from the ignition, throws open her door, and strides off. Sheri is relatively composed most of the time; it's unlike her to be so visibly upset.

"Good job." Popeye tuts as he stiffly steps out of the van to follow her. "You ruin everything, Everett."

I want to help him, but I'm still rammed into the backseat with my parents on either side of me. The three of us watch as Popeye carefully climbs the porch steps, and then disappears out of sight.

"You shouldn't have said that," Mom says stonily, breaking the silence with a disappointed sigh. She glares at Dad. Maybe I'm in the clear, perhaps the subject has changed, but then Mom crosses her arms and stares me down in the most uncomfortable of ways. "So, is that who you were with yesterday? *Blake?*"

"Yes," I answer without missing a beat. My voice may be bold and my expression firm, but inside, my heart pounds in my chest and heat surges through my veins. I rarely ever talk back to my parents, but I refuse to let them decide who I can and can't hang around with. Not now, not ever again. "We went to Nashville with a few other friends. I'm squished. Can we get out of the van now?"

With a huff, Dad gets out first and I slip out after him. Mom walks around the vehicle to meet us, her and Dad lining up in front of me with very unpleasant expressions on their faces.

"Welcome home," Ruben calls from up on the porch, his tone sardonic as ever. "How was church then?"

Without turning around or even taking his fierce eyes off me, Dad loudly and clearly announces, "We learned that Mila is dating LeAnne Avery's son. But not for much longer."

"LeAnne Avery?" Ruben repeats, and then he recognizes the name. "*Oh*. The other woman from your early days." He descends the porch steps and joins my parents, his hands placed sternly on his hips. "Mila, if your father doesn't want you dating this boy, then you absolutely need to stop seeing him immediately. We are trying to contain a situation here, not create more complications. This *relationship* of yours clearly has disaster written all over it."

"Ruben, enough," Mom says, then, only *slightly* less strictly than Dad, "Mila, you can't date this kid. We have history with his family, and you aren't staying here forever. I'm sure you'll find a great guy back home one day. Don't be difficult about this."

I'm still trapped next to the car with my parents and the insufferable Ruben against me – the three of them poised in a line in front of me, all staring back with disapproval and intense pressure. Maybe they expect me to give in to their wishes like I most likely would have done a month ago, but one thing Blake has taught me is that you need to live your own life the way you want to, even if that means causing friction with your parents. It's a good lesson. LeAnne doesn't want Blake to pursue music, to be with me, but does that stop him? No.

"Dad. Mom. *Ruben*," I say, my gaze shifting to each of them one at a time. "I'm dating Blake, and the most I can promise you is that I won't bring him over here."

There's a horrible silence, then: "Your phone," Dad orders, holding out his hand.

"What?"

"Give me your phone."

A mixture of resentment and panic seizes me. "You're kidding, right? No way!"

Dad looks at me, completely unimpressed. "Mila, I have every right. I pay for your damn phone and whether you like it or not, I *do* get to have a say in your life. Now, hand it over!"

"Fine." I grab it from my skirt pocket, and slap it down

117

hard against Dad's palm, hoping it stings. "It's smashed, anyway, so you can buy me a new one. You owe me, after all. I threw it in anger because of *you*."

"Mila!" Mom exclaims, as if appalled by my behavior.

Dad rubs at his forehead in frustration, turning to his annoying shadow. "Ruben, you're to speak with Sheri and figure out how Mila left this place. Then make sure she can't do it again." He glares at me. "Mila, you aren't leaving this ranch until it's time for us all to go home."

I try not to laugh. When will he learn to stop throwing these blanket orders at me? "What, like, together?" I scoff. I'm forcing myself to find this hilarious only because if I don't, I fear my anger will explode until I burst into tears. "How optimistic of you, Dad, to believe everything will be okay when you are literally ruining my entire life!"

"Don't be so melodramatic," says Mom.

"But it's true! You – all of you – are controlling every move I make!" It's spilling out now, all the frustration, and with burning eyes I look at each of them individually. "Not allowed to spend the summer at home, not allowed to leave this ranch, not allowed to have my phone, not allowed to see the guy I like. Blake is the only person who understands the monumental mess that *you* made." My glower settles on Dad.

"Mila, this is for your own good," he tries, and by his side I see Ruben growing increasingly exasperated, waiting for the right moment to jump in.

"No," I snap back, "this is all because you're so goddamn SELFISH!"

Dad, Mom, and Ruben share a hopeless look as I break away from them, propelled by fury. It's like I am a total stranger to them, but how am I ever supposed to figure out who I really am if they're always controlling my life? Ruben might do most of the groundwork, but I'd be naive to believe my parents don't expect me to fall into their plans without question. The more I grow up and make my own decisions – and mistakes – the more they have me believing I'm stepping out of line.

But I'm not.

I'm just becoming Mila.

# 12

As it turns out, being grounded really *does* mean grounded.

Who knows quite what I've done to deserve this level of punishment, but for the past four days, I have had no phone access, no contact with the outside world, and absolutely no sanity whatsoever. And the only thing worse than being grounded at a family ranch? Being grounded at a family ranch where every member of that family loathes one another.

Mealtimes are unbearable. Any attempt at conversation is a disaster. The rift between Dad and Popeye is worse than ever, despite our attempt at a united front at church last week, and Mom and Dad are working through issues together behind closed doors. Ruben spends most of his time criticizing everything while keeping a close eye on my whereabouts and checking the security cameras more often than necessary, thanks to his bullying Sheri into telling him how I escaped the ranch.

It's truly been a miserable few days, and I haven't been afraid to sulk about it.

"I know you're angry, Mila," Dad said last night when he

caught me slamming my bedroom door too aggressively. "But things have the potential to get out of control right now. I know, I know – it's not fair. But it's not safe for you to be running around town with Blake with all the paparazzi swarming around."

Which only angered me even more and resulted in a second door slam.

"Sheri?" I say as I slide the heavy saddle off Fredo's back. "I want to ask you something, but I don't want to be ... well, rude."

Sheri and I are in the stables after our afternoon canter around the fields with some of the horses, a part of our new daily routine to get some fresh air away from the heavy weight of tension bearing down on us inside the house. She guides her horse back into his stall and clicks the wooden door shut.

"Nothing you say will ever be as rude as what comes out of Ruben's mouth," Sheri jokes with an easy smile. She grabs a bucket of straw and hooks it over her arm, turning solemn. "What would you like to ask me, Mila?"

"You were really upset on Sunday," I say, swallowing the lump in my throat. I can't look her in the eye out of fear that I'm about to offend her, so I carry my saddle down the length of the stables to the far wall where all the riding equipment is neatly stored. "Do you wish your life was different? With kids and stuff?" I pause and wait with my back still turned.

"Mila," Sheri breathes softly. She appears next to me, setting the iron bucket down with a *clink*. We glance at each other. "I'd have loved kids, but things haven't worked out that way. That doesn't mean I'm not happy."

"But is this what you wanted?" I press her. "Doing nearly all the work around the ranch and looking after Popeye by yourself?"

"No," Sheri admits, angling toward me, and I return the courtesy. I'm surprised to see that there's a hint of a smile returning to her face. "But there's still time to figure things out. I'm working on it. And what about you, honey? How's the situation with the *boyfriend*?"

My eyes roll in embarrassment, and I head back to Fredo, combing my fingers through his thick mane as he emits a soft neigh of satisfaction. "I haven't spoken to him since church. And that was only for two seconds. Dad took my phone, remember? So Blake is probably wondering why I'm not texting him back." I grimace into Fredo's glistening black eyes and pat his elegant neck.

I'd be lying to myself if I pretended Blake hasn't been on my mind every damn hour. With each day that passes without being able to check in with him, the more my anxiety builds. I probably have a thousand missed calls from him. So many unread texts. I even tried to sneak onto Sheri's desktop computer in the middle of the night to connect with Blake on social media. Hunt him down on Facebook, find his Instagram. But Ruben changed all my passwords, so I couldn't even gain access to my accounts in the first place. I don't know when my parents plan to stop holding me and my freedom hostage, so who knows how much longer I'll have to wait to see him again, let alone talk to him? I've been cut off from the outside world completely. I wish I hadn't warned him not to call the landline.

Sheri approaches and places a hand against Fredo's neck. She strokes him for a moment as she zones out, her gaze hovering just beyond my shoulder, like she's contemplating an important decision. Then her eyes shift to meet mine.

"Here," she says. "Call your boyfriend."

I stare at the cellphone she holds out for me as though it's something rare and unusual. "But I don't know his number."

"Hmm. Well, I have Patsy Bennett's number," Sheri says, forcing her phone into my hand with a mischievous smirk. "Start there. C'mon, Fredo."

As Sheri guides Fredo off to his stall to get him settled, I flip an empty bucket around and sit down, cradling the phone in my hands like a prized possession. The stables are a haven of privacy – neither Mom, Dad, nor Ruben have ventured out here in the time they've been at the ranch. Horses are too "country" for them, which is why Sheri and I escape out here so frequently. It's the only place on the ranch where we feel like we can breathe.

First, I call Patsy Bennett's cell number, and ask her to pass me over to her daughter, Savannah – who is very relieved to hear from me after days of radio silence – and who then very kindly provides me with Blake's number. I nervously drum my fingers against the side of the bucket as I listen to the phone ring.

"Hey. Blake Avery here," he answers.

The sound of his voice alone has me smiling already. "That's how you answer calls from strange numbers?"

"Mila?" Blake says in surprise as his polite, chirpy tone instantly switches back to his usual low huskiness. "I always hope when new numbers call it's someone finally calling me back about my requests for a gig at their bar. But no luck so far. Anyway, where the hell have you been? I've been calling for days."

"Hell is about right, but never mind that." Then I blurt, "I want to see you," but for once I don't feel embarrassed by my upfront honesty.

"I'll come meet you at the wall."

"No," I say. "I can't leave. And they know I climbed the wall last time."

"Then how are you getting out?"

My gaze wanders to Sheri, who is now grooming one of the other horses at the opposite end of the stables. She is already doing too much by letting me call Blake, but a phone call isn't going to cut it. I need to see him, to get out of this toxic ranch and enjoy a normal summer with him. It's going to mean trouble for me. A lot of trouble. But the very sound of his voice fills me with longing. I've had enough. "The same way as everyone else," I finally answer. "The gate."

Sheri knows this is a terrible idea, but surely as my aunt, it's her duty to let me make decisions that my parents would never agree to. She doesn't promise to lie for me or distract Ruben from the security cameras, but she does scrawl her number on the back of my hand in case of an emergency. She knows that my parents are the last people I'd want to call if things go wrong during my forbidden journey outside the ranch – again.

"Are you sure you can handle them on your own?" Sheri asks in a low voice, grimacing toward the gate in the distance. We can hear the faint buzz of voices, the press still here days later, though admittedly the crowd is dwindling as time passes and new headlines steal everyone's attention. That's the one thing about Hollywood you can always rely on: the spotlight is forever moving.

"Head down, lips sealed," I say, pretending to zip my lips shut.

"Okay. I'm off to grab a shower so that I can say I didn't witness you leave," says Sheri. She gives me a hug, brushes the straw off her jeans, then heads inside the house.

This is my moment. Blake should be here by now, my parents are wrapped up in another one of their intense conversations, Ruben is pacing the kitchen on a phone call, and Popeye is upstairs in his bedroom with his head in an old western novel – something he has resorted to doing every day as an excuse to stay clear of Dad and Ruben.

I race down the porch steps and sprint toward the gate, fully aware that my every move is being captured on the Harding Estate's security cameras, but by the time anyone notices, I'll be out of here. Pointing the remote at the gate, I unlock it and tip my sunglasses down over my eyes.

And then I brace, brace, brace.

"MILA, HOW IS YOUR RELATIONSHIP WITH YOUR FATHER?"

I hug my arms around myself, arrange my features into a nondescript expression and force my way through. Cameras flash and the shuttering of lenses drills into me.

"ARE YOUR PARENTS CONSIDERING A DIVORCE?"

Bodies close in around me. I can see Blake's truck idling down the street, waiting. My path gets blocked by a pap barging in front of me, video camera rolling.

"IS IT TRUE YOU'VE BEEN HERE IN FAIRVIEW FOR THE PAST MONTH?"

Obviously, the press has been prowling around town finding locals willing to dish some dirt. Nice. It's unsurprising, really. After all, it's basically public knowledge at this point. But I still don't give the media the satisfaction of having me confirm it.

"Excuse me," are the only words that leave my mouth. My tone is polite, but incredibly firm. There are other phrases I wouldn't mind saying, but I'd like to keep my dignity – and, anyway, Ruben would throttle me if I got caught on video telling the paps to, well, you know.

I only need to reach Blake's truck, and then he'll whisk me off to safety. Only twenty yards to go. So close. I just need this menace of a pap to get out of my way. I can barely take another step and I'm starting to feel claustrophobic, like the oxygen around me is being sucked into a vortex.

"Let her through!"

Through the tint of my sunglasses, I see Blake barge his way through the crowd, elbows pointed outward like weapons. He grasps my hand and pulls me with him, forcing his way forward with me close behind him, protected. I bury my face into the back of his T-shirt and trust his guidance, but someone else has grabbed my arm.

"MILA, DO YOU BELIEVE LAUREL PEYTON PURSUED YOUR FATHER?" a gruff voice yells into my face, so close to me his camera whacks my shoulder.

"Don't touch me!" I scream, freaking out and shaking my arm in an attempt to loosen his grip.

But his fingernails dig into my skin, making me flinch, and my heart skips a beat in panic and fear. The paparazzi usually respect some kind of boundaries, but after days of no activity at the gate, they are clearly growing desperate.

"HOW DO YOU FEEL ABOUT YOUR DAD CHEATING ON YOUR MOM?"

"She said *don't touch her*," Blake growls, and before I can even register what he's doing in time to stop him, his fist spirals through the air.

Blake slugs the guy square in the jaw with such force that he stumbles back a few steps and drops his equipment to the floor. Cameras flash at lightning speed, voices erupt, other photographers surge forward to steady their colleague. My mouth hangs open, stunned, as there's a break in the thickly packed crowd and Blake seizes the opening to haul us both out of here.

We hightail it to the truck, the engine already running, and with the screeching of tires and a plume of exhaust smoke trailing behind us, Blake stomps on the gas pedal. We tear down the country road so fast no one even tries to chase after us.

Terrified, I scramble to secure my seatbelt, one hand

pressed to the dashboard. "Why did you ... Why did you just do that?" I gasp.

It's the one major rule: never, ever, *ever* lay a hand on the paparazzi. But Blake isn't a part of Dad's crazy world. He acted to defend me. He doesn't know the rules.

Still, Blake has gone a shade paler, seemingly in shock at his own actions. He stares wide-eyed ahead at the road as he drives beyond the speed limit. "I don't even know. That guy was grabbing you, I didn't even think, and I just ... Damnit!" He smacks his hand against the steering wheel.

I push my sunglasses up into my hair and place my hand on Blake's thigh. He's panicking over the potentially severe consequences of his lack of temper control, and although I know he *should* be worried, I also want to put him at ease. After all, he *did* just punch a stranger in the face for me. "Honestly?" I say. "I'm just jealous I didn't do it myself."

Blake gives me a sidelong glance, his lips gradually curving into a smirk. "Well, you made it out of there. Now you're all mine."

"I've missed you these past few days," I admit softly. It's so nice to be back in his truck, next to him, watching the rays of sunlight dance across the dimples in his cheeks, and already the stress of my family drama is melting away. "I told my dad about you after church on Sunday, and he was *pissed*. He took my phone, so that's why I've been off the radar. But I'm so glad I'm with you now."

I don't know what possesses me to make such a bold move, especially considering it's a move I have never once made in my teenage life so far, but I grip Blake's thigh a little harder. Slide my hand a little higher.

Blake's quad muscle tenses beneath his jeans and his breath hitches in his throat. "Mila ... can you not do that?" he says with an audible gulp. "I mean, while I'm driving. Not never."

My hand creeps ever closer. I lean over the center console and gaze up at him. In a low whisper, I tease, "Blake ... are you *nervous?*"

And oh, how amazing it feels to have all the power for once. Even though I'm blushing too.

Blake laughs and grabs my hand from his thigh. He closes the short distance between us, pressing his lips quickly against mine, then interlocks our fingers as he focuses back on the road, easing off the gas pedal. "I hope you don't expect Nashville today," he says, "because some of the guys are over at my place, so I'm taking you home with me."

"Is your mom—?"

"Going to kill me? Probably," Blake finishes. "But yeah, she's at home. Don't worry about it, though. We don't care what our parents think, remember?"

"If I did," I say, "I wouldn't be here with you."

# 13

Parking in front of Blake's house fills me with a sense of unease. It was exactly a week ago when I arrived here, full of anticipation, all giddy and happy to hang out with him, but instead got hit with the shattering news of Dad's affair. I ran from this driveway with tears burning in my eyes.

LeAnne's Tesla is sparkling clean and there's a pressure washer and buckets of soapy water at the top of the drive. There's also an old beat-up truck parked out on the road, one I recognize from the tailgate party last month. I think it belongs to Blake's friend Barney.

"I'd just finished Mom's car when you called," says Blake. "I still need to wash mine."

We hop out of the truck, sneak in a quick kiss, and then head around into the backyard. Barney is sprawled out on a sun lounger on the patio, shirtless and trying to catch a tan while tossing a football in the air. Myles is here too, wrestling a rogue stick from Bailey's mouth. Bailey drops it the second he spots Blake and me coming through the gate.

"Hey, Bails!" I call, and I realize it's the first time I've shortened Bailey's name. Just like Blake does. "Come see me!"

Bailey barrels over to us, but I am no longer a new and thrilling stranger to him, so thankfully, he doesn't knock me to the ground again. He calmly nudges his nose into my leg while I scratch the back of his ears, and his fur is warm from the sun.

"*Myles*," Barney hisses. "There's a girl here now, so you better stop moaning about your genital warts. It's disgusting."

"Ha," Myles deadpans, firing Barney a look. "You better stop whining about your intact virginity before you embarrass yourself in front of Mila."

Blake rubs his hand over his face and lets out a sigh. He glances sideways at me as I stroke Bailey, an amused smile tugging at my lips. "Yeah, this is what it means to hang out with the guys," he says with a nervous laugh.

"You don't mind me intruding?" I ask. Blake seems to have dropped everything he was doing to rush across town to pick me up, and I wonder if he'll ever know how much I appreciate it. It feels nice to be put first.

"As long as you don't mind helping me clean the truck," Blake responds with a wink, and I think how I'd clean a whole parking lot of trucks if it meant hanging out with him.

"Hey, Mila," Barney calls, sitting up on his sun lounger. He pulls his shirt back on. "Everyone's been talking about how wild things are over at your place. You think you could sneak me in to get your dad's autograph? A couple hundred of them? And then I can flip them on eBay for some cash to buy new tires." He grins, cocky as ever.

"C'mon, Barney," Blake warns with a stern shake of his head. "Don't joke around. Things *are* wild over there."

"Yeah," I say, giving Bailey one final pat on the head. "Blake just hit a photographer."

Myles straightens his shoulders, and his jaw goes slack as he stares across the yard at us, flicking his mop of blond hair out of his eyes. "You did *what*?"

"He was being pushy. It was a fierce right hook, but ..." Blake groans. "I didn't mean to."

"What if they press charges?"

"Oh, Blake doesn't have to worry about that," Barney interrupts with a chuckle. "Mommy Mayor will make them disappear."

I steal a cautious glance at Blake. He clenches his jaw, takes a deep breath as though to keep himself calm, and then reaches for my hand and leads me back toward the gate.

"We'll be washing my truck," he calls over his shoulder. "Don't destroy anything. And watch Bails for me."

We head out onto the driveway together, and Blake leans into his truck, turns on the radio, and blasts the music at full volume. Country pop, duh. He slams the door shut and smiles at me as the opening melodic beat travels all the way down the street.

"Your neighbors don't mind?" I ask, leaning against the white picket fence.

"They're used to it," Blake says. He plunges his hand

into one of the buckets and retrieves a sponge, wringing the water out of it. He arches an eyebrow at me. "So do you wanna help me, or would you rather admire my truck-washing skills?"

Relaxing in the sun and watching the movement of Blake's muscles as he cleans his paintwork does seem like the perfect way to spend a chilled afternoon, but getting involved could be fun. Especially because ... "I've never, um, washed a car before."

Blake stops wringing out the sponge and lifts his head. "You've never washed a car before?"

"Hey, I'm sixteen, remember? I didn't have a permit *or* a car up until a couple months ago."

"And you haven't washed it yet?"

"Well." I pull my shoulders in, a little shamefaced. "A detailer comes around every week."

"Okay, Hollywood," Blake says, rolling his eyes. "Time to learn a key life skill like a normal person." He tosses the damp sponge straight at me, and I catch it just in time before it hits me in the face.

"Blake!" I whine, pouting.

Blake holds up his hands and innocently widens his eyes. "Accident, I swear."

"This better not become that whole cliché thing where you soak me with that," I warn, nodding at the hose hooked up to the outdoor faucet behind him.

"Nope."

Keeping my eyes suspiciously locked on him, I grab a bucket and move around to the rear of the truck. Moments later, he joins me with the other bucket and sponge, and with the music still blaring from inside the vehicle, we get to work.

"So how are things with your mom?" I ask, covering the tailgate with suds.

I sense Blake shrug next to me. "Bumping into your dad at church really threw her off, so she's been in the worst mood all week, but when have you ever seen her crack a smile?"

I shouldn't snicker, but I can't help it. I don't think I've *ever* seen LeAnne with a genuine smile on her face. I know I'm not exactly her favorite person, but it's kind of … sad, in a way, that she's always so stressed and uptight. Still, she has no right to take it out on others.

"Plus, I was the idiot who tried to discuss college with her the other night," Blake continues, "and as you can imagine, she didn't want to hear it."

"But you'll need to start working on your applications soon, right?"

"I've already started," he says. "I'm applying for an early decision for Vanderbilt, so my application needs to be in by November. I'm working on my personal essay just now, but there's a major problem in that my mom is refusing to sign the agreement when the time comes. I'm set on Music at Vanderbilt – seriously, it's the *only* plan I've ever had – but Mom is adamant that I need to have options, options that include non-creative degrees. I'm getting nowhere with her."

Blake sets to scrubbing the truck a bit more aggressively,

rubbing soapy circles into the paintwork at supersonic speed. I gently place my hand over his, forcing him to hold his sponge steady, and he exhales. We continue washing, easier now, moving our way around the truck.

"So you have three months to convince her?" I ask, quietly wondering to myself what kind of person holds their kid back from their dreams. But then I think of Dad and Popeye ...Popeye isn't a bad person. He loves Dad, but I think he was scared. Scared that his son wouldn't make it, that his dream wouldn't work out and he'd be left with no backup plan. The creative arts *are* a risky career path to take, and Dad *didn't* have a plan B. I don't think Blake does either.

"Yeah, but I've already been trying all year," Blake explains with a hopeless sigh of defeat, like he sees no option but to give up. "The acceptance rate for early-decision applicants is already as low as twenty percent, but do you know the rate for regular-decision applicants? Eight percent. *Eight!* If she doesn't sign it and I have to go down the regular decision route, then she's cutting my chances by over half." He dunks his sponge force-fully into the bucket, sending water droplets flying. "I'm already worried I won't get in, let alone with a damn eight percent chance."

"You'll get in," I tell him, pausing my scrubbing to turn toward him with the most reassuring smile I can muster. It's not fake. I've not heard these plans before, but I do believe in him. One hundred percent. "You're an amazing performer. I don't really know anything about music, but you definitely nail the guitar. You know that from the bonfires – everyone's transfixed by you. And when you sing ... *Your voice*."

I melt even now just thinking about his low, husky tones with his captivating Southern twang. I like Blake's voice when he talks, but I like it even more when he sings.

He turns to me, a prompting smirk on his face. "What *about* my voice?"

"It ..." I try, but any elegant words to describe the way Blake's voice makes me feel evade me. So I resort to my usual blushing instead. "I can't say it."

"Do I sing that bad?"

"No! Your voice ... It gives me butterflies." I close my eyes, embarrassed to have said it out loud, then find the courage to peek at him.

Blake flashes me a smug, cocky grin and steps closer, eyes smoldering. "Butterflies, huh?"

"Don't!" I groan playfully, and then before I can stop myself, I've slapped my wet sponge against his chest. The shy smile is instantly wiped from my face and I gasp, my free hand moving to cover my mouth in surprise at my lack of judgment. "Oops."

Blake parts his lips and stares down at the damp stain in the center of his T-shirt. He's quiet for a moment, unmoving, and then he abruptly springs into action. He throws his sponge to the ground and sprints over to the faucet, turning on the water and snatching the hose from the ground.

"No!" I shriek, diving behind the rear of the truck.

But any attempt to hide is futile. Blake catches me around the other side, points the hose in my direction, and fires a cold stream of water straight at me. I hurl my sponge at him as I run, zipping back and forth across the driveway as he chases me, soaking every inch of me. My hair sticks to my cheeks, my sneakers squelch, but in between my infuriatingly girly screams, I hear laughter. Blake's laughter, *my* laughter.

"Cliché, Blake! *Cliché!*" I yell, and then I grab a bucket of soapy water and throw it over him.

We both stop, drenched. The heart of a country song beats through the air.

Blake drops the hose and shakes his hair out, water spraying everywhere, and then runs his hands through the damp, tousled mess. I wring out the hem of my shirt.

"Hey, can you expect anything other than cliché from a Tennessee kid who dreams of being a country star?" Blake says, breathless.

His smile mirrors mine, and we gaze across at each other as water drips from our clothes, and I'm thinking that now is the perfect moment to close the gap between us and kiss him—

"Lacey," he says.

I blink.

Blake leans into his truck to shut off his music, then walks past me to the foot of the driveway. I turn to find him approaching Lacey, who seems to have appeared out of thin air. I notice a swanky Range Rover parked behind Barney's truck. When did *that* show up? Blake and I must have been more caught up in our water fight than I realized.

"Lace," Blake says again, and I can't help but recoil slightly at the familiarity between them. "What are you doing here?"

"What a welcome for your dinner guest," Lacey says with an eye roll. She's all cutesy, her hair curled at the ends and lips shining with gloss, her hands folded sweetly in front of her. "Your mom invited me! Didn't she tell you?"

"No," Blake admits, but then laughs. "Sorry, come on in. Avoid the ... puddles."

Lacey stealthily pivots around the pools of water on the drive – the hose is still running – and as she passes me, she looks me up and down. "Hey, Mila. Are you staying for dinner too?"

"I don't think so—" I glance, unsure, at Blake.

"Oh, Mila," another voice appears breezily.

I tear my eyes from Lacey and lock them on LeAnne as she emerges from the front door, which increases my irritation tenfold. Why does every good moment have to be ruined? First by Lacey, and now by LeAnne. She strides down the path from the porch, towels in her arms, which makes me wonder ... Has she been watching Blake and me? Did she know I was here the whole time?

"I would ask you to stay, Mila, but Lacey is a friend of the family, and we are having a long overdue get-together. I hope you understand," she says, then pulls Lacey into a one-armed hug and cheerfully exclaims, "Hey, honey!"

The whole scenario is making me feel small and

insignificant, especially when LeAnne won't even make eye contact with me. She pulls back from Lacey and throws a towel at Blake. "Get inside and shower before dinner. Dress nice since we have a guest tonight."

Blake flips the towel over his shoulder. "Yeah, great that you're here, Lacey. But, Mom ... Can't Mila stay too?"

"I'm sorry, there simply aren't enough chicken breasts to go around! Maybe another time," LeAnne replies with a fake smile. She angles toward me and holds out the other towel, her dark eyes full of an emotion I can't quite put my finger on. "Mila, dry yourself off. I called Sheri, and she's already on her way to get you."

"I'll go halves with mine," Blake tries, but LeAnne holds her hand up to silence him.

"No, Blake. Another time," she repeats.

But I know there won't be another time.

"Don't worry about it," I reassure Blake as I reluctantly take the towel from his mom. I swear Lacey displays a hint of a snooty smile as she stands there next to LeAnne, all lofty and righteous as though LeAnne's approval is the greatest gift in the world. To be honest, I can't think of anything worse than sitting down to dinner with them.

"Oh, and Blake," LeAnne adds nonchalantly as she moves to the faucet and shuts off the water, "send Myles and Barney on their way too. Dinner will be ready soon, and I've promised Lacey a nice evening with just the three of us. Like old times!"

Lacey beams, the perfect guest. I wish I wasn't standing here soaked to the bone and starting to shiver. "Thanks so much for having me over again!" she says. "My mom insists we are to return the favor next week. For dessert she's going to make her famous fudge pie just for you, Blake."

"It's my pleasure." LeAnne walks back to Lacey and squeezes her shoulder, a gesture that suggests she's already accepted her as her future daughter-in-law. "Blake, shower, please. Mila, would you mind waiting for your aunt on the porch?"

LeAnne guides Lacey toward the front door, two best buddies, but Blake lingers behind. As always whenever his mom is on the scene, he is disgruntled and fighting back rage by clenching his jaw tight. There's a flicker of guilt across his face.

"Mila—" he says.

"*Now*, Blake," LeAnne orders with a stern glance over her shoulder. "I need you to help in the kitchen!"

"*It's okay*," I mouth, giving Blake permission to accept defeat. This situation is beyond awkward, and it's best for all of us to finish it now.

"See you around, Mila!" Lacey calls from the porch with a pleasant wave, but her whole demeanor is triumphant. She may be a family friend, but having dinner with Blake and his mom is still personal and intimate. "Now, c'mon, Blake!"

"Coming, Lace," he says, then dips his shoulders and frowns at me apologetically. "*I'm sorry*," he mouths back.

Towel over his shoulder, water dripping from his hair, he follows after his mom and Lacey. The front door slams shut behind them and I hear the twisting of the lock, and all of a sudden, everything is quiet and still. From music and laughter and the splashing of soapy water to ... nothing. Nothing but this horrible empty feeling in my stomach.

# 14

Sheri's van never turns up, but Dad and Ruben's rental SUV does.

The all-blacked-out Ford Edge crawls down the street in search of the right address, so slow it's suspicious, and then it abruptly stops outside Blake's home. The thought of Sheri being called out to pick me up makes me feel guilty, but the idea that Dad or Ruben are here instead has me feeling nauseous. With the windows tinted and the sun reflecting brightly off the windshield, I can't tell which one of them is driving. And honestly? I'm not sure which one of them is the least awful option.

The engine shuts off, the door swings open, and out steps Ruben.

He's wearing dress pants and a white shirt, the sleeves neatly folded up to his elbows. It's the first time I've seen him look like his usual self while he's been here in Fairview. Ruben in his business attire is a force to be reckoned with.

He eyes me haughtily as he approaches. "You look like a drowned rat," he observes as he lifts his sunglasses. The smell of cigarettes follows him – he has been smoking way more here in Tennessee than he does back home. The stress must be getting to him.

"Thanks, Ruben. That's the vibe I was aiming for," I say, sarcasm unmissable in my voice. "Where's Sheri?"

"I thought I'd do her a favor and come get you myself," Ruben answers. He tilts his sunglasses back over his eyes and turns his chin toward Blake's house. "Besides, I'd like to meet LeAnne Avery in person."

It should be a relief that Ruben isn't blowing steam at me breaking his absurd rules *again*, but my body remains stiff with tension. Ruben wants to talk to LeAnne. Just great. Their contrasting personalities are a disastrous clash waiting to happen. This won't go down well.

"She's busy," I splutter.

Ruben waves his hand at me, as dismissive as ever. "Be quiet. Busy or not, we have an agreement to make."

He makes his way to the porch, fiddling with the Rolex on his wrist, and I dash after him. My hair is a damp, straggly mess and my jean shorts chafe against my thighs, but no matter how much I plead with Ruben to just take me home for another parental lecture about my newfound acts of teenage rebellion, he barely pays me any attention and goes ahead and rings the doorbell.

It feels like the longest wait in the world for someone to answer, but at last the door opens. The security latch is still on, and LeAnne glares sternly through the gap, looking thoroughly annoyed when she sees I still haven't left her property.

"Mayor Avery!" Ruben declares, holding his hands out

in a polite manner to show he means no harm. "How great that we can finally meet."

"And you are?" LeAnne asks in a voice so cold and disinterested I almost want to high-five her for it.

"Ruben Fisher."

LeAnne instantly slams the door shut, but Ruben blocks it with his foot.

"I only want a quick chat," he says, less amicable now, staring back at LeAnne through the gap in the door. "And I'm not leaving until you open up."

LeAnne huffs at his assumption of authority and reluctantly releases the latch, but she stands firm in the doorway, arms crossed over her chest in a threatening stance. I don't know whose side I'm on, but I do know it feels good to see someone else glare at Ruben the same way I do.

"So, you do remember me. Good," Ruben says, clearing his throat. He steps back from the door to give LeAnne some space, probably because she looks as though she's going to deck him any second.

"How could I forget? You're the class act who sent me that non-disclosure agreement ten years ago."

"Which you didn't sign," Ruben reminds her with a bitter smile. "Even so, it's very relevant right now, isn't it? Your history with Everett."

LeAnne looks at me, almost – and that's a very big *almost* – sympathetically. At this point, these conversations about Dad's affairs feel like they've become part of my daily life. I don't flinch anymore. I don't want to throw up. Instead I listen, soaking up as much information as I can.

"And?" LeAnne pressures him with a hard stare. "You're worried that now would be a good time for me to cash in? Mr. Fisher, you're mistaken. I have more self-respect than that."

"Naturally." Ruben almost grimaces. "I'm here simply to clarify that we're all on the same page," he adds, appearing physically relieved that the Mayor of Nashville isn't about to fire off that specific grenade. "I understand you and Everett got caught up at church last week."

LeAnne laughs, like she can't believe that, after all this time, she has Dad's manager on her porch wanting to discuss something that happened twenty years ago. I don't get the feeling that LeAnne is exactly over it, but if she hasn't told the gossip press by now all about how Everett Harding once cheated on her, then why would she do it now? LeAnne is a piece of work, sure, but she has proven that she's capable of keeping her word.

"You should leave, Mr. Fisher," she says. It's an order. "I have business to attend to, and dinner to prepare."

"Of course," Ruben demurs. "But before I go, if I could just remind you that Everett's financial ... gift ... is still very much on the table, subject to your signature. If you're amenable, our lawyers can get the paperwork over to you before the end of the day." Self-assured again, he inclines his head slightly to the side and subtly looks LeAnne up and down, like the Mayor of Nashville is no match for him. I can read the frustration in his eyes, but Ruben is a pro at acting fake to get what he wants. "I'm sure you'd appreciate the contribution toward your next mayoral campaign. I believe the election is next summer? If I'm not mistaken, now would be the perfect time to receive a generous funding boost."

Now LeAnne is really pissed. She swings the door wide open and steps outside, eyes darting to me. "Mila, if you could kindly remove this despicable man off my porch."

"Me?" I raise my eyebrows at her, relishing this peculiar power play. "Why would you think I can make Ruben do anything?" I ask. Instead, I hand her back the soggy towel, then prod my finger rudely into Ruben's bicep. "The mayor wants you to leave. And she wants me to leave too. So, let's go."

But still, no one moves and then I hear Blake call from inside the house. "Mom?" My ears prick up. "Mila, you're still here?"

LeAnne steps to the side and I see him as he hovers in the hall, fresh out of the shower, wearing basketball shorts and a T-shirt. He's towel-drying his hair while studying Ruben suspiciously. Despite the tense situation, I can't help but appreciate how hot he looks all damp and tousled – and then Lacey pops up behind him. She subtly places her hand on his forearm and peeks around, very obviously being nosy. I'm holding my breath, expecting Blake to move away from her, to shake off her touch, but he … doesn't. Her perfect hand with its cute manicure just stays there, almost stroking him.

What the hell?

"And *you* must be Blake!" Ruben says, sidestepping LeAnne to face him. "I'd very much like to talk to you too."

My gaze flashes to Ruben. "What are you doing?" I hiss, panicked, but he blanks me.

Blake moves forward to stop at the threshold, clearly untrusting of the stranger in front of him. And I think how he's right to have that hunch. But at least Lacey's not touching him anymore.

"I'm Ruben Fisher, Everett Harding's personal manager." Ruben introduces himself in a tone so smug that it gives me a serious case of embarrassment-by-association. I cringe.

"Ruben," Blake says flatly. "I've heard a lot about you." We exchange a look. All I've done this summer is complain about Ruben, so I bite my lip and try not to crack a smile.

"And I've been hearing a lot about *you*," Ruben counters.

"It's really time for you to leave," LeAnne tries, but Ruben actually holds up his hand to silence her, never taking his eyes off Blake.

"I'll get straight to the point," he announces, any pretense of camaraderie gone. "It's very simple. I'm here to tell you that you are not to see Mila again."

LeAnne, unsurprisingly, can't help but look rather pleased with this command of Ruben's. It may be the one thing she and him would ever agree on, but I'm sick of hearing what this man thinks I should do with my life. And so is Blake.

"You guys are funny," he says, glancing back and forth between his mom and Ruben. "We aren't going to stop seeing each other, so why don't you both stop wasting your breath?"

"Listen to me," Ruben almost growls. "You will not come near that ranch again, is that clear? Everett Harding does not want you in his family's lives. Which means that, no matter how much Mila here begs you, you do not, under any circumstances, go near her."

"Like I said, you're one funny guy." Blake narrows his eyes, folds his arms over his chest. "And, unfortunately, I'm not making any promises to you."

He steps forward into Ruben's face at the exact same moment Ruben does the same to him.

"Stop!" I gasp as they almost bump chests and stare each other out like a pair of trash-talking boxers.

"Yeah, *this* is professional, Mr. Fisher," Blake calmly scoffs into Ruben's face, unfazed and unthreatened. Ruben glowers even more fiercely, and I wonder how he thinks he's going to extricate himself from this absurd scene.

"Step away from my son," LeAnne instructs, equally as calm as Blake, like composure runs in their blood. "I'll make sure he stays clear of her. You won't find him over there again."

"Very well." Ruben moves back, taking a deep breath and rolling back his shoulders.

"Are you okay?" I hear Lacey whisper. Yet again, she has positioned herself far too close to Blake and her hand has sneakily found its way to his arm.

"He's fine," I snap.

Lacey looks at me over Blake's shoulder, and the warning glare I fire at her makes it pretty damn clear that she's crossing a line. Does she not know Blake and I are actually official now? If she does, then I can't help but think she's a bitch for making moves on a guy who has a girlfriend – and that girlfriend is standing right in front of her. But if she *doesn't*, then why hasn't Blake told her?

"Well, then!" Ruben brushes down his shirt as if removing an imaginary speck of dust, breaking the tension that's wrapped itself around us. "That's settled. I really must get Mila home now. Thank you, LeAnne, for letting Sheri know where she was."

LeAnne doesn't answer, just stares at him witheringly.

Meanwhile, Blake has taken the tiniest of steps away from Lacey and is now fixated on me.

Things are getting more and more difficult as our parents become increasingly desperate to keep us apart for their own selfish reasons, all to minimize the chances of them having to interact with one another. You'd think *they* were the teenagers.

But despite that, Blake's clear brown eyes aren't full of defeat, but rather a sense of defiance. He gives me a small nod. I return it with a smile. The meaning is clear: we'll still see each other.

Ruben clasps my shoulder and guides me down the porch steps, and I go willingly. We can't stand around on the Avery porch all day shooting daggers at each other, and these wet clothes are starting to get *really* uncomfortable. It may be eighty-five degrees in the sun, but a damp chill runs down my spine.

"Mila, get in the car," Ruben orders, propelling me toward the SUV.

I slide into the passenger seat, my clothes sticking to the leather upholstery, and sigh. All this trouble and I didn't even get the chance to kiss Blake properly. We might have, drenched on the driveway together, if Lacey hadn't turned up. It's a nice thought.

Ruben plugs the Harding Estate into the GPS and drives. No radio. Just silence.

"Why didn't LeAnne sign the non-disclosure agreement ten years ago?" I ask, breaking out of my dreams of Blake. "If she's never going to talk to the press anyway, then why wouldn't she just sign it?"

Ruben gives me a sidelong look and drums his fingers against the steering wheel. "I'm convinced she didn't sign it just to spite your father, even though he tried to apologize to her many years before."

"He did?"

"Apparently," Ruben says with a shrug, and for once he is actually talking to me in a normal tone without all the theatrics. "Back before I ever worked for him, back when he married your mom. So he says."

This is new information, valuable information, yet Ruben sounds doubtful. "You don't think he did?" I press him.

"If he really tried to make amends with her, then why is she still acting this *wronged* after all this time?"

"I suppose."

For once, Ruben makes sense. Surely LeAnne wouldn't still hold a grudge *this* intensely if Dad had given her a sincere apology like he said he did, so I guess that's another lie he's told – and kept on telling. I feel a bit ashamed of him, but I'm no longer surprised.

I look directly at Ruben as I change the subject. "So, are you going to yell at me for disappearing again, or did you just drive out here to threaten my boyfriend?"

Ruben laughs at my dramatics, lowers his visor against the glare of the sun. "Don't you worry, Mila, your parents are waiting for you."

# 15

The next morning, Popeye slaps the Fairview newspaper down on the breakfast table and jabs his finger at the front page. "What in the world is this?" he demands. "Can I not keep my family life private?"

And because we are all sitting at the table together again, Mom reaches across for the paper to check out for herself what exactly Popeye is annoyed about now. Probably another article from the local journalists about Dad still being in town. Popeye is growing sick of having the Harding Estate constantly in the spotlight.

"Mila!" Mom gasps.

I nearly spill my orange juice as I glance up. "What?" I say, innocent.

"You didn't tell us *this* happened!" she accuses, scooting the paper across to me and then pressing her index fingers to her temples.

"What is it, Marnie?" Dad asks. He screeches his chair back from the table and gets up, moving behind me to read over my shoulder.

The sinking feeling in the pit of my stomach is exactly

the same as I had all those months ago in my own kitchen back home when Ruben showed me those headlines about me getting drunk on champagne and throwing up at Dad's movie pre-screening event. Only this time, it feels worse, because I'm not the only person in the article.

Front and center is a photograph, one taken yesterday afternoon, right outside the front gate of the Harding Estate. In the midst of a blur of unfamiliar faces and a sea of cameras, there's Blake and me. I'm pressed close against his back, my pink hair blown across my face, my features arranged in shock as Blake's balled-up fist is suspended in midair. It's the precise moment before Blake punched a pap in the face.

The headline reads:

SON OF NASHVILLE MAYOR LEANNE AVERY
IN ALTERCATION WITH PAPARAZZI OUTSIDE
EVERETT HARDING'S FAMILY RANCH

Dad leans over me and snatches the newspaper to get a closer look. "Great, Mila! You picked a real winner!"

"The paps were being jerks!" I protest, knowing it's not much of a defense.

"They're always jerks, Mila!"

"Let me see," Ruben grunts. Smoothie bowl in hand, he grabs the paper from Dad and leans back against his chair to study it. "Huh. This town *really* is the sticks – even their front-page news articles don't flag up on my alerts."

Sheri catches my eye across the table, her expression ...

disappointed. I doubt she'd have let me call Blake from her phone yesterday if she'd known he would punch a pap in the face when picking me up. I admit, it doesn't make Blake look good, and this is a real dent in my efforts to win my parents around.

"The article mostly sweeps straight over you," Ruben states, looking at me over the top of the newspaper. "This isn't our problem. It's a problem for that *delightful* woman, LeAnne Avery." He sets the paper down and calmly takes a swig of his black coffee – after a week of staying at the ranch, Ruben has stopped complaining about standard filter coffee and learned to accept the offerings here.

"Mila," Mom says, clinking her glass against the table. "Can I talk to you upstairs?"

I nod, and we rise from the table together, leaving the kitchen as Popeye mumbles something about how Dad and Ruben should quit pestering LeAnne after all these years, and we stop halfway up the stairs.

Mom leans against the wooden banister and crosses her arms, studying me intensely. Her demeanor is a lot more relaxed than last night. She and Dad were waiting for me in the living room when Ruben brought me home, and they bawled me out for what felt like hours. Though they are still fighting – quietly, at least – as a couple, they seem to have no problems uniting as parents, and they are growing increasingly exasperated by my behavior.

"Mila, do you seriously like Blake," Mom says now, "or are you just trying to get back at your dad and me for not telling you how we really met? Because you have to understand that—"

"I really like him," I cut in.

Mom sighs at me, thinking quietly for a moment. "But we live two thousand miles away," she says. "C'mon, Mila. This can't be anything other than a little summer romance, so I don't know why you're creating all this havoc just to see some guy."

"And I don't know why you'd date someone who had a fiancée, yet you were the one who ended up marrying him," I fire back. "*That's* havoc." Mom flinches. I know I'm out of line, I *know* I'm being a bitch to my own mother, but she is in no position to give dating advice. "Blake and me … We'll figure something out. I'll come stay here during the holidays, visit one weekend every month. Maybe he could visit me back home some time."

"It's just … so awkward, Mila."

"Not for me it isn't. I really like him," I say again, harder this time so there is no doubt about it. "Can't you and Dad get over yourselves and let me be happy? Maybe call Ruben off while you're at it? Can't you just let me – for once – make a decision by myself?"

Mom's gaze softens. She reaches out to touch the ends of my pink hair, running her fingertips through the strands, and presses her lips together into a sad sort of smile. "When did my baby girl grow up?"

"It's a work in progress," I tell her, lightly reaching up to catch her fingers in my own. "I'm learning that you and Dad aren't perfect, and that means I don't have to be perfect either. Even though Ruben wants me to be."

"You're absolutely right," Mom agrees, and I blink back at her in surprise. I expected this conversation to end up like all of the others with her and Dad this past week, but she's actually listening to me this time. Am I getting through to her? Am I finally making my point clear? "But you're still grounded for sneaking out twice, so under no circumstances are you allowed to leave. Blake will have to wait."

"I know I can't leave." I smile sweetly. "But can I invite some friends *here*? Just Savannah and Tori."

"No."

"*Pleeeease*," I beg, pressing my hands together. "The atmosphere around here is mentally draining, Mom. You and Dad are pretty much locked in nonstop marriage counseling with Ruben at the helm, Popeye does nothing but grump and pick fights, and Sheri's the only sane person around. It's summer. I'm sixteen ... *Please* can I have some friends over?"

Mom mulls it over in her head. "I'd need to check with Sheri—"

"Sheri won't mind."

"*If* Sheri doesn't mind," Mom concedes with a scolding look, "then yes, maybe you can invite your friends over. Your *girl* friends. No boys. No Blake."

Thankfully, the cluster of paparazzi and reporters outside the ranch continues to decrease in size each day. Which means that Savannah and Tori don't have to battle their way through the craziness as they walk down from the Willowbank ranch. As I shield myself behind the ranch walls while the buzz of the gate rings out and it begins to open, I hear murmuring outside. It's the first time all week we've let guests onto the property, and a voice yells, "ARE YOU GUYS FRIENDS WITH MILA?"

Neither Savannah nor Tori reply – I've already asked them to maintain perfect poker faces – and a few seconds later, they slip through the gate and join me. Quickly, I point the remote and close it again.

"Hello, stranger!" Tori says, opening her arms to hug me. "We haven't seen you for *sooo* long!"

"Shhh," I whisper, then gesture toward the house as I briefly hug her. I pull her with me as I start to walk. "No talking until we're away from the gate."

"This is so exciting!" Savannah gushes, and when I look at her, I can't suppress my gentle laughter at today's choice of earrings. Movie clapperboards.

I lead them to the porch, and then I pause before I open the front door. Twisting around to look at the pair of them, I notice how nervous they have suddenly become. And that's saying a lot for Tori, who has the confidence of a lion.

"My mom wants to meet you guys," I tell them.

After Mom let me use the landline to call and invite my friends over, she was insistent that I had to introduce her to them. I don't tell Savannah and Tori that they are about to, essentially, be vetted.

"We're going … inside?" Savannah squeaks, like we're standing at the gates of the freaking White House.

"Should I take out my nose ring?" Tori asks.

"No. Now, c'mon."

Opening the front door, I gesture for Savannah and Tori to follow me inside. Popeye is at the hospital for a follow-up appointment to see if his doctors are any closer to discovering what's wrong with him, and of course, Sheri has accompanied him. Dad and Ruben are talking business upstairs, and Mom is waiting in the living room to meet my friends. I think she's just relieved to have something *normal* to focus on rather than mulling over where her relationship with Dad currently stands.

"Do you think he's touched this door handle?" I hear Savannah whisper behind me.

I glance back and Tori shakes her head pityingly at me. "Can we kick her out?"

Savannah blushes and holds her hands up, embarrassed to have let her fangirl persona slip out once again. If she knew Dad was in the room directly above her, I think she'd faint.

"Mom?" I say, peeking into the living room. Mom jumps up from the couch and I move into the room to join her. "You remember Savannah Bennett and Tori Coleman, right? We were all in grade school together."

Savannah and Tori shuffle in after me.

"Of course!" Mom says with her dazzling red carpet smile. "Hi, girls!"

"Hey, Mrs. Harding," says Tori. "Thanks for letting us come over to hang out."

Mom is supremely glamorous again. Her hair is in a

perfect blow-dry, her cheekbones are bronzed, and her lips are painted a cherry pink. She looks like her usual self – the stunning, talented makeup artist who works on some of the biggest movies in Hollywood, and the gracious, supportive wife of Everett Harding. It's nice to see her like this, even though it's all an act. I know my mom – and she simply can't wear sweatpants to meet guests.

"I'm glad Mila has been able to spend time with her old friends," she tells them. "Savannah, please tell your mom I said hi."

There's a little knock against the doorframe. "What's all this?"

Dad hovers outside the living room, his expression curious but with a hint of suspicion. He's never been a fan of strangers in his home. Looking at us all, his gaze rests on Mom.

Savannah is suddenly close to hyperventilating. I can hear her murmuring under her breath, "*Oh my God, oh my God, oh my God!*"

Mom moves toward Dad and touches his arm, and I find myself fighting hard not to roll my eyes. Even if they've mostly been civil with one another while they work through what Dad's affair means for their future, it's definitely not been to the point of affectionately touching one another. But I know what's going on here – they can't give anyone the impression that their marriage is on the rocks. And they obviously expect me to play my part too. I try not to let it get me too annoyed.

"Mila invited some friends over. They all went to

elementary school together. Isn't that sweet?" Mom tells Dad, and he raises an eyebrow at her as though wondering what part of me being grounded does she not understand.

"Hi. *Hi.* Mr. Harding. Everett," Savannah breathes.

"Savannah is a big fan," Tori says. "In case you haven't noticed."

Dad smiles, as dazzling and as enchanting as Mom – it's his professional smile. "Well, thank you, Savannah. So, you're a childhood friend of Mila's?"

Savannah nods, gulping.

"She can't speak right now," Tori answers on her behalf, stepping forward, as chill as ever, "but I know what she's dying to ask, so I'll ask for her: Could she maybe have a photo taken with you?"

"Tori!" Savannah hisses, mortified. "Shut up!"

But Dad lets out a polite, friendly laugh. He gets this all the time. "Sure," he says, and advances toward Savannah.

Hands shaking, she passes her phone to Tori. Dad is way taller than her, so he hunches forward and puts his arm around her shoulders. He grins, and for a moment it's easy to forget that he lives a life full of secrets and tension. Of lies. Like everyone else, I used to believe Dad was a movie star enjoying all the benefits of the high life without any particular problems.

As I watch him pose next to Savannah, putting her at her ease while Tori snaps a photo of the pair of them, my throat feels dry. I'm guilty of putting Dad on a pedestal too. *Of course* he's going to make his own mistakes in life.

Right now, they seem so much more shocking because I always expected him to be perfect.

"Well, you girls have fun," he says as he breaks away from a near-swooning Savannah. "Nice to meet you. But Mila has to stick around the ranch, so please don't encourage her to leave."

"We won't, sir," Savannah promises, and Tori scoffs. I'm also trying not to laugh. Savannah is adorable, an over-excited puppy desperate for approval, just like Bailey. It's hard not to love her.

"Marnie, I need you for a sec, please," Dad says. He slips his hand into Mom's and together they leave the room as though they're a flawless, happy couple.

"I'm totally trembling!" Savannah says once my parents are out of earshot. She holds up her hands to show the tremor in them, and then she grabs her phone back from Tori to check out the photo of Dad and her.

Tori gives me a strange look. "So, what's going on with your parents? They seem … together."

"I'm as confused as you are," I say with a sigh. "I know they're working on stuff, and they keep talking about when we all go back home, so … I guess things might be okay again at some point, but I've stopped speculating for now."

"Oh, I forgot about that," Savannah admits, tucking her phone away as she calms down and tunes into the conversation.

"Forgot about what?"

"That you'll eventually go home," she says, and the way she seems genuinely disheartened by this realization tugs at my heart. I'm pretty sure Savannah and I would have grown up as best friends all through middle school and high school if I hadn't moved away. "What about Blake?"

I sit down on the couch and throw myself back against the cushions, sighing. "We haven't really talked about it yet, but I'm sure we can make it work. I'll just visit more often, so I'll get to see you guys too!"

"No! You can't leave," Tori protests, dramatically throwing her hands up in the air as she adds, "Lacey Dixon will swoop in and steal your man the second you're out of those gates and across the state border, girl."

"She's already trying," I grumble. "In plain sight." I pick at a frayed edge on one of the cushions and glance at Savannah. "His mom seems to be a real advocate for her."

Savannah sighs and settles on the couch opposite. "Yeah, my aunt LeAnne has always loved Lacey. After all, she's the perfect girl-next-door. Plus, her parents are close family friends, so she wasn't impressed when Blake dumped Lacey over Christmas break."

I sit up so fast it actually hurts my abs. "Wait. They *dated*? I thought you guys said he wasn't interested in her."

Tori shoots Savannah daggers. "Nice one, Savannah."

It's back again, that awful feeling of my heart sinking into the pit of my stomach. Back at the bonfire a few weeks ago when I first laid eyes on Lacey, Tori gave me the impression that Lacey was interested in Blake but not vice versa, but if they actually *dated* ... And yet Blake always tells me they're just friends. Now Lacey's discreet little advances toward Blake seem so much more malicious. And he calls her by a nickname ... *Lace* ... which feels a whole lot more significant than it did before.

"Oops," Savannah squeaks, chewing her lip. "But it is kinda better that you know, Mila. Honestly, it's no big deal. They were only official for a month or two, and I'm pretty sure Blake just gave in to her after she pursued him the whole year."

"*Ooookay*, change of subject!" Tori announces. She claps her hands together and positions herself in the center of the living room, her gaze moving rapidly back and forth between Savannah and me. "Did you guys see the news this morning? Mila, you didn't tell us Blake practiced his boxing skills on a photographer."

"Because I still haven't gotten my phone back," I groan, tossing the cushion I was picking at to the side. The headline from this morning flashes through my mind, accompanied by that unflattering picture of Blake turning aggressive. "But yeah. His mom won't be pleased about that."

I'm worried about him. We haven't talked since Ruben picked me up from his house yesterday, but I imagine there has been a big fallout in the Avery home this morning. LeAnne is strict even if Blake is on his best behavior, so this stunt of his – justified or not – won't go down well. But I'm also wondering how the dinner with Lacey went. When was he going to mention to me that she's his ex?

"Myles talked to Blake an hour ago," Savannah says. "He's dropping Bailey off at our place soon and then going out of town."

My body stiffens. "He's leaving?"

"Yeah. He's going to Memphis."

"*Memphis?*" I repeat, jumping up from the couch. Goddamn, why did my dad have to confiscate my phone? I need to talk with Blake now more than ever. "For how long?"

Savannah shrugs, unsure and a little uneasy.

"You know what would be romantic?" Tori muses, gazing dreamily up at the ceiling. "If you went with him."

I stare at her. "To Memphis?"

"Well, yeah. Why not? Both of you are in trouble with your parents, so why not take off together until things cool down?"

"I'm in trouble with my parents *because* I keep taking off with Blake," I point out, but her idea fizzes inside of me, a playful suggestion that grows bigger and bigger. "I snuck out with you guys to go to Nashville last weekend, and then I snuck out *again* yesterday to see him."

Tori smirks. "So, what's a third time?"

"Tori, you are the *worst* influence," Savannah tuts, shaking her head disapprovingly as her earrings dangle wildly.

"I'd rather be a bad influence than an Everett Harding superfan," Tori fires back, grabbing one of the cushions next to me and flinging it across the living room at her. "When you post that photo on Instagram later, please mention in the caption that you were a stuttering mess."

Savannah launches the cushion back at her, but Tori bats it away and then dives toward Savannah on the couch, wrestling with her. The two of them are in fits of giggles as they play-fight, poking each other in the ribs and trying to shove the other to the floor.

But I'm not part of this easy friendship. My mind is all out of focus, foggy but with the idea of Memphis sparking little fires of possibility. I stare at a smudge on the TV screen as my head thumps with thoughts of Blake. I'm already in everyone's bad books. There's not much more my parents can do to punish me at this point, so Tori's joking suggestion poses a valid question. What *is* a third time in the grand scheme of things? How much worse can it get?

"Guys," I snap, and Savannah and Tori abruptly pause their gentle wrestling to look at me. "I need to borrow one of your phones."

# 16

"They're going to kill me this time for sure," I murmur.

Wedged in between Savannah and Tori, I sprint down the dirt track toward the gate. We have to move quickly and escape out to the other side of the gate before my parents or Ruben discover I've left the house. There's a small duffel bag over my shoulder that I threw together in five minutes flat, because Blake plans to spend the night in Memphis. So not only am I sneaking out, but I may actually be running away, at least for twenty-four hours. I've left a note promising that I will, indeed, come back.

"I *hate* when they make us run track at school,"Tori says, wiping sweat from her brow. "I can't believe I'm doing this for you, Mila."

"You hate everything at school, Tori," Savannah points out.

We stop just in front of the gate to inhale a gulp of fresh air before the real cardio workout begins. We need to race to the Willowbank ranch at full speed, not only to avoid a barrage of questions from the press outside, but also because Blake is waiting for me there. Myles is looking after Bailey for the night, because there's no way LeAnne would ever take sole responsibility for a dog she never wanted Blake to get in the first place.

"Ready?" I whisper, but I don't wait for the thumbs-up. I point my remote at the gate and open it. "Go!"

And like a bat out of hell, I take off running, my strides long. Savannah is close on my heels, though Tori lags behind a little, panting and muttering, "Why would anyone do this for *fun*?"

The paparazzi scrambles to grab their cameras and a few of them chase us, but they quickly realize a boring picture of the sweaty back of Everett Harding's daughter isn't what they're holding out for, so they soon back off. But we don't stop running, just in case.

"I see Blake's truck!" Savannah pants as she sprints alongside me, pointing a shaky arm out toward her ranch as we approach.

I squint through the tinted lenses of my sunglasses. Blake's truck *is* parked outside Savannah's home, ready to make a getaway. Even though my energy is running out, I find my legs moving faster, leaving even Savannah in the dust.

"Thanks, guys!" I call back to my friends as I slow into a jog up the dirt track, heading through the Bennett property toward the truck. "I'll use Blake's phone to keep in touch!"

"You owe me! BIG TIME!" Tori yells back, doubling over with her hands on her knees, gasping for air like she's just run a world-record marathon.

"Have fun!" Savannah says with an enthusiastic wave.

"Make it worth the trouble you guys are going to be in when you get back!"

Breathless, I jump into the truck, place my duffel bag down at my feet, and turn to Blake with a smirk so mischievous it could compete with his. "Hey, boyfriend. You thought you'd go to Memphis without me, huh?"

Blake leans over and kisses me, one hand cupping my jaw and his lips forming a soft smile, a promise against mine. He was more than happy when I called and asked to join him. This might be the craziest thing I've ever done, but I think I like the feel of crazy.

It's a straightforward, three-hour drive down the highway to Memphis from Fairview. We have the windows cracked open and the breeze ruffles my hair, but it's refreshing and I stick my arm out every once in a while, feeling the wind whistle through my fingers. As always, there is a constant stream of music that Blake can't help but sing along to.

"Wait, can I hear you *humming* the lyrics?" Blake asks, cutting off the volume to catch me in the act.

I immediately stop my bumbling attempt at singing. "You play this song all the time! I know the chorus by now."

"Hit it then," he says, blasting the volume back up as the song enters its chorus for the final time.

"No! I can't sing."

Blake turns his head to pout his lips sweetly at me. "C'mon, it's just me. I bet you're not that bad."

Rolling my eyes, I begin to sing as eloquently as possible,

trying to pull off a low Southern tone. I get a mere few seconds in when Blake cuts to the next song on his playlist.

"Never mind," he says. "You do suck."

I gasp and whack his arm, mortified, then we both burst into laughter. We can't *all* be performers like him – some of us aren't blessed with perfect vocal cords. He cranks up the music as if to drown out any further attempts at singing from me, but I only raise my voice, belting out the now-familiar lyrics. Blake competes against me, singing so loud he's practically yelling at the top of his lungs, and then as the song comes to an end, we catch each other's eye and collapse into laughter.

"So, what are we doing?" I ask once we've settled down. "Where are we going?"

Blake leaves the highway and I gaze out the open window as Memphis slowly begins to unravel around us. The buildings around us seem a lot older, more historic, and there's not much in the way of glamorous modernization. I've never been to Memphis before – or maybe I have as a kid, but I can't remember.

Blake gives me a sideways glance of disapproval and shakes his head. "You really are bad at this whole Tennessee thing. We're going to Beale Street. Where else?"

It may be Friday, but the streets are fairly quiet as it's still early – just after five – so the night hasn't quite started yet. We continue downtown and the volume of pedestrians begins to multiply on the sidewalks once we start passing hotels and restaurants, arriving at the heart of the city. We drive under a large, arched sign that reads "BEALE STREET" in electric blue letters, then Blake turns into a parking lot.

We've been in the truck for a few hours, so I'm relieved to get out and stretch my legs. It's a sizzling hot summer evening here in Memphis, with only a slight breeze to cool things down, and like in Nashville, already I can hear the alternate clashing and harmonizing of different music from nearby bars and am, of course, enveloped in the smell of freshly cooked food. I glance back to the Beale Street sign and realize the reverse side reads "HOME OF THE BLUES." People stream underneath it, headed in one direction to where all the action begins.

"So, was this always your plan?" I ask Blake as he locks the truck. "Drive all the way to Memphis to ... listen to music? Why didn't you just go to Nashville?"

"I need some breathing space," Blake answers. "Mom's staying in the city tonight, but I really needed to put a few hundred miles between us. I'm so glad you're with me," he whispers and leans in for a kiss.

I meet his lips and mirror his smile while I slip my hand into his, interlocking our fingers, and we follow the crowd.

Beale Street, at first glance, seems like an older, more run-down version of Nashville's Broadway. It's more rustic and perhaps in need of rejuvenation, but in an old-school sort of way. The low brick stone buildings are brought to life by colorful store fronts and funky signs that jut out over the pedestrianized street, which I imagine will electrify the area with bold neon colors once the sun sets and night rolls in.

I don't imagine blues music being that popular among

younger generations, so it's no surprise to see that Beale Street attracts an older crowd that's a bit rough around the edges. The street is kind of seedy with a definite party vibe, and between the panhandlers and the police presence, I find myself gravitating closer against Blake.

"Are you sure this is safe?" I whisper, hugging his bicep.

Blake tilts his chin down to look at me, holding back laughter at my tight grip on him. "We're going for food, Mila. We'll be out of here before the real nightlife starts. Relax!"

"I didn't know you liked blues music," I think out loud, gazing at all the different bars with their live music spilling out onto the street.

"I don't. That's why I'm not taking you to a blues bar," Blake says, his stride confident as he continues to lead the way. "I'm taking you to the Tin Roof! They host country performers there."

"Have you been before?"

"Yeah. Me and Lacey found it last year," he tells me, casually. "Best place on Beale Street!"

Ugh. *Lacey* ... the apparent ex-girlfriend. Obviously no thanks to Blake for that knowledge.

My stomach knots and I bite down hard on my lip to suppress the urge to ask him about her.

*Don't say anything, don't say anything, don't say anything.*

"There it is!" Blake announces, pointing ahead.

And I'm not even surprised that this is Blake's venue of choice. The Tin Roof is basically the Memphis version of Honky Tonk Central back in Nashville. They are both right on the corner of the block with wide-open windows on the second floor, showing off the irresistible atmosphere that waits inside.

"You are *so* predictable," I say. "But in a good way." I squeeze his arm a little tighter, pushing all thoughts of Lacey away.

As it's still early, there isn't a line yet and there's no one manning the door, so Blake and I go straight through. Excitement fizzes in my stomach, the same way it did when Blake took me to Honky Tonk Central for the first time. Bars like these in cities so far from home are just so out of my world. All those swanky, five-star restaurants with perfectly aligned silverware and suited waiters that my parents always choose to dine at seem so stale and stuffy in comparison. The finer things in life aren't necessarily the most fun.

The Tin Roof is, honestly, a bit of a dive bar. There are old bicycles hanging from the rafters, multicolored Christmas lights wired all around the ceiling, Americana memorabilia all over the walls. There's a guy playing keyboard up on a rickety stage in the corner, and people are crowded around the bar, already tipsy and in high spirits as they order their next round. The second floor is a mezzanine level with balconies that overlook the stage below.

"Here," Blake says, pulling me across the cracked concrete floor to an empty table with red and blue retro-leather diner chairs. He pulls one out for me. "Let's sit down, Miss Mila, and enjoy a taste of Memphis freedom."

I settle into the chair and feel the coolness of the AC above us. Despite all the interesting, quirky things to observe around me, my attention remains only on Blake as he sits opposite me. He has his sunglasses pushed up into his hair, his forehead creased in concentration as he skims over the menu, and under the colored lights, he looks as gorgeous as ever. When he notices my stare boring into him, he glances at me over the top of the menu with a perplexed look.

"What? You don't like it here?" he asks.

I laugh and reach across the table to touch his hand, mindlessly examining his calloused fingertips. "I was just thinking how hot you looked."

Blake lowers the menu and arches a brow, a tantalizing smirk toying at his mouth. "Seriously, Mila, *where* has this confidence come from? You would have never said that out loud a few weeks ago."

"I've learned something about myself," I say. Letting go of his hand, I slide off my chair and move around the table. I step behind him and lean down to wrap my arms around him, then with my lips hovering dangerously close to his ear, I whisper, "I'm only shy at first."

I give his jaw a little kiss and then release him, floating back to my seat feeling like an absolute queen. My cheeks burn and my pulse races, but a sense of pride falls over me, because Mila Harding is making *moves*. Blake stares back across the table at me open-mouthed, then gulps and buries his head back into the menu.

"I'm gonna get the, uh, wings," he forces out.

My smile widens into an amused grin. I could get used to this, this feeling of power at being able to make Blake

– cool, self-assured Blake Avery – nervous. Oh, how the tables have turned. It fuels my confidence.

I reach over and lower the menu to reveal Blake's blushing expression. "I was thinking this morning ...I'll be going home eventually. What do you think will happen?"

Blake's features rearrange themselves into a more serious expression. "To us?"

"Yeah."

Before Blake can voice his thoughts on the matter, we are interrupted by our waitress. Blake orders his wings with spicy Nashville hot sauce, and I flick through the menu at lightning speed and opt for some classic chicken tenders with simple BBQ sauce. Blake tuts in disapproval at my basic choices as soon as the waitress has left to put in the order.

"Leave me alone," I say, with a mock growl. "Can't a girl just eat some tenders without being judged?"

"Your palate kind of sucks. Aren't you used to, like, French cuisine and exotic dishes with names that no one can pronounce?"

"Exactly. I never get to eat this stuff, so let me take advantage." I point my knife threateningly at him. "You haven't made an assumption like that in a while. Please don't start again."

Blake holds up his hands. "My bad, Hollywood."

I glare playfully as I brandish the knife closer to him, and then he breaks out into his hearty laughter that instantly melts away any irritation. I place the knife down, then lean back into my chair and frown.

"But seriously, Blake," I say. "How are we going to make things work?"

"Do we even have to think about it?" he asks with a hint of aggravation in his tone, which takes me aback. "Can't we just have fun *right now*?"

The keyboard player finishes up his set to a round of applause from the Tin Roof's clientele, silencing Blake and me for a few moments until the commotion dies down. The waitress drops by our table with our drinks.

"Of course we have to think about it," I say quietly, dropping my eyes to my lap.

Blake *does* want this to work out, right? I know it's still very, very early in our relationship, but what's even the point of being together otherwise? I'm dating Blake with every intention to keep seeing him, but it suddenly dawns on me, right here in this dive bar, that maybe Blake only sees this as a summer fling. Maybe he doesn't want to talk about our plans for the future because he doesn't care if we even have one.

"Yeah, but …our options are pretty limited." He looks at me with a mix of uncertainty and exasperation. "You live so far away, so I guess we'll just have to try and visit each other as much as we can. Can't we just focus on enjoying tonight and work this out later? It bums me out thinking about it."

"I don't like thinking about it either," I agree, "but we kinda need to have a plan."

"Our plan is to have fun right now," he shoots back impatiently.

"Okay," I say in a mixture of both defeat and relief. I guess we'll have to pick up this conversation another time, but will there *ever* be a right time to discuss us being apart?

One of the waitresses hops up onto the stage, grabbing hold of the mic. "Who's ready for some country?" she yells, her voice vibrating through the speakers, and the crowd *whoops* and thumps the tables in response. "Here to get your feet tapping for the next hour, give it up for Jason Cox!"

Suddenly, there's a clatter as Blake knocks over his drink. The glass rolls across the table, his soda spilling everywhere and ice cubes crashing to the floor.

"Whoa," I exclaim, scooting my chair back from the table to avoid the splash zone. I begin reaching for napkins and force myself to joke, "You can't be *this* enthusiastic about country music!"

But Blake doesn't laugh. In fact, I stop blotting the table dry when I notice he is frozen stiff in his chair, eyes wide and locked on the stage. It's an expression I've never once seen on him before, like he's shocked to his core.

"Blake?" I nudge him with my elbow, gently.

"That guy—" he rasps, diverting his panicked eyes back to me.

"Which guy?" I prompt. "Where?"

"The one walking out onto the stage." He nods over at a tall guy, casually waving to the crowd. "That guy is my dad."

# 17

Jason Cox tosses his guitar strap over his shoulder and connects the amp cable. "How are y'all feeling tonight, Memphis? Let's get rocking!"

With an electrifying opening strum, he breaks straight into the deafening tune of a country rock song, his hands dancing over the fretboard. His long messy hair whips around his face from beneath a cowboy hat, and his style is seriously vintage – red flannel shirt paired with faded, torn jeans and clunky Timberlands.

"That's your *dad*?" I tear my eyes away from the performer up on stage and back to Blake, who seems locked in a trance. "But I thought you said your dad gave up on music."

Blake doesn't even blink. "He did."

I grab another stash of napkins and hastily dry the table, then duck to the floor to scoop up the handfuls of ice that Blake has spilled. It's all I can do to keep my hands busy as I wrap my head around the fact that Blake's dad is in this random bar in Memphis playing music again after he had, apparently, long quit.

A waitress rushes over with a mop bucket to take over

cleaning the floor while I apologize profusely on Blake's behalf. When she leaves to fetch another drink, I sit back down and watch Blake watch his dad.

Like Blake, Jason is a country musician, armed with an acoustic guitar and a husky Southern drawl that melts hearts – only it seems Jason prefers rock, while Blake leans more toward pop. And they both sing with their eyes closed.

Jason's tone is deeper, edgier as he belts out the lyrics into the standing mic, losing himself in the feel of his guitar beneath his hands, one foot rhythmically thumping the ground. Under the intense spotlight, I notice his face break out into a sweat.

"Luke Bryan," Blake says in a quiet voice, barely audible over the music booming through the speakers above us.

"What?"

"'Move' by Luke Bryan. That's the song he's covering," he explains. His eyes never leave the stage, and his expression is still so unfamiliar, so eerily unmoving and full of consternation.

I realize then that I know nothing about his dad. I know Blake has an old, treasured guitar that belonged to him once, and I remember Blake mentioning that he'd moved to Memphis with his side chick, but the mostly resounding silence regarding his dad never had me pushing for more. "Do you ever talk to him?" I ask, leaning right into him so he can hear me.

"Every once in a while." He thanks the waitress as she returns with his drink, and he instantly chugs several mouthfuls of soda, like his throat has turned to sandpaper. He sets the glass back down with a *clink* and relaxes his shoulders. "I haven't visited since last year, and we haven't talked in several months. He has a drinking problem, and he hasn't … he hasn't played in years. Not since he left."

We both glance back at the stage at the same time. Jason hasn't missed a chord, screwed up any lyrics, or even made a single out-of-beat foot tap. He is very in control of his performance with a sincere smile spread across his face. He doesn't look much like a deadbeat alcoholic to me.

I avert my gaze back to Blake. "Are you guys close?"

"No," Blake answers honestly. "But we get along, and I always looked up to him as my musical inspiration growing up. He's just not much of a father." His eyes cloud with disappointment and he glances away.

Before I can even try to sympathize with him, a hand touches my shoulder and I jolt in surprise. An older guy with a jawline laced with stubble and the bitter scent of beer on his breath leans in uncomfortably close to me and says, "Hey, you look like the kid of that guy in the news. That ain't you, is it? Something Harding."

"Sorry, my name is Savannah Bennett," I lie smoothly, and the guy scratches his head and saunters away.

When I turn back to Blake, his features have transformed into their usual arrangement – raised eyebrow, dimpled cheeks, and a smirk that sends shock waves through my body.

"First name that popped into my head," I tell him, then wrap my arms sheepishly around myself. I nod to the stage.

"Are you going to let him know you're here, or should we slip out as soon as we've eaten?"

"I'll talk to him once he's finished his set. Don't wanna throw him off his game." Blake mocks ducking down low and shielding his face with his hand, then angles his chair so that he isn't facing the stage directly. It brings him closer to me.

"Hi, Blake," I say.

"Hi, Mila."

"Are you sure you're okay?"

"Yeah. I mean, my dad rocking out again was the last thing I imagined seeing tonight, but it's kind of … great," he says, glancing over his shoulder. "Watching him perform again."

I rest my head against his shoulder, the two of us intimately close together, and we listen to Jason smash out song after song with some intervening joking with the crowd.

After a while, I glance up at Blake. "You seem happy to see him, but I thought … Well, I guess I assumed by the way you talked about him at the bonfire that you didn't like him all that much."

Blake tucks an arm around me and leans his jaw against the top of my head, the pair of us still huddled close. "It's complicated. He's always been my musical inspiration, but I also thought he was a coward for giving it all up just because Mom thought he needed to grow up."

"She didn't support him?"

"Does that honestly still surprise you at this point?"

"No," I admit. "Is that why he left?"

"Yup," says Blake. "Quit his music, walked out and left me his guitar when I was twelve, moved here to Memphis, and acted even more carefree than he did before. He wasn't really cut out to be a father. He was always boozed up whenever I saw him. Not, like, flat-out drunk or anything. But he always had a buzz on, kind of drifting his way through life. I'm just relieved he seems to have some motivation again."

"I just can't see him with your mom. They're—"

"Polar opposites, right?" Blake finishes, and I nod shyly against him. I don't know if he would prefer not to talk about this stuff, but I figure he doesn't mind when he continues: "I remember my mom was fun for a while when I was younger. Dad encouraged her to let her hair down, I think that's why she liked him, but then she got more involved with her work for the city council and the idea of becoming mayor. Her fun side was short-lived. Dad was still acting like a free spirit, so Mom didn't have a choice but to step up and be the serious one."

I lift my chin to look at him. "You're like them, you know. Your parents."

"What – an alcoholic politician?" Blake asks, a hint of tease in his words as his eyes dip to meet mine.

"No." I stifle a laugh and snuggle in closer against his arm. "You're easygoing and talented like your dad, but you're composed and single-minded like your mom. At least when you need to be."

"Hmm," he says, then goes quiet as though pondering this observation.

We remain pressed close to one another for a few more songs until our food arrives. I dive straight in, but Blake picks slowly at his wings, his mind evidently elsewhere.

His plate is still half full when his dad reaches the end of his set.

"That's all from me this evening, folks!" Jason declares in between panting breaths as he wipes the back of his hand over his brow, having given his all up there. As the Tin Roof rumbles with applause, he unplugs his guitar and chugs a glass of water, then hops nimbly off the stage.

Blake pushes his plate away and gets to his feet. "Time to let him know I'm here," he says with a deep breath. "Are you coming?"

I scramble after him as he takes off, easing his way around tables and bar patrons in the direction of his father. Jason is over by the bar, laughing with a guy who seems to be the manager of this joint, and he nestles his guitar protectively into its case and slings it over his shoulder. One of the girls behind the bar passes him a bottled water, and he gives a little salute of a thanks before he swaggers toward the exit.

"Hey!" Blake picks up his pace and intercepts his father. "Hey, Dad."

Jason is knocked for six. He stiffens into position as he squints, like he's shortsighted, and takes in the boy standing in front of him. His strong, rugged features shift from shock to joyful disbelief. "Blake! What the hell are you doing here?" He awkwardly throws his arms around Blake, thumping him a little too hard on the back.

"I could ask you the same thing," Blake replies as he pulls away. Although he is happy to see his dad again, he's also extremely wary, like he knows there's potential for this to turn into a catastrophe. "Are you seriously sober in a bar? *And* performing again?"

Jason holds up the bottle of water in his hand with a shrug. "Hey, let's not rat me out in front of strangers." He then gives me a clipped nod and curiously asks, "Who is this, Blake?"

"How about we sit down, Dad?" Blake suggests instead, clapping a hand on Jason's shoulder and guiding him back to our table across the bar. Blake and I sit back down in our seats, and Jason pulls up a nearby empty chair. He sets his guitar case down at his feet with the same delicate handling Blake uses with his own guitar, and then whips off his cowboy hat and shakes out his damp hair.

"This is Mila. She's—" Blake introduces, but he catches my eye and grins before he can get the words out.

I plant my elbows on the table, cup my hands innocently around my chin, and taunt him with a smoldering gaze. "Say it, Blake."

Blake narrows his dark eyes back at me, a seductive smile on his lips. "She's my girlfriend."

"Well, hey, missy!" Jason says, briefly lifting his hat from the table as a polite gesture. "Nice to meet ya. So, what brings you two lovebirds here to Memphis?"

"Got into a fight with Mom again," Blake says with a slightly petulant shrug. They may not have a close relationship and it may have been many months since they last spoke, but there's a sense of understanding between them, however ill at ease it may be.

"About school?"

"No. I did something stupid and ended up in the Fairview paper," Blake admits, not quite looking at his dad. "I, uh, threw a punch at one of the paparazzi guys outside Mila's family ranch."

Jason spins the cap off his water and takes a swig, looking at me inquisitively. "Paparazzi?"

"My dad is, um, kind of famous. Everett Harding," I whisper, and as soon as his name leaves my lips I'm reminded of just how much I hate saying those exact words out loud. It's rarely something I broadcast, who my father is. The statement makes me internally cringe, like I've just bit into a bitter lemon.

*My dad is Everett Harding.*

"Oh," Jason says, and then: "*Ohhh.*" He runs a hand through his long hair, pushing it off his face, and slumps back into his chair. "This conversation calls for a beer, but y'know, I'm staying clear of alcohol right now."

"Yeah, about that," Blake says, looking at his dad as if he's not quite noticed him before. "You look ... better. Have you stopped drinking completely?" His tone rises to an optimistic note, and I can see the hope in his body language; his shoulders pulled back, his gaze full of anticipation.

Jason's shoulders pull back too, an exact mirror of Blake's. "Ain't had a drop of bourbon, beer, or anything else in months." He sighs, cupping his long fingers around the water bottle. "It was getting out of hand, and well ...

I decided to really kick that shit altogether not long after I last saw you," Jason announces, pride creeping into his voice now as he beams at his son. "I didn't mention it to you yet. I'm trying to get back on my feet first." He drops his gaze shyly to the floor.

"That's great, Dad. I'm honestly impressed. But ... are you still dating Marissa?" Blake asks, and I search for purpose by haphazardly stacking our dirty plates and silverware in an effort to be helpful to the waitress. It doesn't stop me from noticing the hard edge to Blake's voice all of a sudden. "Because maybe you shouldn't be around her if you're trying to clean up your act. She's—"

Jason firmly waves his hand in the air. "Don't worry. She's out of the picture. You're right, I need to keep my focus and, well, we weren't really in the same place with the drinking ..." His voice trails off, a little subdued.

But Blake appears rather pleased by this information. He drums his fingers against the table, like he's full of the jitters. "And you're ... you again. Playing music. You sound just as good as I remember."

"Hey, I needed a distraction, huh? Check out the new baby." Jason straightens up and retrieves his guitar from the floor. He lugs the case onto his lap and opens it to reveal ... well, a guitar. But to Blake, it may as well be a million dollars in cash.

"Nice! You stuck with Gibson." He jumps off his chair to examine the guitar up close, stroking his fingers along the fretboard and over the head, his touch light and feathery. "Mila, this is a J-45. A classic!"

Blake knows I don't know a damn thing about guitars, but his contagious enthusiasm has me nodding back in acknowledgement. It seems that music is the only topic that comes naturally between Blake and his dad.

"Yeah, but it ain't got a thing on that old Hummingbird of mine," Jason says with a wink as he clicks the case shut again. "Not bored of it yet?"

"Never," Blake says, forcing himself back onto his chair in an effort to calm his energy levels. "I never thought I'd see you perform again, though. Why'd you get back into music, Dad?"

"Ah, I guess I never wanted to give it up in the first place." Jason shrugs, but I can see the flicker of sadness in his brown eyes, the same emotion Blake has in his whenever LeAnne shuts down his dreams of being a musician. "Just took me a few years to realize it. That and it's a much better friend to me than a bottle of JD ever could be. I've only been gigging for a few months, seeing if I've still got it in me. I may have been known in Nashville back in the day, but here in Memphis, I'm pretty much a new kid on the block, y'know. I had to call in a lot of favors to get my first slot."

Blake lets out a satisfied sigh. I get the feeling he's genuinely proud of his dad. "You have no idea how awesome it is to see you on stage again. Do you remember you used to take me to all of your gigs, even on school nights, and Mom would lose her damn mind?"

"Does she let you use that language?" Jason asks, tilting his head sternly to one side, and Blake scoffs. "Those were the good days. You used to sit by the side of the stage playing air guitar like the most badass ten-year-old kid in the world." He looks at me and Blake, suddenly animated. "Hey, how about you guys come back to my place, and we can jam out together? That's if Mila doesn't mind."

Blake looks to me with bated breath. "Mila?"

It might be a change to the evening I envisioned with him, but this might be even better. As though I would ever deny a chance to watch Blake lose himself in music. I laugh and say, "Let's do it!" And in my head, all I can imagine is a young Blake playing air guitar, dreaming of the day when he too would be performing on stage like his father.

We call over the check, which Jason puts up a fight to pay for on our behalf, and then the three of us head outside into a bustling Friday-evening Beale Street. It's busier now, louder. I can see how quickly the area has transformed into catering toward an adult crowd as the night draws in. There are far fewer kids around now.

Blake's hand gravitates toward mine as though he can sense my apprehension again.

Jason strolls slightly ahead of us with his guitar over his shoulder and his head held high. It's like the famous Beale Street is his own personal playground, but then I suppose it is, considering he lives in the downtown area. I hold on tight to Blake as we walk the ten minutes to his dad's home, only a few blocks away, Jason pointing out various bars and venues as we go.

It's a large, modern apartment building and as we huddle into the elevator, Jason jokes, "My neighbors keep putting notes under my door asking me to shut the hell up. I try to oblige, but I reckon they're not big fans of me fine-tuning my riffs at midnight."

He brings us to his apartment, unlocks the door, and gestures for Blake and me to head on in. Blake guides me in by my elbow, and I glance around, immediately wondering how Jason was ever married to LeAnne.

The apartment is bright, spacious and neutral-toned, with vintage gig posters and a wall of vinyl adding color, but it's also kind of a mess. There's dishes stacked in the sink, empty milk cartons and food wrappers cluttering the granite countertops, and the couch with its sad, flat cushions is in desperate need of being plumped. It's a studio apartment, so there's no hiding the unmade bed at the other side of the room and the guitar picks littering the side table.

It's so different from the spotless, glitzy house that Blake lives in with his mom, where one would be hard-pressed to even find a speck of dust, let alone misplaced objects or a jumble of slightly dog-eared album sleeves. It's evident that Jason is way more carefree and laid-back, like he's still young and reckless at heart, whereas LeAnne doesn't even seem to know *how* to kick back because she is too busy overseeing the running of Nashville while also having raised Blake on her own. I honestly don't see it – them as a double act. Like, at all. Just from this brief encounter, I'm not surprised the two of them weren't compatible in the long run.

"You aren't hitting the road again tonight, are you?"

Jason asks, hooking his hat on the back of the door and then setting his guitar case down on the coffee table in the lounge area. It's warm in here, and he switches on the ceiling fan.

"Tomorrow," Blake says. "We're gonna sleep in the truck, and then I was gonna come see you in the morning, but you beat me to it by rocking up at the Tin Roof."

Jason places his hands on his hips and stares him down, then shakes his head pitifully at me. "I'm so sorry, Mila, this boy of mine clearly doesn't possess an ounce of chivalry. Making you sleep in a truck!" He makes a deep huffing noise, then adds, "You two can spend the night here."

"Are you sure?" I ask, exchanging a glance with Blake. His shoulders sink in unison with my own. Sure, spending the night in his truck isn't the most comfortable of options, but it's definitely romantic, and private, and full of unspoken possibilities. Tonight was going to be our first night alone together, but it would be awkward to turn down Jason's offer.

"Absolutely!" Jason says, then in disbelief, he mumbles to himself, "*Sleeping in the truck.* Idiot." As he walks past Blake, he playfully torments him by flicking him in the back of the head, then he grabs sodas from the refrigerator and gathers us around the couch, though he sits on the edge of the coffee table. "Blake, give the J-45 a whirl."

Blake's face lights up with pure delight as his dad nudges his guitar case toward him. "Seriously?"

"Seriously. Give me some Keith Urban."

"I only know 'Somebody Like You.'"

Jason smiles. "Then play 'Somebody Like You.'"

Blake sets his phone on the coffee table and carefully removes his dad's guitar from its case. He nestles it against his body, the curves unfamiliar to him, and spends a minute adjusting to the feel of a new guitar in his arms. With the utmost precision, he aligns his calloused fingers along the fretboard.

Jason tosses him a pick out of his pocket and then says to me, "Mila, you can chime in with some backup vocals."

"*No*." Blake's eyes flash up from the guitar in mock-panic. "She can't sing."

I playfully swat his arm. "He's right," I say with a sheepish grin. "I really can't."

"*And* she's new to the country scene," Blake points out. "The Tin Roof was another step forward in her musical education."

Jason furrows his eyebrows at me. "Mila, you don't even know one of Keith Urban's greatest hits?"

"No," I admit, then sink back into the couch and tuck my knees to my chest, feeling my cheeks grow hot as I try to keep my laughter at bay. I see where Blake gets it from now, that ingrained notion that every person on the planet *must* love country music as much as they do. It's too cute.

"Ah, you and me, Blake, always picking the wrong girls," Jason teases with a wink, then he gives him the go-ahead nod. "Take it away."

Blake inhales a deep breath, closes his eyes, positions the pick over the strings, then begins to play. The opening strums are fast-paced, and I notice Jason's gaze shine with pride as he watches Blake's fingers move flawlessly across the guitar, entranced. Blake's eyes flicker open and he parts his lips, diving into the song's lyrics, his voice deepening and his twang strengthening.

It's an upbeat, happy song that builds nicely into its chorus, and that's when Jason joins in.

His husky, low pitch laces around Blake's smooth, deeper tone, and although their voices are both uniquely different, they blend together perfectly. The atmosphere around us intensifies as they carry on together, their voices in sync and their gazes latched onto each other, and it feels like something truly magical.

I sit cross-legged next to Blake on the couch, a glowing smile across my face as I watch the joy dance in his eyes. God, he looks so happy, so at peace with himself. It makes me want to yank the guitar out of his arms and throw myself into them instead, but I resist because this intimate little gig in front of only me is way too perfect.

Then the lighting up of Blake's phone screen on the table next to me ruins this moment. It's nosy, I know, but I can't help myself – I squint at the screen and my smile falters when I see a new text from Lacey, of all people.

It reads: *Hope you're having fun in Memphis, but this tailgate blows without you here!*

My head spins. Why is she messaging him? I glance at Blake to see if he's noticed, but he's absorbed in his performance. Do they text often? I know he insists they're nothing more than friends, but I also know he's not told me about their dating history. I hate the churn of jealousy it triggers, but it feels super weird for Lacey to text him like this. Her message will probably seem innocent to Blake, but to me, it is so obviously flirtatious. Will he reply? Will he ignore her?

*Will he tell me?*

I try to focus back on Blake as he sings alongside his dad, lost in their shared world of music, but bitter nausea lingers in the pit of my stomach for the rest of the night.

# 18

I wake up to the smell of cooked bacon, the sizzle of a frying pan sounding around the apartment. Morning sunlight streams in through the open blinds and I peel open my eyes, adjusting to my unfamiliar surroundings. Sleeping on the couch has left my bones stiff and my neck rigid, but at least I didn't volunteer to sleep on the floor like Blake did. I glance over the edge of the couch and find him asleep on his stomach, face pressed into a cushion. At some point during the night when I stirred, I thought about joining Blake on the floor and snuggling up against him beneath the blanket, but I promptly remembered Jason's presence in the room when he let out a snore.

"Wakey wakey!" Jason yells, banging a pair of pans together. "Breakfast is served!"

Blake jolts awake and smacks his head off the edge of the coffee table. "Ugh! What the hell, Dad?" He sits up and rubs the back of his head, tired and disgruntled.

Jason sets out plates on the breakfast bar while shooting Blake a stern look of disapproval at his use of bad language again. "I have to be on site in thirty minutes. You think I wear these cargo shorts and steel-toed boots for the fun of it?" He motions at his work attire, that of a construction worker, then grabs the frying pan full of bacon from the stove. "Alexa, play Florida Georgia Line on shuffle."

The device on the countertop lights up and begins to play some music on a low volume in the background as Jason plates up breakfast for the three of us.

"Morning," Blake says, and I glance down at him, taken aback by just how attractive his raspy, quiet morning voice is. He yawns and runs a hand through his bedhead hair. "Did you sleep okay?"

I prop myself up on my elbows. It feels nice waking up next to him, even though I'm on the couch and he's on the floor. There's something so intimate about seeing a person in those first few moments after they've woken and haven't quite come to life yet.

"I did," I answer, then weave my fingers through his messy hair. "I hope you didn't just give yourself a concussion."

Blake laughs and tilts his head back to kiss my hand. He jumps up from the floor, shirtless but still in his jean shorts from last night, the waistband of his white Calvin Klein boxers visible. The silver chain he never takes off is dangling around his neck, and I have to remind myself that his dad is in the room to keep my mind clear of thoughts verging on the edge of dirty.

I'm wearing an oversized Champion T-shirt that reaches my knees, and I pull my hair back into a ponytail as I follow Blake to the breakfast bar. Jason has filled plates with bacon, eggs over easy, and crispy hash browns, and it looks greasy, high-calorie, and delicious – something my parents would *never* let me eat for breakfast.

"Dig in, kids!" Jason waves at the plates, urging us to eat. I look at the feast but search in vain for some silverware. For some reason I feel shy about asking, but luckily Blake beats me to it and starts opening drawers around the kitchen table.

"Dad, where do you keep the knives and forks?" he asks.

Jason looks a bit self-conscious and shuffles over to the kitchen sink. "Let me just clean some off for you. Sorry, I'm not really used to looking after anyone but myself," he answers with a half-embarrassed smile.

Something about this rather innocent statement seems to shift the atmosphere. Blake and Jason suddenly both seem uncomfortable, and though I have not known either of them for very long, or know much about their relationship, it is clear to me that there are many things unsaid between them. No, Jason is not used to looking after anyone but himself, and he hasn't been the father that Blake needed.

The awkward moment breaks when Jason busies himself with cleaning and Blake dries off the silverware then settles in with me at the breakfast bar.

"You're sounding really great, by the way," Jason compliments Blake as he carries his plate over to the couch so that we aren't all crammed around the breakfast bar. He lies back, boots propped up on the arm of the couch, and again is much more at ease discussing music than anything else. "Still no luck getting yourself a gig?"

Blake stabs his fork into a strip of bacon. "They all say I'm too young," he grumbles.

"But you're *amazing*!" I tell him.

"Mila is right. You are," Jason says. His plate rests on his stomach, and he shovels a mouthful of crispy hash brown into his mouth as he thinks. "I have some connections in Nashville again. I'll talk to them. Try to get you a slot. Once they see how good you are, you'll be on their weekly lineup."

"Really?" Blake asks, his voice rising with elation. "That'd be amazing."

"I'll make some calls tonight," Jason promises with an easy smile.

Blake looks at me, overjoyed, and I squeeze his hand in support. I know how badly he wants to perform, not just to his friends around a bonfire, but to a real crowd of strangers. It's the ultimate test of one's talent. Friends can be biased, but strangers won't hesitate to tell you if you suck.

We all wolf down our breakfast, leaving behind empty plates, and Blake carries the dishes over to the sink. His dad joins him.

"Thanks again for letting us spend the night," I tell Jason.

"Yeah," adds Blake. "It's been real nice to see you. Maybe I could visit more often, or maybe I could just ..." The gears in his mind churn, and he looks at his dad out the corner of his eye with apprehension. "Stay here. With you."

"What?" I say, straightening my shoulders. Blake glances over to me, uncertain, but his eyes don't linger. Instead, they divert back to his dad, anxiously waiting for an answer.

As Jason dunks a frying pan into the sink, his hands freeze beneath the soapy water. He turns his head toward his son, his expression pensive. "You can't stay here, Blake."

"Why not? I've stayed here before when I've visited."

"Sleeping on the couch is only okay for a couple nights. Not permanently," Jason says, then gestures around the apartment with a wet hand covered in soap suds. "It's a studio apartment, Blake. Not even a one-bedroom. Don't be an idiot."

"But we could jam out together every night! Imagine how awesome it would be. Just you and me and our guitars!" Blake says, bordering on manic. "Every night could be like last night."

"Blake ... your life is in Fairview," I point out.

"It's not about that, Mila," he says dismissively, and my feelings are instantly hurt, like my opinion doesn't matter. Where is this coming from? Out of nowhere, or so it seems to me, Blake is suddenly desperate to stay in Memphis with his father who he barely keeps in touch with?

"Blake, I'm serious," Jason states, abruptly turning to face Blake head-on. It's weird seeing him so earnest after how easygoing he's been. He seems more like a parental figure rather than Blake's cool rock-star buddy. "You're going home to your mom. That's where you need to be. You can't get carried away just because we jammed together last night. Don't be stupid, son."

At that, Blake slams a plate down hard on the countertop, gritting his teeth as hurt flashes across his dark eyes. "Why don't you want me?" he growls, but his voice cracks with a pain I've never heard before. "Why have you *never* wanted me? I don't care that you never fought to have me in your life, but I'm telling you now that I *want* to stay with you, and yet—"

"Look, now is not the time or place to get into all that. I know your mom is hard on you. She was hard on me too," Jason interrupts calmly, and I realize that he's deliberately keeping his voice steady and empathetic. "But it comes from a good place. She wants the best for you, and she's a much better influence on you than I'll ever be."

"You're wrong," Blake says, refusing to be appeased and shaking his head fast in disagreement. "I look up to *you*. You understand what music means to me. Mom won't even sign my early-decision application for Vanderbilt! She's a bitch."

"Hey!" Jason snarls, pressing his finger into Blake's bare chest. "Don't you dare talk about your mom that way."

"Blake …" I murmur, pivoting around the pair of them, reaching for his arm in an effort to calm him down, but he only shakes me off.

"Well, she is," Blake counters, nostrils flaring. "What kind of parent doesn't let their kid chase their dreams?"

"The kind of person who watched her husband throw his life away chasing music," Jason says in a steely voice. His eyes are locked on Blake. "I didn't make it, Blake, and you know where I've ended up? Building condos! I should have pursued a real career instead of fooling around, always thinking my big break was round the corner." He slams the last of the dishes into the draining rack, wipes his hands on a cloth, and murmurs almost to himself, "Maybe then I would have been a better husband and father."

This is getting way too heavy and personal, and I know this conversation isn't meant for my ears. But Blake and his dad are oblivious. I retreat a few steps, removing myself, but in a studio apartment, there's not exactly anywhere to go.

"So what you're saying is that you don't believe in me either," Blake says in a small, defeated voice. "You agree with Mom. You think I should study something else."

"No, I just want you to be smarter than I ever was." Jason turns to look at his son, his eyes gentler now. "Of course I believe in you, Blake. You have way more talent than I ever had."

Blake's expression shifts in an instant to become painfully eager. "I have?"

"Yes. And you're doing things right; getting a degree. If it's what you want, *I'll* be the parental signature on your course application. Get it over to me when the time comes. You only need one parent's signature, right?"

"Yeah."

"Well, there you go," Jason says. "You're officially applying for early decision for Vanderbilt. Congratulations, buddy."

Blake is speechless, caught off guard by the turnaround of events. His expression is despondent and ecstatic all at the same time – half disappointed that his dad won't let him stay here in Memphis, but also massively relieved that he'll get the signature he needs to get his foot, hopefully, in the door of the Vanderbilt campus next fall.

Jason grabs the plate Blake slammed down on the countertop and dunks it into the sink, calmly continuing washing the dishes. Blake walks around me, avoiding eye contact, and collapses onto the couch with his head in his hands.

I sit down next to him and put my hand on his thigh. He's breathing deeply as he runs his fingertips back into his hairline.

"Hey," I whisper gently, lowering my head to catch his eye. "Are you okay?"

Blake inhales a sharp breath and drops his hands from his face, nodding. But it's obvious he's not. His eyes shine, bloodshot. I'm not sure why he's so upset, but as his empty gaze fixates on the window ahead, I scoot in closer to him, wrapping my arms around his bare torso. He's hot to the touch, and I can feel his heart beating fast beneath his skin. He rests his head atop mine.

"I need to jet off now," Jason says, wiping his damp hands on his cargo shorts. He walks over to the living area and sits on the coffee table in front of us, and Blake and I pull apart. "You call me when you get back to Fairview, okay, Blake? Drive safe, and I'll see you again soon. Mila, it was great to meet you."

"You too," I reply. "I loved watching you perform last night."

"Ah, thanks," Jason says, humbly waving me away. He extends a closed fist to Blake. "Put it here."

Blake sighs and reluctantly fist-bumps his dad. "We'll lock up when we leave."

Jason ruffles Blake's already messy hair, then leaves the

apartment. Silence falls over Blake and me as we're left alone.

"You'd rather stay here in Memphis?" I ask him. It's such a surprise to me – Blake has always raved about Nashville and how much he loves the city.

"I'd rather stay with my dad," Blake says, his hardened gaze rising to look at me. "I don't care where, as long I'm out from under my mom's roof. Here, Nashville, Alaska. It doesn't matter. He gets what I'm about. He gets that music is my life. He won't treat me like a kid and walk all over my ambitions."

"But Vanderbilt is in Nashville."

"So? That doesn't mean I couldn't finish senior year *here*." He gets up to grab a T-shirt from the backpack he ran to his truck to retrieve along with my duffel bag last night.

My heart sinks even lower than it did yesterday when I brought up this subject, yet I do it anyway. "But what about us?" I say, trying to keep the whine out my voice.

"Mila, what do you want from me?" Blake snaps, slipping the white T-shirt over his head, his movements clearly fueled by frustration. "*You* don't even stay in Fairview. You can't just expect me to stay there forever."

"You sound like you don't care," I say, not even trying to hide the disappointment evident behind each word.

Blake squeezes his eyes shut as he relaxes his tight shoulders, and he exhales loudly. "I *do* care, Mila. I'm mad *because* I care," he retorts, exhaling loudly as he starts gathering our stuff. "I'm mad because I don't *know* what will happen when you go home. Every time I start thinking about it, the whole situation just seems impossible."

Growing exasperated, I stand in front of him. "We'll make it work," I say sharply. Then in the heat of the moment, I fire accusingly at him, "And when were you going to share with me the news that Lacey is your ex?"

Blake's hands freeze over my bag, and he lifts his head, his expression bleak. "Why does it matter?"

"Because you keep insisting she's just a friend, yet she comes by for dinner? Texts you? *Flirts* with you?" I fold my arms, frustrated by the irritation flickering in Blake's eyes. "A friend can do that, sure, but your ex? No. That's too weird, Blake."

"Mila, I've known the girl my whole life, and the only reason she still hangs around me is because her parents are close friends with my mom. You know that already; I'm not hiding anything," he explains, then lets his weary sigh fill the air around us. "I didn't say anything about her being my ex because we only dated for a short while, and it was never anything serious."

"For you, maybe," I mumble, wishing I could stop myself pushing him on this. "Lacey, however, she—"

"Mila, stop. I'm not doing this." He grabs my bag and shoves it into my arms, then nudges his shoulder against me as he walks away. "Let's just go home. We have parents waiting to yell at us."

# 19

The two hundred miles between Memphis and Fairview seem to stretch on forever on the drive home. Blake and I aren't talking much, at least not the way we usually talk. No teasing glances, no head-bopping to the latest country tunes. In fact, it's the first time I've ever been in Blake's truck with the music at a respectable volume. That's how I know he's lost deep in his own head. The trip had its fun moments, but it hardly turned out like I envisioned. And now my future with Blake seems much more uncertain.

By the time we roll up to the Harding Estate, the muscles in my neck are strained from napping against the window. I untangle myself from the seatbelt and sit up with a yawn. It's just after noon and of course, there's still a handful of stragglers pitched outside the gate. In a day or two, they will all surely have given up. Dad's affair is no longer breaking news in the world of fame.

"Start opening the gate. I'll drive you to the house," Blake says in a subdued voice, pulling down his sun visor as we approach. I doubt he wants the paps to remember him from his lapse in self-control the other day.

I sluggishly fish the remote out of my bag and point it out the windshield, timing the opening perfectly just as the truck reaches the gate. We are on the other side, safe behind the ranch's protective walls, before any of the paps can even pull the lens caps off their cameras. The gate closes automatically behind us, and the truck creeps nearer to the house, but I notice Sheri's van is missing. Only the rented SUV is parked outside. Mom and Dad haven't left the ranch since our trip to church.

The moment I allow myself to think of Mom and Dad, they appear at the front door with faces like thunder. They must have spotted Blake's truck arriving. As they move outside, Mom presses her hands against the porch railing and stands rigid while Dad marches down the porch steps and stands threateningly at the foot of them, arms crossed, waiting.

Blake swallows hard and slowly brakes to a stop. We exchange a look of dread, then he says, "I guess I should meet your parents."

Here goes nothing.

I swing my bag over my shoulder and hop out of the truck first, braced and ready for yet another episode of *Mila Versus Her Parents*, but despite the fury on their faces, neither of them immediately says anything. Blake's truck door thuds shut, and he moves around the hood to join me, then we make those dangerous few steps toward my father.

"Memphis," Dad says in a steely voice. So, they got the note I left. "*Memphis.*"

Blake edges protectively in front of me. "I'm sorry, sir. Memphis was my idea."

Dad isn't wearing sunglasses today, despite the blinding sun shining down into his eyes, so it feels extra dramatic the way he slowly turns his attention to the boy by my side. "You're brave coming onto this ranch, Blake."

"I'm brave dating your daughter in the first place."

I glance fiercely at Blake and purposely step on his foot. Is he serious? In what world is talking back to my *dad* ever a good idea when he already disapproves of Blake as it is? Does this boyfriend of mine have a death wish?

A brief flash of curiosity crosses Dad's face and he tips his head to the side inquisitively. "I assume your mom has told you about our history."

"Yes, sir. I've known for a couple years," Blake says, keeping his voice steady. "But that's between you and my mom. It has nothing to do with me."

Dad, in his best badass tone of voice he reserves only for on set, challenges, "So you aren't dying to throw a punch at me like you did to one of those guys outside the other day?"

"No, sir."

Dad drops his folded arms from his chest and places them on his hips instead, his eyebrows drawing together. "Why?"

"Because I know how it feels to have her stand in your way," Blake says without missing a beat. He holds Dad's gaze, completely unfazed by his superstar status. Neither of them is breaking eye contact, so I step forward.

"Blake wants to be a musician," I tell Dad. "He plays guitar. He sings. He's really, really good."

"Huh," is all Dad says. He looks Blake up and down with the most peculiar expression on his face.

"Mila, I want you to get in this house," Mom orders from up on the porch, gesturing over the railing. "Blake, I think you should go home."

"Yeah," Dad agrees. "I'm sure your mom must be worried about you too."

"She's in Nashville for the weekend." Blake shrugs. "I doubt she even knows I left."

"Still. Go home," Dad says. He takes my bag from my shoulder and throws it over his own, then gestures toward the house with a clipped nod. "Mila. Inside, please."

I bow my head and brush past him, making my way up the porch steps to Mom. She turns to face me and releases a weary sigh. I'm not sure how much more worry I can put my parents through before she develops permanent wrinkles.

Dad remains rooted to the spot, patiently staring Blake down until Blake finally cracks under the pressure and returns to his truck. He pulls open the door, steps one foot inside, then pauses.

"Please don't be too hard on Mila. She's just trying to live her own life. It's not easy feeling like you're nothing but the secondary character in someone else's story." His eyes travel to mine and he frowns.

"Mila will open the gate to let you out," is all Dad replies.

Blake nods grudgingly and slides into his truck. Mom and I watch, unspeaking, from the porch as the engine rumbles to life and Blake U-turns back down the dirt road. When he nears the gate, I electronically open it for him and feel an ache in my chest as I watch him disappear, wondering what lies ahead for us.

Dad spins around to look up at Mom and me. "I quite like that kid," he says.

That tightness gripping my chest suddenly loosens. "What?"

"I like him." Dad shrugs casually, joining us on the porch.

"What?" Mom echoes, just as surprised as I am.

Dad is unbelievably indifferent, his expression cool and composed. "I imagined him to be more—"

"Like LeAnne?" Mom finishes, and a dark look is exchanged between them. I get the feeling their history with LeAnne was sort of swept under the rug all those years ago, never to be spoken of again. Until recently... which means it's lost none of its sting.

"Yes. Like LeAnne," Dad says. "He has her boldness, that's for sure, but he seems like he has his head screwed on. Wasn't afraid to own his actions and his thoughts. I like a kid who can look me in the eye, unlike that boy you dated last year. Jack, wasn't it? He shriveled up into a ball of nerves every time I entered the room."

"So I can keep seeing him?" I ask optimistically, crossing my fingers behind my back.

"No," Dad answers bluntly. He pats me on the shoulder

and gives me the smallest of smiles as he says, "Because you, Mila, are grounded for about the millionth time. And I'll be enforcing it this time."

There's something in his dark eyes, something forgiving and humane, and my heart soars. I can't see Blake because I'm grounded and *not* because Dad dislikes him. It feels like a monumental step forward, and I'm pretty sure Mom was already swaying toward throwing in the towel over this battle. They are realizing that I really like him, and that he doesn't represent his mom. It's not fair for them to write him off just because of his DNA. He deserves a chance, and the gentleness in Dad's expression leads me to believe that he might just give him one.

"I can't believe you went to Memphis," Mom says as she presses her hands flat on my back and guides me inside the house. "Everett, give us a minute, please."

Dad nods. "Mila, I'll put your bag in your room," he says, then heads off upstairs.

I'm still wondering why no one is yelling at me yet. Have my parents spent the past twenty-four hours going through a reality check? It's like I have returned home to two totally different people, but so far, I have no complaints.

Mom leads me to the kitchen and gently pushes me into a dining chair. She pulls out the chair opposite, but is too fidgety to bother sitting down. She shifts her weight from one foot to the other. "Mila ... I was your age once. I know how easy it is to rush into things, and you definitely shouldn't be taking overnight trips with boys yet, and I just want to make sure—"

My cheeks burn. "Mom, nothing happened. I didn't have sex with Blake."

Mom visibly relaxes enough to actually take a seat. "Last night? Or ever?"

"Ever," I say, my face feeling like it's on fire as she analyzes my expression for any hint of a lie, but there isn't one. Just pure mortification at having to spell this out for her.

"Okay." Mom nervously laughs and twirls a piece of hair around her finger. I guess it's pretty embarrassing for her too. I notice that she's wearing her usual immaculate makeup again today, which also makes me wonder if things are maybe improving around here. "But if the moment ever ... arises ... just remember you're only sixteen. You haven't known this guy all that long, and he's about to be a senior, and high school seniors can be ... pushy. Don't ever do anything you aren't comfortable with. Maybe don't do anything, period. I'd feel much better that way."

"*Mom*." I give her a fierce look. "I understand. Please stop already."

"Okay, okay, I'm done!" Mom holds up her hands, then lets them drop back to her lap as she gazes at me. "You know I'm always here for you, right? I don't appreciate all this rebellion and attitude, but it's nice to see you ... well, be you."

Ruben enters the room with a theatrical wave aimed at me. "Ah, the teen delinquent returns!"

"Alive and well, as always," I mutter with a sarcastic smile.

Ruben grunts, then helps himself to a root beer from

the refrigerator. He pops the cap and leans back against the countertop, one leg crossed in front of the other. "Hey, Everett, your daughter decided to grace us with her presence," he says as Dad enters the kitchen, pointing his root beer at me. "I don't know what more you expect me to do with her at this point."

"I'm sitting right here, Ruben," I remind him.

Dad crosses in front of him to get to the refrigerator, pulling out a jug of sweet tea, then fixes him with a sharp look as he shuts the door. "I can see that, Ruben. Marnie and I are handling it."

"Handling it?" Ruben snorts. "She keeps running off!"

"True," Dad says, glancing at me for a moment. Then he broadens his shoulders and overshadows Ruben as he reaches over him to fetch a glass from the cupboard. "But Marnie and I will handle it from here. We need to get through this as a family. And that means we as her parents will deal with any situations that arise. Not you."

Clearly aggravated, Ruben nudges Dad away as he straightens up and slams his root beer down on the counter. "Quit it with the holy act, Everett. A month ago, you were the one having me send her out here. *You* were the one who didn't trust her to leave this place."

"Yes, I know. That was a mistake," Dad says. He remains calm and oddly quiet, like his voice is fragile and he doesn't want to risk raising it. He pours himself a glass of sweet tea and then sits at the table right next to Mom. "I know I've been selfish, Mila, and that I've let you and your mom down, but I'm trying to work things out."

Ruben indignantly rolls his eyes, then takes his root beer as he strides past us all. "Everett, I'll be upstairs when you remember what you pay me for."

"That's another relationship I have to fix," Dad says with a sigh once Ruben is gone. He glances between Mom and me, abashed. "I can't blame Ruben for everything that's gone wrong, but I know I don't appreciate that style of management anymore."

"I think that's a wise thought," Mom says.

But I only stare blankly at the two of them, wondering why I no longer feel that tension that's enveloped them for the past week. "Why are you guys being so weird? What did I miss while I was gone?"

Mom wipes the smile from her face and turns serious. She glimpses at Dad, seeking validation, and he nods. Beneath the table, I catch his hand moving to her leg.

"We were thinking it might be time for us all to head home soon," Mom says carefully.

"Like, together?"

"Together," Dad confirms.

Whoa. It takes a minute for this information to really sink in, mostly because I'm in two minds. Half of me is overwhelmed with relief that my parents' marriage seems to be salvageable, but the other half of me doesn't want to go home yet. It's inevitable, I know that, but I guess I thought I had more time.

"When?" I ask, biting the inside of my cheek.

"Next week," says Mom, glancing quickly at Dad. "I need to get back to work, and I think life will be better for us all if we're in our own home while we try to sort things out."

"But don't you still need to clear the air properly with Popeye too, Dad?" I ask. I know the purpose of Dad's visit was to save our family, but our family is more than just him, Mom, and me. There are wider cracks that need fixing. "Talking about Popeye … where is he? And Sheri?" I glance around the kitchen as if expecting them to magically appear.

Dad's expression turns grave. "Your grandpa took a fall yesterday."

Oh my God, what else have I missed while in Memphis? I jump from my chair in a blind panic, wondering why a fall yesterday means that he's not here *now*. What if he broke a hip? Old people always break hips when they fall.

"Don't worry, Mila," Dad reassures me. "It wasn't too serious. He tripped on the porch steps, but they kept him in overnight for observation and rest. They think the clumsiness may be connected to his ongoing health issues. Something degenerative, but he's still insisting there's nothing really the matter. Sheri is bringing him home later."

I lower myself back into my chair, my mind racing. This is all too much for a girl who slept on a couch last night. It's like I've returned to a parallel universe where *everything* has changed. Popeye being in hospital somehow casts my delinquent behavior in a different perspective.

"Poor Popeye," I mumble, anxiously fiddling with my hands in my lap, imagining him bundled up in a hospital bed, confused and grouchy, hoping that Sheri is by his side to reassure him. "Maybe we can make him his favorite dinner when he comes home? He loves a pot roast."

"That's a great idea," Mom says. "We can all make it together. It's been a long time since any of us cooked anything more than an egg."

Dad clicks his tongue with a *tsk*. "Oh, and before I forget, Mila ..."

I glance up. "Yeah?"

"Here," he says. He stuffs a hand into the pocket of his jeans, pulling out his phone and sliding it across the table. Except it's not his phone, unless Dad has traded his black iPhone for a lilac version.

With apprehension, I pick up the phone and examine it in my hand. It's brand new – I know because there's not a single scratch on it yet. I raise an eyebrow at my parents. "Why are you giving me a new phone?"

"You asked for one," Mom reminds me.

"Ruben transferred everything over for you already. He has his uses sometimes," Dad says.

"Yeah, but ..." I quickly lay the phone back down on the table, half expecting it to zap me with an electric shock. This seems like a prank, some sick punishment. "Usually when someone breaks all the rules, their parents don't buy them new phones."

"That's true," Mom agrees. "But your dad and I discussed it, and we realized yesterday that we would have much preferred if you'd had a phone with you when you took off so that we could have at least known you were safe. So, grounded or not, we wanted to give you your phone back. But you wrecked your old one pretty bad, so …"

"Thank you," I say in disbelief, my gratitude sincere.

I get up and move toward my parents, squeezing Mom in a tight hug. Dad watches me closely, nervously, and I hug him too. He kisses my cheek, and for the first time all summer, I feel like things might turn out okay.

# *20*

None of us go to church that weekend. Popeye has been instructed by his nurses to take it easy for a few days, and he's sporting a giant bandage around his forehead from where he bumped it. He's in good spirits otherwise, and I can tell because he's grumbling constantly about being treated like a wounded soldier and insisting he's perfectly fine.

"I survived the Vietnam War and you lot think I can't handle tripping down a couple stairs? I can make myself my own damn coffee!" he snapped at Dad at one point for daring to offer to make his early-morning coffee for him. He's so incredibly stubborn, and as bad-tempered as an old dog that just wants to be left in peace, though not really with me. I'm pleased that there's still always a twinkle in his eye when I'm around.

Early Tuesday morning, while Mom bickers with Popeye over why it's a terrible idea for him to go digging up weeds in the fields, my phone rings with an incoming video call. At the sight of Blake's name on my screen, I excuse myself from the living room and sneak off to my bedroom for some privacy. All my parents told me on the weekend was that I'm officially, seriously-we-mean-it-this-time, grounded.

So I may not have seen Blake in a few days, but that doesn't mean we haven't been video calling each other late at night. Something about keeping my voice low as I hide beneath my comforter and speak with him feels intimate and personal, bringing us closer than ever, but Blake's dismissive words in Memphis are niggling at me. We know time is running out and that we need to have *that* talk soon, but it's almost too scary to broach the subject again. Our options *are* limited.

"Hi, Blake," I answer as I collapse onto my bed, holding my phone above me as I flash him a cheeky smile.

"Guess what?" He grins, but doesn't even give me the chance to reply before he says, "My dad came through! He got me a gig!"

I bolt upright, beaming at the excitement vibrating from him, his features lit up. This is the opportunity that Blake has been waiting for. "Amazing! Where?"

"Honky Tonk Central!" he blurts in a frenzy, and is so high on adrenaline that he can't stop pacing. "Can you believe it? He got me a gig at my favorite honky tonk! It's next week. Monday. I need to figure out what I'm gonna play."

My smile instantly fades. "Next week?"

"Yeah! You'll be there, right? I expect you front and center, cheering the loudest."

Oh no. My heart sinks to the pit of my stomach. Blake

doesn't know yet that I may not still be here next week – I can't stand the idea of our last week together being tainted by arguments.

"Of course I'll be there," I lie, feeling my chest constrict, like my head is telling me to just be honest with him. But my heart is telling me not to ruin his moment of euphoria, so I force my smile to return. "I'll be your best groupie. Well," I try to flirt, "your only groupie." I get a sudden, very unwelcome flash of the annoying Lacey in my mind. All my instincts tell me she has her eyes firmly on Blake, no matter how good she is at hiding it.

"I'd love that," Blake says, then leans back against the wall and groans. "When can I see you? Bailey misses you too."

"My mom may have hinted yesterday that if I don't put a foot out of line this week that they *might* just let me make plans for the weekend." I don't tell him the "if we're still here" part of Mom's conditions.

"Great. I'll think of something. Keep Saturday night free, and expect to spend it with me."

Butterflies, butterflies … goddamn butterflies.

"Then I guess I'll see you on Saturday," I say in a hushed tone, smiling to myself alone in my room.

Blake's dimpled smirk beams at me. "I'm counting the seconds," he says, and then hangs up.

Tossing my phone – *carefully* – behind me onto my bed, I blow out a breath of air and weave my hands into my hair. I need to hang on around here for just a little longer. At least until Monday. I need to be there for Blake at his first proper gig in his favorite music bar. There's no way I can miss it.

And I know it's a stupid idea, but I sneak next door to the bedroom my parents have been sharing – though one of them has obviously been sleeping on the old couch beneath the window that's made up with spare blankets – and spot Mom's purse on the dresser next to Dad's wallet. Heart thumping, I grab both their IDs and tuck them into the back pocket of my jean shorts, then I skulk back downstairs and peek into the living room.

Popeye has resigned himself to repairing a loose handle on one of the coffee-table drawers, his toolbox open next to him, while Mom watches in defeat from the couch. She notices me at the door and shakes her head hopelessly, and I stifle a laugh. Popeye just doesn't listen. "Relaxing" isn't in his vocabulary.

I head out the front door into the fresh morning air and freeze in my tracks as Dad and Ruben both turn to look at me. Ruben rocks back and forth on the old wooden chair that resides in the corner of the porch, and Dad leans against the porch railing with his arms folded stiffly across his chest. I get the impression that my arrival has immediately silenced their conversation.

"Good morning, Mila," Dad says, his hard expression morphing into a smile.

"Morning."

"Where are you going?"

"To see the horses," I say, and Ruben snorts. I ignore him and continue down the porch steps, leaving them to get back to business, though I do glance at them over my shoulder as I walk away and notice Dad's hands moving irritably.

I haven't encountered Sheri this morning yet, which means there's only one place she can be, so I head for the stables in search of her. It's another glorious day here in Tennessee, as always, and I'm growing to love roaming the fields under the clear blue skies in peaceful serenity. It's like my daily detox from the real world, a breath of fresh air in the midst of all the crazy. The thought of returning back to Thousand Oaks, where there's no respite from city life, feels suffocating.

As I approach the stables, I spot Sheri's curly blond hair inside, but I also spot a flash of strawberry blond belonging to a girl with her own unique taste in earrings.

"Savannah?" I say, stepping into the stables. "What are you doing here?"

Savannah and Sheri both pause. Savannah is wading around in rubber boots with a shovel, looking way too delighted to be cleaning up manure, and Sheri is sifting through paperwork at the small desk against the far wall where all the equipment is kept.

"Hey!" Savannah says. "I'm helping out your aunt!"

I glance at Sheri, intrigued, and she gets up from the old stool and shakes off the dust from her pants. "Having your help around here has made me realize that I can't take care of these stables all on my own when you leave, Mila, and Savannah is great with the horses, so I thought she'd be perfect."

"And I'm totally free labor!" Savannah chirps in. "This is my dream volunteer role. I can use this on my college applications next year. *Savannah Bennett, senior stable-hand at the Harding Estate*," she intones dreamily.

"I *did* offer to pay her," Sheri tells me, but Savannah declining payment is the most Savannah Bennett thing ever, and I have to laugh.

Sheri is right, though, Savannah is the right person to assist her, even though seeing her here makes me feel … well, jealous. I've been the one helping out over the summer, and I've enjoyed working alongside Sheri, but I have to leave, and now Savannah will be the one exercising the horses around the fields alongside Sheri instead. Life in Fairview will continue, but I won't be part of it. I don't like the way my throat turns dry at the thought of it.

"I was just telling Sheri that she should totally open a riding school," says Savannah, leaping past me to gesture outside the stables to the rolling green fields. "Look at all this free space! All these empty fields that you guys don't use!"

"And *I* was just telling Savannah that I'm not qualified to be an instructor," Sheri says dismissively as she stacks folders away into a battered filing cabinet and slams the jerky metal drawers shut.

"But you could be!" Savannah protests. "You'd be a natural at it."

I move to Fredo's pen and he pokes his head over the door and nuzzles my neck, his hot breath tickling my skin. As I stroke his soft nose, I look at Sheri. "Savannah's right. Why *don't* you do something more with this place?"

"Oh, not you too, Mila!" Sheri exclaims. "This hasn't been a working ranch for years, and the only reason we even still have the horses is because my mother loved them dearly. I do too, but I honestly owe it to her to keep them around."

I scratch Fredo behind his ears. "These were Mawmaw's horses?"

"Of course, Mila. Don't you remember her out riding them every morning when you were young?" she asks, walking over. She leans back against the door to Fredo's pen and looks at me over his long, expressive face. "Dad never wanted stables. It was only ever cattle and sheep we had here when your dad and I were kids, but Mom persuaded him for their wedding anniversary to build her these stables and line it with stallions."

"Relationship goals," Savannah says with a sigh, gazing off into the distance as though planning how one day she too will eventually twist her future spouse's arm into building her her own personal stables.

"Dream on, sunshine," Sheri snorts and pats Savannah on the shoulder. "I'll be back in a second. I'm just going to check on Popeye."

"I saw him rifling through his toolbox earlier," I warn her, and she releases a groan of exasperation and takes off toward the house, though I doubt she stands any chance of getting him to put the screwdrivers down and his feet up instead.

"Will you take good care of Fredo for me when I'm gone?" I ask Savannah, pouting sadly. "He's my favorite. We've really bonded this summer." And perfectly on cue,

Fredo whinnies into my ear, lovingly nudging deeper into my neck. "Yes, Fredo, I'll miss you too."

"I promise," Savannah says, and she holds out her pinky, which I interlock around mine. We exchange a smile and then she gets back to work in an empty pen, the shovel scraping the concrete floor.

"Blake called this morning," I tell her, lingering at the door to the pen she's working in. "He has a gig next week. Monday at Honky Tonk Central, so we all need to be there to hype him up."

"*Finally!*" she says, flashing me the biggest grin. "That's so cool. Some of us were hoping he'd perform at the tailgate last weekend. It was so boring without him taking charge of entertainment."

"Yeah, how was that?" I ask, as casually as I can. Thanks to Lacey, I'm fully aware that the July tailgate party took place on Friday night, but of course, Blake and I were hours away in Memphis. The night may not have gone as planned, but I'm still glad I was there with Blake, rather than stuck playing games at the tailgate.

Savannah drops the shovel and nearly throws herself against the door, reaching over it to grab onto me in a flurry of excitement. "Nathan Hunt talked to me! Like, *talked* to me. Not just 'Hey, can you pass me a soda?', but a real conversation. Then he liked my Instagram post the next morning! I was going to message him, but Tori said that would be lame and desperate, but if she's such a feminist, why would she think it's lame for the girl to make the first move? You know?"

"Caaaaalm," I say slowly, placing my hands on her shoulder. I take some deep breaths, nodding for Savannah to copy, and her cheeks flare with color. How will I ever survive back home without a babbling Savannah in my life?

"Sorry," she apologizes. We let go of one another and she heads back to continue her shoveling, telling me over her shoulder, "But yeah. Barney took Blake's role as host, and Lacey was clearly annoyed that Blake wasn't there because apparently he told her he would be? I don't know. She didn't smile the whole night. Meanwhile, Myles and Cindy suspiciously disappeared onto the baseball field for twenty minutes, but I don't even want to *imagine* what they were doing." She shudders.

"I'm really starting to dislike Lacey," I gripe, grinding my teeth in frustration.

I'm so sick of this girl and her sweet, angelic smiles. Blake is *my* boyfriend, and although she may have dated him before me, he dumped her at the end of the day. It feels seriously twisted how she's still pursuing a guy who's with someone else, and I don't like knowing that soon I won't be around. My being gone might give Lacey the nerve to parade herself around Blake even more. And considering she doesn't hesitate to make moves on him in front of my face, I dread to think what exactly she will do when I'm not here. I trust Blake, I do, but he just doesn't seem to notice that Lacey has an agenda when it comes to him.

I'm hoping and praying I can stay in town for a little while longer. I really want her to get the message that, in spite of LeAnne's cozy dinner invites, she's no longer part of Blake's life.

Savannah has turned back to cleaning the stall and while she's hard at work, I stealthily creep toward the back of the stables. Saddles, helmets, and reins all hang from the wall. Grooming and cleaning tools overflow from dusty trays, and on the old rickety desk, I zero in on a folder that Sheri has left out. I flip it open – it's insurance paperwork for the horses, all neatly organized in plastic sheet protectors – and scan my way through each page until I find Fredo's paperwork. With a quick glance over my shoulder to ensure Savannah isn't paying attention, I grab the IDs from my back pocket and slip them inside the sheet protector, then slam the folder shut and file it away in the cabinet.

"Do you need some help?" I offer as I return to Savannah, and when she nods, I hunt down another shovel and join her in the pen.

After a minute, she gives me a suspicious look. "Why are you smiling like that?"

"No reason," I say.

And I'm not smiling because I find pleasure in shoveling horse crap – no way.

I'm smiling because no one will be boarding a flight out of here anytime soon.

# 21

Engrossed, Mom's gaze travels the length of the shelf and back again, entranced by the drugstore makeup options on offer. She plucks a six-dollar mascara from the rack and examines it between her fingertips. "People really use this?"

"Yes, Mom," I say, pressing my lips into a firm line and snatching the tube from her hand. I place it back on the shelf and grab her elbow, pulling her away before she has a heart attack when she discovers that two-dollar lip gloss exists. "Don't be such an elitist. You weren't *always* a sought-after Hollywood MUA," I remind her.

"I know, but it's just been such a long time since I've—"

"Stepped foot inside a Walmart?" I finish with a judgmental tilt of my head.

Mom has always been the one to instill humility in me, more so than Dad, but sometimes she loses sight of where she came from in life. It's rare, but it happens. Sometimes when you live a life of luxury for so long, you forget it's exactly that – luxury.

Mom lowers her head, shamefaced, perfectly aware of how snooty she's been acting ever since we pulled up in the parking lot in the rental SUV. But she didn't expect to be in Fairview for so long, and she needs supplies. Specifically, a conditioning hair mask that – no surprises here – Walmart doesn't stock. Still, it feels otherworldly, browsing the aisles of Walmart with Mom. Okay, it's not where we usually hang out, but checking out cosmetics together is such a normal thing for people to do, and I'm just glad to get us both out of the house. Plus, there's no crowd of paparazzi swarming outside the Harding Estate anymore, so Mom is free to leave without fear of being harassed. That doesn't mean she isn't maintaining a low profile still – she's draped in a baggy, unflattering sweater with a pair of sunglasses resting on her head, ready to hide behind at any moment if anyone were to recognize her.

"Can we go by Dunkin' on the way home? I *need* a hazelnut iced coffee right about now."

"Sure," Mom says, glancing into the blue Walmart handbasket I have resting in the crook of my elbow. "Is there anything else we need? Maybe we should bring something back for your grandpa."

"This way," I say, making a sharp U-turn and directing Mom down the candy aisle. "He loves Jolly Ranchers."

Mom abruptly halts. "Oh! I forgot dental floss. I'll be back in a second."

As she disappears, I weave my way around some kids eyeing up M&Ms and search for the largest bag of Jolly Ranchers I can find. Popeye is always sucking on those damn things, so I reach out for a bag that should last him until the end of the year.

"Mila?"

I twist around and my heart momentarily stops beating, like a glitch in the system.

"I thought it was you! Hey!"

I force myself to say, "Hi, Lacey."

Lacey brings herself closer to me, her brunette hair in a high, smooth ponytail that swings around her shoulders as she walks. It's the first time I've ever encountered her while alone, and the shine of those red streaks in her hair beneath the fluorescent lightning sends a ripple of total indignation through me. Who does this girl think she is?

"We missed you at the tailgate, but how was Memphis?" she asks, and as always, her voice is sweet yet with a subtle undertone of falseness.

"I loved it," I answer with a bright, emphasized smile. "Blake and I had a blast."

Lacey props an elbow up on a shelf of Hershey's and keeps her expression placid, but the corner of her mouth twitches. "Did he take you to the Tin Roof? I love that place. He kissed me up on the balcony once."

"Are you kidding me?"

She wipes the complacent smirk from her face and widens her eyes in mock innocence, feigning confusion. "What?"

My resentment rears its ugly head and I drop the handbasket to the floor. I slam the bag of candy in my hands back onto the shelf and take a step toward Lacey, my pulses racing with hot anger at the image of her lips against Blake's. "That was then," I remind her in a cold voice. "He's not yours."

"No, but he was," she says calmly, "and who knows what will happen when we head off to college together?"

I screw up my face, wondering how this girl was voted student body president at Fairview High. She is truly delusional. "You're applying to Vanderbilt?"

"No. Tennessee down in Knoxville, and LeAnne will ensure that Blake applies there too." Her smile is back, more composed than ever, while I have my jaw clenched rigid in an effort to control myself.

"Do you know how twisted that is? For you and his mom to manipulate him like this?" I shake my head in disbelief, unable to comprehend how underhanded they both are. "He doesn't want the University of Tennessee. He wants to study music at Vanderbilt. Why don't you and LeAnne get that?"

"Mila." Mom clears her throat from behind me and I snap out of it, instantly feeling a surge of shame for venting my jealousy. I can't let Lacey manipulate me too. Mom narrows her eyes at me, bewildered, and then leans across me to grab the bag of Jolly Ranchers. She drops them into the basket on the floor, then swoops down to pick it up. "Let's go," she says.

Lacey dares to wave goodbye, but I don't give her the satisfaction of letting her turn me irate again. I don't think I'm an aggressive person. Most arguments have me crying in two seconds flat. I can't *bear* animosity, but there's something about Lacey that pushes my buttons. Or maybe it's something about Blake that brings out a territorial streak in me. Whatever it is, I don't like that I'm capable of getting so riled up.

"Who was that?" Mom demands to know as soon as we've turned the corner toward the checkouts. "And *why* were you talking to her like that?"

"Blake's ex-girlfriend," I mumble. "She likes to remind me of the *history* between them."

Mom begins unloading the basket's contents onto the conveyor belt, but not without looking at me in disapproval from beneath her thick, false lashes. "Mila, if there's one thing in life you need to bear in mind, it's that you should always remain calm when confronted. You never win by fighting fire with fire." Then her tone softens a little in sympathy. "Truly, however sly she might be, don't let her get the better of you."

I sigh and take the bags, then we head outside into the parking lot. I might have had a run-in with Lacey, but I'm honestly rather amazed we made it through an entire Walmart shopping spree without anyone bothering Mom or interrogating us about Dad.

"By the way," says Mom as we stroll toward the SUV, "we were thinking of going home on Friday."

My feet stop moving. "*This* Friday?"

"Yes, this Friday. As in two days from now."

Even though their IDs are safely hidden, there's a seed of anxiety that somehow my parents and Ruben will still manage to get me on a flight. I need to at least appeal to Mom. Maybe if I explain just how badly I want to stay until the summer is over, they'll let me stay put, even if that means they go home without me.

"Mom—"

A Tesla pulling into the lot catches my eye. As it draws closer, my first thought is proven to be true – it is, indeed, LeAnne Avery's car. What was supposed to be a quick trip to Walmart for hair products has turned into the worst outing possible. First Lacey, now LeAnne. Small towns really are a curse when you're trying to keep a low profile.

"Uh, Mom, you should get in the car," I say as I speed-walk over to the SUV where Mom is throwing the bags into the trunk. "Like, *now*. LeAnne Avery just pulled in."

Mom slams the trunk shut with way more power than necessary, and lifts her head to scan our surroundings. "Where?"

"That Tesla," I hiss, subtly pointing as LeAnne's car makes its way down the same row we're already parked in. "C'mon. Let's go."

But Mom doesn't budge. She locks her eyes on the Tesla as it comes to a standstill in a parking spot, then LeAnne steps out. Even doing the grocery run, Mayor Avery is elegant and classy, like a total boss who isn't afraid to let the world know she is in charge. Her impeccable outfit highlights her gym-toned figure, and her heels click with authority against the asphalt as she walks.

"LeAnne," Mom says loudly, and my jaw falls open as I gape at her. We had a clear getaway – LeAnne hadn't noticed us yet. *Why* would Mom want to get her attention?

LeAnne halts and looks back in search of the voice

that's called her name, and I see her shoulders stiffen when she spots Mom and me. However, she maintains her composure and confidently approaches.

"Marnie," she says in a clipped voice. "Mila."

"Everett already told you," Mom says, immediately confrontational, rooted to the spot in her refusal to get in the car, "but I'd like to remind you one more time. You had no right to share our history with Mila, and if you ever, *ever* ambush my daughter like that again—"

"Mom, let's just go," I plead, trying to fish the car keys out from her enclosed fist, but her fingers are sealed tightly around them.

LeAnne rests her hand on the strap of her purse, her cool expression as dauntless and intimidating as ever. "That sounds like you have more secrets to hide, Marnie."

Is there anything trashier than calling each other out in the Walmart parking lot? Sure, I've just had a less than edifying encounter with Lacey inside, but Mom knows better than this. Hell, so does LeAnne. But despite their high-profile public images, they're both women who wanted to be with the same man twenty years ago. Two decades – and a distance of two thousand miles – don't seem to have leveled out the tension between them. The atmosphere is off the scale with friction. And when I catch sight of the wrath barely concealed within LeAnne's steady gaze, I wonder if perhaps she hates Mom more than she hates Dad. After all, Mom *knew* Dad was engaged, yet she got involved anyway. She owed LeAnne nothing, but still her behavior feels shabby, treacherous.

I think of Lacey leaning so coolly against the shelves and the rage that coursed through me, and for a terrifying split second, I understand LeAnne. I get it. The anger is irrational, uncontrollable. LeAnne has every right to be hostile.

"You haven't changed," Mom openly sneers, and again I recoil at the venom in her voice.

"Neither have you," LeAnne fires, then narrows her eyes as she looks Mom up and down, scrutinizing the huge hoodie she's wearing. "Except maybe your fashion sense. Is *oversized* how they dress in Hollywood these days?"

Mom purses her lips and takes great, callous pleasure in announcing, "Oh, this old thing? It's Everett's. Boyfriend style at its best, I guess."

"*Mom!*" I hiss, mortified.

I have never seen my mother act this way. What happened to not fighting fire with fire? She is always so caring and supportive, sweet and polite, but this person standing next to me now is ... immature. Taunting and cruel. It's so jarring, and this stand-off is straight-up embarrassing. It feels like I'm suddenly the parent and she's the teenager, because I have to step in front of her and push her back, forcing her toward the car. Thank God we're at the back of the parking lot and no one has witnessed this encounter. But I doubt LeAnne would have come near us if there was any possibility of witnesses.

"I'm sorry, LeAnne," I say with a chagrined glance at Mom, and perhaps it's the genuine feeling in my voice that finally cracks her indestructible demeanor.

LeAnne stares at me as I climb into the SUV with Mom, and then I catch her eye in the side mirror. She seems rather stunned that I may have just, however briefly, taken her side. It almost feels like a betrayal against my parents, and a niggle of guilt settles inside me as I pull on my seatbelt. LeAnne gathers herself and, as though nothing unusual has happened, struts off toward the store.

Mom, on the other hand, is livid. She grabs hold of the steering wheel and squeezes hard, her head tilted back as she glares out the panoramic sun roof to the blue skies above.

"How that woman *ever* got elected mayor is beyond me!" she mutters, exhaling slowly as she lowers her chin and starts the engine. "I can't stand that superiority complex of hers. I don't care if she was the damn president. I'd still think she was a bitch."

With a reproachful look, I shake my head. "Remind me again what you were just saying about keeping calm when confronted?"

# 22

There's a knock on my bedroom door as I'm getting ready for bed on Thursday evening. I continue massaging cream into my face as I skip toward the door, expecting it to be Mom checking in before she goes to sleep too, but my relatively upbeat mood diminishes at the sight of Ruben on the other side of the threshold.

"Oh," I say. I immediately turn back around without another word and sit down on the edge of my bed, not making eye contact with him as I peacefully moisturize my forehead. Sometimes it's easier to completely deny his existence, otherwise my blood pressure gets too high.

Ruben strides into my room and peers around. "Change of plan. It's time to get this show on the road!"

"What?" I pretend to be surprised at his barking.

"I've booked us all a one-way ticket out of this God-forsaken town. Our flight is early tomorrow," he explains. "I need you packed and ready to leave first thing."

"Well, *you* can board that flight, but I'm not leaving yet," I tell him, unthreatened.

"I'm serious, Mila," he insists. "Where's your suitcase?"

When I stare expressionless at him, he has the nerve to march over to my closet. He finds my empty suitcase inside and drags it out, flinging it open on the floor.

Calmly, I wipe my hands together and remain perched on the end of my bed, like having Ruben storm around my room is perfectly normal. "What's with the attitude?"

"Because I know you don't want to go home and I know you're going to argue with me, and quite frankly, I'm not here for your whining." He places his hands on his hips and nods down at my suitcase. "So please just get going with it. I can't have you holding things up tomorrow."

"No." I gesture to my sweatpants. "Can you leave my room? I need to change into my pajamas."

"*Mila*," he growls, fixing me with one of his infamous threatening looks that would have worked on me before. I never would have challenged Ruben's authority and control, but I no longer take orders from him. "Just pack the damn case."

"No," I repeat. Keeping my temper in check, I act as though he's not even in the room. I flip my head upside down, gather up my hair and secure it into a messy bun, refusing to let my nightly beauty routine be disrupted.

"Then I'll damn well do it for you," Ruben bristles, and starts yanking my clothes from their hangers. Recklessly, he tosses them into my suitcase in a messy heap. He pulls some shirts out so aggressively that he snaps a couple hangers, but still, I remain unflinching. "Are you sure you don't want to do this yourself?" he asks, purposely scrunching up one of my blouses into a ball and aiming it into my suitcase like a basketball player shooting hoops.

I shrug, unconcerned. "Whatever. You think I care about a creased blouse?"

My lack of reaction only drives Ruben deeper into his rage. I've never seen him quite so rattled and it's almost fun to watch.

"Agreeing to send you out here for the summer has been the worst decision I think I've ever made, and I can only hope that once we're back home, you'll lose this attitude and start acting like your normal self again."

"And what was I like before, Ruben? A pushover? Easy to control?" I lean back on my hands and cross one leg over the other, knowing that my disinterested act is only making him more enraged, like he knows he's losing his grip on me with each passing day. "You aren't *my* manager."

Ruben starts grabbing pairs of my sneakers now, bundling them into the suitcase. "Your father doesn't have time to deal with your teenage crap, Mila. He's a busy man, with more than enough on his plate, and for what it's worth, I do think you're being incredibly selfish acting out the way you are."

"You're right, he doesn't have time to deal with my *teenage crap*," I say, "because he's busy dealing with his own short-comings. Like, let me think, his affair." Ruben glances up, eyes narrowed and sharp, and I blink innocently as though I've said nothing out of line. "You should be helping him make amends for that, but then again ... Dad is a saint in your eyes, isn't he? It's just the rest of us – the ones he hurts with his crappy behavior – who you like to yell at."

"That's enough," Ruben snaps, pushing my suitcase across the carpeted floor with his toe. He points a finger at me. "I'm serious, Mila. You'll be on that flight home tomorrow."

"But, Ruben—" I sit up straight and widen my eyes with a tiny lift of my shoulders. "I'm so sorry, but I believe my parents may have mislaid their ID cards."

Ruben glowers down at me. "Mila."

"Ruben."

"Stop fooling around. What have you done with their driver's licenses?"

"I just told you," I say. "Perhaps they misplaced them somewhere?"

We stare at each other in a tense standoff till I break it with an aggravating grin. I almost giggle and that sends his temper skyrocketing, his nostrils flaring as a fury consumes him. Ruben gets angry, sure, but he usually knows when to reel it back. He's always been professional; mannered and icy. Now, however, he is like a spoiled toddler throwing a tantrum when he can't get his way. He moves to the dresser first, pulling open drawers and rifling through each one, only to slam them shut again when he doesn't find what he's looking for. There's no luck in my bedside table drawer either, so he starts raiding my purses. It's totally inappropriate for him to be going through my stuff like this, but I sit back and let him lose his mind for sheer entertainment value anyway.

I yawn and pretend to examine my nails, pushing back the cuticles while he flies off the handle. I only look up when I notice he's found my wallet. He pulls out dollar bills, throwing them on the floor, and tosses my Dunkin' Donuts loyalty card onto the bed in disgust. Eyes fierce, he storms over and thrusts the empty wallet in my face.

"Mila, *where* are the IDs?" he hisses.

Again, I shrug. "Who knows?"

Ruben lunges. He grabs my arms and pulls me to my feet as my breath catches in my throat. Holding me steady in front of him, his fingers tighten around my forearms and his nails dig into my skin. He brings his forehead level with mine and glares furiously into my eyes. I pull away as much as I can. It is the first time I have ever, ever felt truly fearful of him.

"What the hell?"

Dad bursts into the room and in one fast movement shoves Ruben away from me, grasping my arms. He runs his eyes over the scratches and the redness from the pressure. His shocked eyes lock with mine, and then he turns.

"*Ruben!*" he snarls. "What the hell are you *doing*?"

Ruben backs away, flustered, and points at me. "She's hidden your ID! She's playing us all for fools!"

"I don't care!" Dad snaps, closing the distance between the two of them and pressing his chest against Ruben's. Their faces only inches apart, Dad warns in a low, frightening voice, "You don't ever lay a hand on my daughter."

"I know, I know," Ruben relents, attempting to retreat.

"It won't happen again. Mila, I can only apologize." But Dad sticks to him like glue until Ruben is backed up against the wall. He is always so bold and confident when he's the only one in charge, but I notice that he's not so brave around Dad. He tucks his shoulders in, seemingly aiming to make himself smaller. "I was simply asking her to pack her bags."

"Bags be damned," Dad spits. "You're right it won't happen again. In fact, you can pack *your* bags. You're fired."

"Now, now, Everett, let's not be hasty," Ruben says, but the panic in his voice is unmistakable.

Dad puts his hand on Ruben's shoulder. "I said you're fired. Why are you still here?"

"Everett, c'mon!" Ruben pleads, gently shrugging away Dad's grip. "I've worked with you for over ten years! You aren't just going to throw that away because I raised my voice at your kid, are you?"

"You laid a hand on her!" Dad barks, and I flinch as he curls his hand into a fist. "You have ten seconds to get out of my face before I do something I *won't* regret, Ruben. Get your stuff and leave. Now."

Mom rushes into the room, having heard all the commotion. "What's going on?"

"Ruben is leaving," Dad tells her, then sets his fierce eyes back on Ruben and begins to count down. "Ten. Nine. Eight—"

"Okay! I get the message," Ruben mutters, succumbing to defeat perhaps in order to save his nose from being broken. He stomps to the door, but looks back at us with a look of intense betrayal. "You won't find anyone else in this business who's as loyal as I am."

"Luckily, I don't need a manager for what I intend to do next," Dad says. "Now go."

Ruben marches off down the hallway to his guest room, and Dad and Mom both rush to my aid, one at either side of me. Mom cups my cheeks in her hands and examines every square inch of my face in a frenzied state, while Dad takes a closer look at my arms. They are so full of concern, you'd think I'd just been mauled by a tiger.

"I'm okay," I reassure them. "Seriously. He just …grabbed me a little too hard."

"That man is a disgrace!" Mom says, pushing my hair gently from my face to plant a kiss on my forehead. "He has no right to grab you at all."

There's a cough at the doorway, and the three of us look over to find Popeye and Sheri peering around the frame, like they're afraid to interrupt.

"Did we just overhear you firing that son of a bitch?" Popeye asks, and Dad laughs. A genuine laugh, which I never thought I'd hear from him around Popeye.

"It's been a long time coming," Dad says, taking a deep breath. When he releases it again, he is visibly more relaxed, like he's exhaled the tension out of his body. "I know I've made a lot of bad decisions and that Ruben did the groundwork for me, but that doesn't excuse his behavior recently, and especially not tonight. We're not a good team anymore, and I wish I'd seen that sooner."

"So, he's leaving?" Sheri asks as she enters my room with Popeye by her side.

"Dad," I say in a quiet voice, and everyone looks at me, but I lock eyes with only my father. There are questions in my head. "What do you mean you won't need a manager for what you're going to do next?"

Dad presses his lips together. He regards me carefully, then lets out a sigh. "It's probably time that I told you," he says in a low voice, nerves laced around each word. He sits down on my bed and interlocks his hands between his knees.

"Should we leave?" Sheri asks, already taking Popeye's hand.

"No, we should all hear this!" Popeye protests, moving forward to avoid being dragged out of the room by Sheri. He is back to his usual self now that he's mostly recovered from his fall. He is clearly relieved we have all stopped pestering him so much, though sometimes I still bring him a glass of sweet tea in the mornings and help him remove the wrapper from a Jolly Rancher every once in a while. He doesn't seem to mind help so much so long as it comes from me.

"Yes, both of you. Stay," Dad says. His dark eyes are gentle as they glance between his father and sister. "I need to share this with you too."

My heartbeat picks up speed and my stomach knots. Dad never gets nervous. Even before red carpet events, he's as relaxed as ever. This is something big, and I have no idea what's coming, except that it feels like impending doom. "What is it?" I urge, voice cracked.

Dad exchanges a look with Mom, and she nods encouragingly as she places a hand on his shoulder. He reaches up to place his hand over hers, then he swallows the lump in his throat and announces, "I've decided to step back from acting."

There's a long moment of silence as this news travels around my bedroom.

"But you can't stop acting, Dad!" I tell him, scrunching up my face in confusion. "You love what you do!"

"I don't intend to leave the industry," he says. "I'd like to try my hand at producing, and eventually maybe directing. It's been on my mind for a while now, and I have deliberately been turning down new offers of work so that I'm off the hook as soon as the remaining promotion for the Flash Point movies are done. I've kept Ruben in the dark about all of this. He thinks I'm just holding out for better offers."

Mom shifts uncomfortably from one foot to the other. "Mila, when your dad first discussed this with me, I wasn't ready to listen," she admits. "I wasn't sure this would be the right route for him to take, so I wasn't what anyone would call supportive."

"And I made the mistake of letting the stress get to me," Dad says as he lowers his eyes to the floor, shamefaced. "There's no excuse for what I've done, but Mila, though your mom and I still have work to do, we honestly believe that we are going to be okay, and things are going to be different when we go home. Better."

"He's right," Mom agrees with a nod.

I glance between the pair of them, dubious. This seems

like too much of a united front, as if all their issues have been neatly ironed out. Are they just feeding me a spiel of what I want to hear? But I sense a glimmer of truth in there somewhere that I grasp onto.

After an awkward moment of silence, Sheri chews her lower lip and says, "I'm glad to hear that, but you're really giving it up, Everett?"

"It's not the life I want anymore," Dad says. "Not when it's having such an impact on everyone around me, and I've gotten far too wrapped up in it all. Whereas producing won't have me in the public eye so much." He anxiously catches Popeye's gaze. "So maybe we could visit more often without causing such a ridiculous stir."

Popeye is skeptical. He rubs his hand over the bandage on his head as he contemplates Dad's offer, then grunts in what I think just may be acceptance. "Well, *Everett Harding, director and producer* sounds a lot better than *Everett Harding, actor.*"

Dad wipes his forehead. "We still need to work on your criticism of the creative arts."

Popeye scowls, but there's a good-natured glint in his eye. "C'mon Sheri, let's show that Ruben fool where the door is."

Sheri follows Popeye out of the room, placing a hand on Dad's arm and offering him a smile – which has a hint of forgiveness in it – as she passes. It's like some much-needed oxygen has been injected into the air, because the atmosphere suddenly isn't so pressurized. A weight has been lifted. I get the sense that redemption may be possible for not only Dad, but all of us. *Maybe*. If we can learn to trust one another again, however long that may take.

Mom takes my hand and pulls me down onto the edge of my bed with her, stroking my cheek. "Are you sure you're okay, honey?" she asks, doubtfully eyeing my arms again. But the sting of Ruben's touch has faded.

"I'm fine," I reassure her once more.

Dad crouches down in front of Mom and me so that he's level with us. He pulls his wallet out and scans through his cards, raising a stern eyebrow when he realizes his driver's license is, in fact, gone. "What really happened to our IDs, Mila?"

"Well, I don't know exactly," I lie, biting my lip as a smile threatens to expose me, "but I have this feeling that they might show up on Tuesday."

"Tuesday? Why Tuesday?"

"Okay, just hear me out," I plead, pressing my hands together in a begging gesture. "Blake has his first ever gig in Nashville on Monday night, and I *have* to be there. Please, please, *please* can we just stay here for a few more days? I promise I'll come home after that."

"Mila ..." Mom says, frowning.

"*Please*."

I hold my breath as I watch my parents silently check in with one another, wondering which of them will give in first. Surprisingly, it's Dad.

"Tuesday," he says firmly. "Not a day longer."

"Thank you, thank you, thank you!" I stammer, and I fight the urge to break out into dance. *I'm going to see Blake perform live to a real audience. I'm going to be the one cheering the loudest.*

Dad tilts his head. "Now where are our IDs?"

And with a devious grin, I don't even hesitate to tell him. "Inside the sheet protector containing Fredo's insurance paperwork in the green folder in the filing cabinet in the stables."

# 23

"Do you *have* to drive like an idiot?" Savannah mumbles as she shoots her brother a deathly look. "You just ran a stop sign. Are you trying to get pulled over? Cindy will think you're *so* cool if you get your driver's license suspended."

Myles rolls his eyes and looks at me in his rearview mirror. "Mila, tell her to stop being such a wuss."

"But I agree with her," I say, clinging to my seatbelt a little tighter. "I'd prefer to make it to Blake's in one piece, so can you please slow down?"

Myles scowls and eases off the gas as we cross through a lively – well, as lively as a town with a population of less than ten thousand can possibly get on a Saturday night – downtown Fairview. We are en route to Blake's house. LeAnne has conferences in the city this weekend, so she's staying at her Nashville apartment again, which means Blake has the house to himself. He's invited us over to eat pizza while he rehearses his set ahead of Monday, and he says we are all more than welcome to sleep over in the cabin. It feels amazing not to have to sneak out for once. My parents came to the joint decision that I should at least enjoy my final few days here in Fairview before we go home on Tuesday.

Which is a fact I have yet to share with anyone. Especially Blake. The longer I keep this from him, the more the stress piles up, but I'd rather shoulder it all myself than burden him with it during the lead-up to his big gig.

"Are we gonna tell him if his set list sucks?" Myles asks as he parks on the driveway next to Blake's truck. "Because Mila, you're the girlfriend, so I think it has to be you to break the news to him."

Savannah smacks Myles's arm. "His set list won't suck."

"I agree with Savannah again," I comment from the backseat. "Blake knows what he's doing."

"Here's the rock star now!" Myles says, gesturing ahead through the windshield.

Blake swings open the gate to the backyard and Bailey bounds out onto the driveway, circling all of our legs as we jump out of Myles's car. He races back and forth between each of us, unsure of who to sniff first, overcome with joy, but eventually settles on clambering all over Savannah.

I stroll over to Blake with my usual giddy smile that I'm unable to suppress. "Hey," I say in a breathy whisper, burying my head into his chest and wrapping my arms around him.

"Longest week ever," he murmurs, resting his chin atop my head and holding me close to him, protectively and securely. Then he pulls back, pushes my hair behind my ears, strokes my face, and kisses me.

"Why the hell did you even invite Savannah and me

over here?" Myles jokes, and Blake and I both grin over at him. "We can leave if you'd prefer privacy."

Blake drops his hands from my face down to my hip where he interlocks his fingers around mine. "Get your ass in here, Myles. You too, Bailey!"

We all move into the backyard, because despite Blake having the entire house to himself, he still prefers his private cabin outside. It has everything he needs out here, and the weather is too nice to be indoors. Plus, Bailey enjoys digging up dirt and rocketing around the lawn at full speed.

"Puppy zoomies!" Savannah cheers as she chases after him.

After ten minutes of deliberation over which pizza toppings we can all agree on – and ending up ordering two, anyway, because Savannah refuses to eat pepperoni – we all stretch out on the grass. Myles lies flat on his back, eyes closed. Savannah sits cross-legged next to Bailey, who has settled down from the initial thrill of having guests arrive, and calmly strokes him.

"So I haven't finalized anything yet," Blake begins, restless and unable to focus on anything but his guitar in his lap, "but I've picked out most of the songs I plan to cover. I just need to figure out which order to perform them in."

I'm sitting close to him, my knee pressed against his, and I can't wipe the smile from my face. I'm so in love with everything about him, from the dimples in his cheeks to the tremor in his fingertips as he lines them up on the fretboard. He notices my gaze latched onto him, but I don't bother denying that I'm staring. I don't look away, only smile wider, and he flashes me a suggestive grin.

"So I was thinking," Blake says, "that I should open with something fun and upbeat. Something modern, something more my style. I'm set on 'Home Sweet' by Russell Dickerson. And then I'll follow that up with some of my favorites, like Mitchell Tenpenny and Thomas Rhett, all of your more mainstream country pop. And then I was thinking I could do some older rock classics, like the kind of stuff my dad plays, like Keith Urban and Luke Bryan and Blake Shelton, and then cover some female artists. Trusty old faithful, Taylor Swift. Or maybe Carrie Underwood. And then I'll cover some bands. Rascal Flatts. The Chicks. And then I need a finisher."

"You talk like that as though we understand you," Myles says, sitting up from the grass. "Taylor Swift? Really?"

Blake pings his guitar pick at Myles. "Hey, Swift's older work is classic. It sounds really cool when a different gender from the original artist covers a song. People respond well to it."

"I, personally, can't wait to hear you perform a Taylor Swift song," I tell Blake, "mostly because I actually know her music."

Myles flings the guitar pick over to me now and it bounces off my chest and lands in between my crossed legs. "Mila, you couldn't wait to hear Blake perform even if he was getting up on stage with a musical triangle and some maracas," he teases, and Savannah snorts.

"Oh, wait! I have a good finisher," says Blake. He leans

over my leg to fetch his pick, and then places it between his lips as he hoists his guitar into position. From his open guitar case on the grass behind him, he pulls out an odd-looking clip and clamps it around a very specific fret on his guitar. "This, Mila," he says teasingly as he taps the object in response to my intrigued expression, his voice muffled from the pick in his mouth, "is a capo. It changes the pitch. Makes it higher."

"Ohh." I still don't understand, but I nod anyway.

Blake takes his pick from between his lips and hovers his hand over the strings. "What do you guys think about 'I Want Crazy' by Hunter Hayes? It's fun, and it kind of makes me think of you." His smoldering gaze is on me, and for the thousandth time this summer, my body temperature rises and my face burns.

"Barf," Myles remarks, lying back down on the grass.

"I *love* that song!" Savannah says. "Let's hear it."

Blake doesn't wait. He breaks out into song in sync with the opening strum and under the evening sunset, I lean back on my hands and close my eyes, absorbing the mesmerizing sound of his voice. I could sit here forever, entranced, like I'm living in a dream. His voice is so gorgeous, it triggers goosebumps all over my skin, and my body tingles as the music moves through it.

He performs a few more songs for us, seeking our opinions on whether or not we think the crowd at Honky Tonk Central will appreciate them, and then the show is halted when the pizzas show up. And I would pick this over a tail-gate party or a bonfire any day of the week – eating pizza on the warm grass while Bailey works his way around the four of us, pawing at our arms with glistening puppy eyes, but to no avail.

As the sun dips in the horizon and the night goes on, we shift ourselves from the grass into the cabin. Blake takes a break from rehearsing his covers to play a mean game of foosball against Myles, which results in a lot of swearing and yelling. Savannah tucks blankets around Bailey as he settles in his bed in the corner, then kisses him goodnight on his furry, golden forehead.

"*Boop*," she says, tapping his nose. She makes her way over to the couch where I'm basking in the ambience of a late summer's night in a cabin, then she lifts my legs out of the way so she can sit next to me. "I am *so* bloated from all that pizza. I feel like I'm going to throw up every time I take a breath."

I laugh and throw my head back against the couch with a satisfied sigh. "This has been really fun. I never do stuff like this back home. Music, pizza, a cabin … It really does feel like summer."

"*Cheat!*" Myles growls, punching the edge of the foosball table, startling Savannah and me. He raises his fist threateningly at Blake.

"You can't accuse someone of cheating just because you have no skill in those flimsy hands of yours," Blake taunts.

Myles smirks. "Cindy doesn't have a problem with the skill level of my hands."

"Yup, definitely gonna throw up," Savannah mutters while holding her breath, then gags.

"Talking of Cindy," Myles says, "she's waiting for me to drop by, so Savannah, let's get moving."

I sit up and crane my neck to look at Myles, suddenly on high alert, snapped out of my relaxed stupor. "You guys aren't staying over?"

"Not if Myles isn't," Savannah says as she gets up. "I don't want to be a third wheel."

So Savannah and Myles are leaving, which means I'm the only one spending the night …with Blake. Just the two of us, alone. My heart skips a beat and a flurry of nerves cascades through me, full of anticipation.

Blake appears behind the couch, gazing down at me with a smile. "Is that okay, Mila?"

"Yeah," I say, feigning nonchalance, but glad of his consideration. My stomach is in knots, and it's not from the pizza.

Blake leans over me and kisses my forehead, then takes my hands and pulls me up from the couch. With his arm slung over my shoulders, we escort Savannah and Myles out to the driveway, but they hop into the car and wave goodbye without dithering. Luckily, I remember to grab my bag from the backseat before they take off.

"Looks like it's just you and me," Blake says with a flirty glint in his eyes as we stroll back to the cabin. He shuts the door behind us and flicks on the dim lights now that it's starting to grow dark outside, and Bailey lifts his head from his bed to survey his surroundings before curling up and returning back to sleep.

"Just us two," I murmur, sitting back down on my spot

on the couch, which is still warm. My entire body feels tense and every single movement I make feels convoluted and unnatural. I'm overthinking this and I'm fully aware of it, but there's this unspoken agreement swirling in the air between us, like we both know exactly what kind of thoughts are running through each of our heads.

Blake sinks down on the couch next to me and scoots closer so that our thighs touch. "Just us two," he repeats, gaze twinkling, and his lips crash against mine.

It feels like I've waited all night, all *week*, to kiss him. *Really* kiss him. Our mouths are locked together, and his hands are on my neck, his thumbs skimming against my jawline, and I press my hand to his chest and grab hold of his T-shirt. I pull him up against me, then snake my hand down his spine to the hem of his shirt, tugging at the material.

Blake breaks the kiss to give in to my silent commands. He whips his T-shirt over his head and tosses it over the back of the couch, revealing his toned stomach and the V lines that disappear into the waistband of his boxers. Biting my lip, I lightly trace the contours of his abs with the tips of my fingers, but it must tickle, because he releases a breathy laugh and brings his mouth back to mine.

Our chests together, Blake pushes down on me, lowering me onto my back so that he's on top, but I like how I feel like I'm the one in control as I wrap my legs around his hips and lock his body in place. I grab hold of his hair, weaving my hands into his hairline while he drags his lips along my jaw, down my neck. As I tilt my head back and close my eyes, I feel his hand slip under my shirt and brush over my stomach, the warmth of his fingers making me flinch as he skims over my naval piercing.

Blake tears his lips from my neck and his hand from beneath my clothes. He hovers over my body, his hands pressed flat to the couch on either side of my head, supporting his weight. It's so sexy, that sweet, caring shine in his dark eyes. "We don't have to," he says.

"I want to," I whisper. Reaching out for his hand, I guide it back under my shirt and to the edge of my jean shorts. Then, delicately, I grasp the silver chain dangling from his neck and pull him back down against me.

He trails kisses along my collarbone that send shock waves all through me, to the point where I'm trembling from the energy of it. It suddenly feels like it's a hundred degrees in here, which is a perfect excuse to take my top off. Blake assists me, swiftly pulling my shirt over my head, and then he runs the tip of his index finger down the center of my chest and over the lace of my bra. I arch into him.

"Do you want to move inside to my room?" he asks.

I shake my head, my hands on his broad shoulders, and murmur, "No. Here is perfect."

Blake nods and slides his hands underneath my back, releasing the clasp of my bra, and as he slides it away from my body, I fumble with the button of his shorts rather uselessly. He grabs my hand and moves it above my head, locking our fingers together. With a soft peck against my lips, he gets off the couch and undoes his zipper and steps out of his shorts, kicking off his sneakers. It's an image I think will be ingrained in my mind forever: Blake Avery in his fitted white boxers, his tan skin, and that damn sexy silver chain necklace. He finds his way back to me, resuming our position on the couch, our bodies entwined. My heart is thundering and the sweat beading across Blake's smooth skin feels like the most irresistible sensation in the world. I have never felt more wanted as his hands follow the curve of my waist up to my chest.

"Mila," he says breathlessly, his voice seductively husky and extra twangy, "I just want to tell you ... before we—"

I cup his jaw in my hands. "I know, Blake. I feel the same way."

And we leave the words unsaid, because we say it in the way our mouths move in sync, in the way we passionately explore each other's body, in the way we smile every time our gazes lock.

We don't need to say out loud that we've fallen in love with each other.

# 24

A direct ray of sunshine irritating my eyes forces me awake. That's the downfall of the cabin – it is lined with windows but no blinds. Luckily, there's AC installed and it's been running all night, so at least I don't wake up in sweltering heat. I yawn and try to roll over on the couch, but I can't move far because of Blake.

He's tucked next to me, his arm resting over me, and he's only wearing boxers. I shyly bite my lip and glance down at myself. I'm wearing his T-shirt and I take a quick whiff of it, inhaling the scent of his cologne.

There's a scuffle of noise across the cabin, and I bolt upright and peer over the back of the couch. Bailey stretches out his legs, shakes out his fur, then pads over to his water bowl. My sudden movement has jerked Blake awake too, and he groans, still half in a slumber.

"Oh my God," I say, horrified. "I totally forgot Bailey was in here."

"Yeah," Blake says in that morning voice I remember so well from Memphis. "He was here the whole night. We should have probably put him in the house." He stretches out his chest and sits up, hands in his messy hair, which I may or may not have played a role in creating.

Our eyes meet and we both instantly look away, blushing.

"How about – uh – some breakfast?" Blake offers. "I can make a mean stack of pancakes."

"Perfect," I say, and I quit trying to suppress my grin and decide to own it instead. I'm beyond the point of being shy around Blake by now, and I really am happy this morning. Waking up next to Blake … wearing his T-shirt … fresh pancakes …

Can life get any better than this?

Answer: yes, yes it can, because Blake kisses me.

He takes my hand and pulls me to my feet, then we dash across the lawn toward the French doors with Bailey nipping at our heels, thinking we're playing chase. We head inside the grand kitchen, as spotless as ever and as though no one actually lives here. How the hell LeAnne runs a city *and* her home at the same time is beyond me. Maybe they have a maid.

We pass the dining room where I joined Blake and his mom for that awkward lunch one Sunday, and then we head deeper into the house. It's the furthest inside I've been, and I examine the elegant art on the walls and inhale the scent of fresh linen as I follow Blake upstairs to his room, which is surprisingly tidy for a teenage guy. The walls are plain white, his navy bedsheets are neat and crease-free, and there's not a single out-of-place object. I wonder if he even spends time in here, or if he just prefers the more relaxed solitude of the cabin.

"Here," he says, pulling open a drawer and tossing me a pair of gym shorts. He grabs some sweatpants for himself and slides them on. As he passes me on his way out of the room, he catches me in his arms and passionately kisses me, his hands pressing against me. "Now, pancakes. Extra fluffy just for you."

Back in the kitchen, I play tug-of-war on the floor with Bailey over a stuffed rabbit while admiring the dips in Blake's spine as he works shirtless at the stove. I'm wearing the gym shorts he passed me, along with his T-shirt I slept in, and my hair is gathered into a messy bun on the crown of my head, but I wouldn't change this morning for anything. Blake turns to me, a cocky smirk on his face as he confidently flicks a pancake into the air and smoothly catches it again in the pan.

"Okay, I get it, Blake," I say, lifting my hands in a gesture of defeat, "you can sing, you can play guitar, *and* you can perfectly flip a pancake. What *can't* you do?"

He sets the pan back down on the stove and winks at me over his shoulder. "I can't help falling for you."

Fireworks rip through me, exploding in my chest, brightening my world with color. His words fill me with so much joy that I give up my fight with Bailey and let him bolt off with his toy in victory. Hoisting myself up from the kitchen floor, I sneak up behind Blake, wrap my arms around him, and press my head against the warm skin of his back.

My heart clutches tight when I remember these are our last few days together. Just two more days of flirtatious smirks with Blake ... *Two*. And I still haven't told him yet.

I just can't bear to ruin these perfect moments, and I fear that if Blake knows we are on a very, very short timer, things will be different.

"Can you grab some plates? Top cupboard over there," says Blake.

I nod against his shoulder blade and unwrap myself from him. While he cooks the pancakes, I get plates and silverware, and then dice up some strawberries. I do have to admit, his pancake-making skills are extraordinary – he makes a stack on each plate, sprinkles strawberries over them, then smothers the pancakes in maple syrup.

"This is way better than the cereal breakfasts I've been having at the ranch," I tell him as I sit at the dining table, and he sets the pancakes down in front of me. I'm practically drooling.

"*Bon appétit!*" he says with a dramatic chef's-kiss gesture.

He collapses into the seat next to me, and together we dig into our romantic breakfast. This is all new to me and I wasn't sure what to expect this morning, whether or not it would be awkward, but I only feel closer to Blake than I did before. I trust him, I feel safe with him. We keep glancing at each other as we eat, unable to break out of our permanent smiles. I almost want to cry at the injustice of it, I want to wake up in his arms every day.

"By the way," I say, engaging in conversation before I end up hurling myself across the table at him, the urge to touch him almost too strong to resist, "did your mom tell you about the run-in she had with *my* mom on Wednesday? In the Walmart parking lot."

Blake scoffs, like he too thinks our parents are immature and embarrassing. "Yeah, she did. They really hate each other, huh? Mom actually ended up telling me something she hadn't mentioned before. About your dad."

"Oh?" I say curiously, dropping my fork on my plate with a clatter.

"Apparently, he tried to apologize to her once. A few years later after he married your mom," he says, "but she wasn't ready to forgive him yet, so she didn't accept his apology. She needed more time or something."

My features slacken. The day Ruben confronted LeAnne on her porch, he mentioned during the car ride back to the ranch that Dad tried to smooth things over with her, to fix the mess he'd made. Neither Ruben nor I believed that was true, but if LeAnne herself admits he tried ... then I guess he must have.

"Why does she still hold such a grudge against him then?" I wonder out loud, feeling defensive. Surely Dad isn't so callous that he *wouldn't* have tried to make things right with LeAnne, and I'm angry at myself for thinking he could be. "He tried to apologize."

Blake takes my empty plate and stacks it on top of his, standing up. "Yeah, but she wanted to forgive him when the time felt right for *her*. That didn't really happen until she married my dad and had me. She left your dad a voicemail, asking him to meet her so they could talk things over, because I guess she was tired of the awkwardness or whatever. Kind of hard to keep avoiding each other in a small town like Fairview, you know? But he never showed up, and a week later, she received a letter in the mail."

I furrow my eyebrows. "A letter?"

"Yeah," Blake says with an uneasy laugh. "Coward's way out, right? Believe it or not, she let me read it."

"Wait. She still has it?" I ask in surprise. Blake is seventeen, which means ... she's held onto this letter for seventeen years? "Can I see it?"

Blake carries the plates over to the sink and glances back at me, debating my request. It's a total invasion of privacy, I know that, but I need to read for myself what my dad wrote in the letter that resulted in LeAnne holding a lifelong grudge against him.

"Yeah," Blake eventually agrees. "But just pretend you don't know it exists."

"I promise."

He hesitates another moment, perhaps wrong-footed at the odd turn our morning together has taken. "It's in her office," he says at last, then gestures for me to follow.

For being the mayor of a major metropolitan area, I'm surprised LeAnne's home office doesn't even have a simple lock on it. What if someone broke in, ransacking the mayor's private home in search of important campaign documents? But then I remember she has her real mayor's office in Nashville, so I guess the files kept here are of a more personal nature. Like Dad's letter.

Blake sits down on the luxury leather desk chair, wheeling it around the room from filing cabinet to bookcase, stealing quick peeks into each one as he tries to remember where exactly he saw his mom store the letter. Meanwhile, my heart is pounding in my chest.

"Here!" Blake says at last, slamming a drawer shut and circling around in the chair to present me with a folded piece of paper. "Are you sure you want to see this, Mila? It's short, but definitely not sweet."

I nod as I anxiously take the dog-eared letter from him and unfold it, revealing a mere few sentences scrawled in blocky letters. My breath is caught in my throat as I read:

Leanne,

I got your voicemail, but I don't ever want to see you again. You had your chance to accept my apology, but you didn't take it. I don't want you in my life. It's why I broke free of you in the first place.

Do not contact me ever again.

Everett.

"Pretty harsh, huh?" says Blake, breaking the uncomfortable silence my shock has created.

It's nasty. My blood runs cold. "Oh my God."

"I know," Blake agrees, and I see that he's angry too. "And then he had the balls to get that Ruben guy to send her a non-disclosure agreement years down the line, even though she'd already tried to make her peace with him! To be honest, she felt that was a total slap in the face, so I can understand why she refused to sign it," he adds, slipping the letter out of my hands and carefully folding it back up. "You know I rarely ever see eye-to-eye with my mom, and I always thought she was being melodramatic, but your dad *is* a serious asshole. At least in that respect."

My throat is like sandpaper, and I can feel my complexion turning pale under my freckles. I swallow and try to put my thoughts in some kind of order. "No, Blake, you don't understand—"

"What?" he says, his tone defensive. "I know he's your dad, but don't try and justify—"

"No," I whisper. "This isn't my dad's handwriting." I glance up at him with wide eyes. "It's my mom's."

Blake's lips form an "O", almost as shocked as I am by my revelation. We stand there, looking at each other, still in our morning-after-the-night-before clothes but with the romance of our morning pancakes draining away.

Then we hear the click of the front door, and we both jump in alarm at the sound of heels working their way down the hall.

"Shit," Blake mutters, leaping up from the executive chair toward the filing cabinet. He pulls open the drawer to tuck the letter back in its place, but he's flustered and panicky, nowhere near quick enough.

LeAnne appears at the door of her office, a purse over one shoulder and a laptop bag over the other, wearing her usual professional attire of a pencil skirt and elegant blouse with stilettos. She's caught off guard at the sight of Blake and me in her office. It's probably the last thing she expected to arrive home to, but her surprise immediately diverts into rage.

"Blake!" she gasps, dropping her laptop bag to the floor and striding into the room to pluck the letter straight out of his hand. She clearly knows exactly what it is. "I showed you that in confidence! How dare you?"

"LeAnne," I interrupt in a quiet, empty tone.

"And you!" she snaps, pointing the letter in my direction as she glares fiercely at me, taking in the clothes I'm wearing. They aren't mine. They're Blake's. "Do I even want to know what you're doing here so early in the morning? Well, I guess it's pretty obvious." I can't help but blush and dip my gaze as she shakes her head at Blake in disgust, her defined cheekbones sharp as she clenches her jaw.

"No, LeAnne, please. Listen to me," I beg as sensitively as possible, moving toward her and gesturing at the letter in her hand. "I'm pretty sure my dad didn't write this."

LeAnne eases up on her fury for only a moment to hear me out. "What?"

I swallow hard and tell her, "My mom did."

LeAnne wordlessly looks at Blake, then back at me. Her breaths are shallow and she lets her purse slide off her shoulder as she sits down heavily into her desk chair. She opens up the letter with trembling fingers and reads it again, though I have no doubt that she's read it a million times over the years. "Mila, what makes you think your mom wrote this?" she asks in a subdued voice, and for once, the expression she turns to me with is raw and unfiltered.

It's honest and real, it's pained and confused. There's no venom in her tone, no scorn in her eyes.

"The way *Everett* is written," I say breathlessly, moving closer to her and pointing down at the letter in her hand. We are on the same side. "He doesn't cross his Ts like that, not in his own name, but my mom does."

"You're absolutely sure?" she whispers, and I nod.

As I confirm it to LeAnne, it dawns on me just how sickening this is. How could Mom write such a cruel, deceitful letter to LeAnne? It's not the mother I know, but that woman in the Walmart parking lot, the one making snarky comments to LeAnne, that wasn't the mother I know either. So maybe I don't know Mom at all. Dad has been the one I doubted, the one I placed so much pressure on to be perfect, but I never thought that maybe Mom had her own dirty secrets too.

My mind is racing, trying to make sense of who knows what, trying to piece together a timeline of events that happened long before I was even born. I can already feel a migraine probing.

So, Dad tried to apologize to LeAnne after the affair happened, because clearly he does have a conscience... but LeAnne wasn't ready to forgive him just yet, so his apology was rejected and that was probably a dent to his ego. Then, when LeAnne decided she *was* finally ready to forgive him and move on, she left him a voicemail asking to meet, but he never showed up, and instead received a horrible letter – which was actually written by Mom. But if LeAnne had gone to the effort of trying to call him in the first place, why would Dad, years later, try to buy her silence with that stupid NDA? He shouldn't have been worried about her still. He should have known that she'd forgiven him.

Unless he didn't ever know about the voicemail.

*Oh no.* Nausea churns in my stomach and I hold my hand to the wall, steadying myself as the thoughts keep on pressing down on me from every corner of my mind.

Dad has remained angry at LeAnne all these years, hostile because he thinks she rejected his apology and never forgave him. LeAnne has remained angry at Dad all these years, because she thinks he shunned her when she tried to offer an olive branch, to be reasonable and adult. They both have it wrong. Their attempt at a civil existence around each other was intercepted by Mom, who then made sure to destroy it.

"That voicemail you left my dad," I say, meeting LeAnne's appalled eyes. "I don't think he ever heard it."

LeAnne regains her strength, composing her features and drawing her thin, dark eyebrows together. "There's only one way to find out," she says fearlessly, rising from the chair. "Blake, pull on a shirt – you're coming with me."

"Mom," Blake says unsurely, scratching the back of his neck. "Are you sure you wanna do this?"

"I'd like answers." She closes her fist around the letter, her knuckles turning pale.

"I'd like some answers too," I say, moving to the office door.

LeAnne and I lock eyes once again, just like we have

done so many times this summer, but her stare isn't piercingly threatening this time. It's gracious and empathetic with a hint of remorse, and I can almost see it dawning on her, the realization that I am not my parents. I don't represent the mistakes they have made in the past. I'm just Mila, and I think LeAnne knows that now.

She grabs her car keys from her purse and takes a deep, affirmative breath. "Let's resolve this once and for all."

# 25

Blake drives. LeAnne's emotions are too conflicted to focus on anything but digging her way to the core truth of her history with my parents, determined to uncover every nitty-gritty detail. Meanwhile, in the backseat, my nerves are completely shattered as we pull up outside the closed gate. I point my remote out the truck window and open it.

My parents have only just started trusting me again and granting me freedom, yet I'm about to roll up alongside their nemesis and confront them. I've spent the ride over here doubting myself, wondering if I'm betraying them by throwing Mom under the bus like this, but I have to do what's right. Mom played a bigger role in the whole scandal of their relationship than even Dad knows, and if he finds out the truth that LeAnne did try to reach out to him to forgive him, then maybe they can move forward. And, more to the point, maybe Blake and I can date without our parents being at each other's throats.

As Blake parks outside the house and we step out of the truck, I spy Sheri making her way over to us from the stables. She blows a strand of hair out of her face and wipes her hands together, nonplussed.

"LeAnne," she says. "Is everything okay?"

I imagine LeAnne hasn't stepped foot on the Harding Estate property in twenty years, so although Popeye and Sheri are friendly with her in public, a personal home visit is disconcerting. Sheri shoots me a wary glance and doesn't even give the boyfriend clothes I'm wearing the five seconds of judgment they deserve.

"Morning, Sheri," LeAnne says coolly, her manner back under her usual icy control. "I need to talk to Everett and Marnie. Urgently. Are they here?"

"Is this about Mila and Blake dating?" Sheri questions with a dubious grimace, most likely assuming LeAnne has dragged us both here because we're in trouble for breaking some unspoken rules. "It's so clear they like each other, and I know it's not my place to get involved, but—"

Blake clears his throat. "This isn't about Mila and me," he says.

"Oh." Sheri is even more perplexed now as to why LeAnne is here, but she's clearly reluctant to query further. "I'll let them know you're here."

"We'll come with you – if you don't mind," LeAnne says.

Sheri looks to me for a hint to what's going on, but I only nod reassuringly, urging her to just go with it. This won't be pretty, but it might redeem Dad, even if it means shining a less-than-flattering spotlight on Mom.

As Sheri hesitantly makes her way up the porch with LeAnne following close behind, Blake grasps my wrist.

"You sure you wanna be part of this?" he asks.

"This whole thing between our parents has been a nightmare," I answer, pulling free of his grip. "It needs to be resolved."

He seems unwilling to believe that this blowout will do anything other than make things worse, but we follow after Sheri and LeAnne, anyway. He's close on my heels as we barge into the house behind them, straight to the living room.

Mom is filing her nails on the couch, rollers in her hair, and Popeye is aligning a shelf that has slipped from its bracket, holding it straight while Dad drills it into the wall. They all snap their heads around.

"LeAnne—" Dad accidentally releases his grip on the shelf as he shuts off the drill, one side swinging downward.

LeAnne doesn't waste a second for the shock of her arrival to sink in. She nods at Mom and Popeye, then she's across the room in nanoseconds, thrusting the folded letter into Dad's chest. "Good morning, Everett. Do you remember this?"

Dad pulls the letter out from beneath her hand, staring suspiciously down at the paper as though he's just been presented with a toxic substance.

"What are you doing here?" Mom asks, flustered. She's on her feet and encroaching LeAnne's personal space, but LeAnne's not going to take her seriously with those rollers in her hair. She dismissively regards her for now.

"Does this look familiar, Everett?" LeAnne asks again, her whole demeanor like a force of nature; she is not a woman to be messed with.

Dad opens the letter to reveal the offending words written inside, and he starts shaking his head in denial before he's even reached his name signed at the bottom. "I don't know what this is," he says, eyes flickering up. "Why are you showing me this, LeAnne? I didn't write this."

"Let me see that," Popeye demands, leaving the shelf half dangling from the wall to snatch the letter from his hands. He squints extra hard, bringing the words up close to his face, and then gapes in disgust. "Good Lord, Everett. What kind of an excuse for a man are you!"

"Give me some credit, please," Dad protests. "I didn't write that!"

"That's what I'm here to find out, Wesley," LeAnne tells the room. "I received it seventeen years ago in response to a voicemail I left for Everett – and for some reason, whether sentimental or stupid, I didn't throw it in the garbage where it belongs."

And I keep my focus solely on my mother, gauging her reaction to LeAnne's words, while I hear Dad ask, "What voicemail? When?" However skilled an actor he might be, it's obvious his innocence is genuine. He has no idea what LeAnne is talking about – and not simply because it was all nearly two decades ago.

But Mom ...Mom has backed away from LeAnne. Her complexion has changed, all of the color draining from her cheeks, and grim fear flashes in her eyes. It tells me everything I need to know, and my heart cracks. How could Mom do something so shabby and underhand? I think, again, how she and Dad really have got some serious trust issues poisoning their relationship.

LeAnne holds out her hand to Popeye and he carefully gives her the letter back.

We're all watching, in an awkward semicircle of anticipation, as she tears the flimsy paper into dozens of tiny pieces right there in front of us, letting the tatters cascade to the floor. She angles her body toward Mom and says, "Maybe you should ask your wife."

Dad shifts his intense eyes to Mom, a catch in his voice. "Marnie?"

I tense, holding back unexpected tears. My parents have only just started to get their marriage back on track, but this will derail them all over again, a total breach of loyalty and respect once more, but I can't keep quiet about something like this. This has to be dealt with, but knowing that doesn't make it hurt any less.

Blake edges closer to me, his pinky finger wrapping around mine in support. This can't be easy for him to watch either. LeAnne may seem to hold her composure, but there are cracks appearing, years of hurt bubbling to the surface.

"Everett ..." Mom mumbles pleadingly. She crosses the room and puts a hand on his arm, her expression drooping into middle age in a matter of seconds as she's overcome with guilt and humiliation as the jealousies and meanspiritedness of the past are exposed.

Dad takes a guarded step back. He's still waiting for an explanation.

Sheri stands by Blake and me at the doorway, gnawing at her nails in anxiety. Popeye waits, too, arms folded in angry amazement, his good eye trained on my terrified mom.

"*You* wrote that so-called letter, Marnie?" Dad asks, the rasp in his voice making it clear he doesn't want to believe it.

But even if Mom was able to reply, she has no chance to.

"I have wasted years *hating* you, Everett. Years!" LeAnne erupts with a gesture of pure exasperation. "All because I was courageous enough to reach out to forgive you, out of human decency, nothing more." She catches her breath, steadies her voice to a more neutral tone. "This entire time I believed you'd sent me that absurd, childish letter in response to what I believed to be a gesture of goodwill."

All eyes turn to Mom.

"You have some explaining to do, Marnie," Popeye says.

"I'm so sorry," Mom splutters, desperately trying to grab Dad's hand, but to no avail.

He turns to her, aghast. "No, Marnie. Explain."

I watch as Mom makes a monumental effort to compose herself. "I got to the message on your phone before you did, and I didn't ... I didn't want you to fix things with her!" Her voice is so broken I think she may actually burst into tears from the embarrassment of being caught after all this time. "I worried that if the two of you worked through things that ... that maybe you would, I don't know, miss her."

"*Miss* her?" Dad shakes his head fast and backs away from Mom. "Are you *that* insecure?"

"Of course I am! How could I not be? Think of how we met, Everett!" Mom appeals to him. "And I was so young, so naive when I sent her that letter. I was scared."

"Marnie, you have some real nerve. *I* was the victim," LeAnne snaps, "not you."

"Come on, you guys. You really shouldn't be listening to this," Sheri whispers, nudging Blake and me, ushering us out of the room. She forces Popeye out with us too. However, despite her best intentions, we all hover by the door, intrusive eavesdroppers, not wanting to miss a single word.

"LeAnne," we hear Dad say, his tone sincere, "I'm sorry for everything I put you through when we were young. I'm sorry we never got the chance to leave all this resentment behind."

LeAnne must be rendered speechless, because she takes a few seconds to muster a reply. "Thank you … Everett." Her voice is clipped but tinged with emotion, and then she clears her throat. "Marnie, is there anything *you'd* like to say?"

Blake's expression is strained as he catches my eye. Popeye's hearing must be going, because he has his ear pressed up against the wall, blatantly tuned into the private conversation continuing on the other side, but he's not the only one. We are all hanging onto every word.

"What did you expect, LeAnne?" Mom responds defiantly. "I was protecting my marriage. I didn't want you back in our lives."

Finding her iciest tone, LeAnne doesn't hold back as she says, "You, Marnie," with a pause for effect, "are one unbelievably selfish, manipulative bitch."

Any response Mom might be able to muster falters, her voice drowning in sobs. And suddenly I can't stand all this chaos anymore. Mom is falling apart – and, as much as this might be her fault, it's not nice to listen to. I don't know if Dad comes to her defense or not, because I'm already halfway up the stairs before I can listen to another word.

Blake is quick on my heels, reaching out for my waist as he follows me into my room, and my throat tightens as I fight back tears. It's the first time Blake has been inside the house, let alone my *room*, but he doesn't even give it a second glance. He spins me around to face him and pulls me in close, enveloping me in a comforting hug. I squeeze him back, my face buried in his shoulder, and we hold each other steady until the dust settles on the feud raging downstairs, and LeAnne calls him away from me, only to drag him from the house.

# 26

Honky Tonk Central feels even more atmospheric than usual. It may be a Monday evening in August, but the excitement in this bar right now would fool one into believing it was the Fourth of July. All of Blake's friends are here to support his honky tonk debut. I recognize most of their faces from the tailgate party and the bonfire weeks ago, all his Fairview High classmates, and the place is packed with teenagers. Minors are only allowed inside until eight, so Blake's set is scheduled at seven. There are twenty minutes to go until his opening cover.

"Which one of you dares me to whip off my bra and throw it on stage?" Tori teases with an expression that's just a bit *too* serious.

Savannah fans herself with the menu. "*Stop*. We just have to make sure we cheer really loud. He'll kill you if you embarrass him, Tori."

"Aw, but teasing Blake is my second-favorite hobby after teasing you!" Tori says, sticking her tongue out at Savannah.

I'm tuned out, my focus fixated on a spot on the floor

as the current performer rocks out an old-school country ballad. All I can think is that I really am going home in the morning. The flight is booked, my parents' IDs have been retrieved from the stables, and my bags are packed. I want to enjoy tonight more than anything, but I can't relax until I get my imminent departure off my chest.

"Guys," I say, lifting my head. My tone has enough of an edge to it that Savannah stops mid fry-throwing and Tori cocks her head suspiciously when she hears me take a breath. "This is actually my last night here in Tennessee. I fly home tomorrow."

"No!" Savannah gasps. "What!"

"I'm lucky I even got to stay until now," I explain, but the saddened look in both of their eyes makes me dread boarding that flight more than ever. "My parents wanted to go home last Friday, but I couldn't miss tonight."

"Okay, but ... why didn't you tell us?" Tori asks, offended. "Are you *relieved* to get away from Savannah Bennett? Because I would be."

Savannah gives her the stink-eye, then puckers her lower lip at me. "When are you coming back?"

"I've got my fingers crossed that we'll be back next month over Labor Day weekend," I say optimistically, even though so far Dad has only promised me that we'll come back for Thanksgiving. But that's in November, and I can't wait three months to hear Savannah ramble, to laugh at Tori's witty remarks, to feel Blake's hands on my body.

"Does Blake know?" Tori asks. "That you're leaving in the morning?"

"Not yet—" I begin, but then over Savannah's shoulder, Blake himself appears. I immediately cut off the conversation and straighten up. "Heeeey!"

"Hi, Miss Mila," Blake says with a gorgeous, slightly nervous smile. He's been off talking logistics with the tech guys for the past fifteen minutes, and he seems even more jittery now than he did before he left. He pulls me into a brief hug and behind his back, I fire Savannah and Tori a quick throat-slashing gesture to signal that the topic of my LA homecoming is over. "You guys good?"

"Yup! We just can't wait for your set to start." I pull back from his embrace and run my hand down his red flannel shirt, undoing the top button to reveal his chain necklace. "Mmm."

"Mmm," Blake echoes, biting his lip seductively and bringing his forehead to mine.

"Hi, we exist, by the way!" Tori interjects, and Blake and I break our intense eye contact with sheepish laughter.

He throws his arm over my shoulder and wiggles his eyebrows at Savannah and Tori. "Do you guys mind if I borrow Mila for a sec?"

"No, go ahead! Take her!" Savannah says, enthusiastically waving us off.

I slide off the barstool and let Blake guide me away from the table, snaking our way through the crowd. A lot of Blake's friends are already up on the dance floor, standing around yelling in each other's ears over the blaring music, and several of them fist-bump him and wish him good luck as we pass.

"Why are we going outside?" I wonder as Blake leads me to the door.

"Because," he says, "I need fresh air."

Even though it's a Monday, Broadway in Nashville is alive with tourists. The sky is a clear, dim blue, the sun starting to dip, and electric neon signs strung along the street are ready to light up as the day fades. Live music can be heard on each block as performances spill out from bars, and when I steal a peek at Blake, I notice him wiping a trickle of sweat from his brow. As his own live set draws closer, his nerves continue to heighten.

"You aren't chickening out, are you?" I ask when we dip down a side street toward the parking lot where we left his truck. Blake has waited what I think may be his whole life for this moment. There's no way he's going to abandon the opportunity and make a quick getaway.

"No!" he says, managing a laugh. "I just wanted a minute alone with you."

Through the packed parking lot, we weave around vehicles until we reach his truck. He lowers the tailgate, then before I can process what he's doing, he clasps my waist and sets me down on the truck. My legs dangle over the edge of the tailgate and Blake stands directly in front of me, his body pressed against my knees. He is tense.

"*Breathe*," I tell him soothingly. "Did you hear back from your dad yet? Is he going to make it?"

"No, he had to work late, so he wasn't going to make it here in time," he says. I can tell he's disappointed, but he's keeping his spirits deliberately high. I feel for him; it would have meant a lot if Jason had been here to watch him perform. I know Blake would've trusted his opinion above all others.

I push his hair back off his forehead and then let my hands fall to his jaw, where I hold his face steady as I gaze into his eyes. "You're going to kill it."

"Mila," he says, running his hands over my thighs. "Just kiss me already."

Beneath the shifting colors of the sky, I press my lips to his. The kiss is passionate and blinding, his hands moving to my waist to pull me closer against him. If we weren't in the middle of a parking lot right now, I'd burst those buttons of his shirt straight open. His touch leaves me breathless, and as he pulls away, he runs his thumb over my bottom lip.

"I think we should continue this after your set," I whisper.

"Yeah, I think we should," he agrees, desire sparking in his eyes, and then he slides his hands beneath my thighs, running them up to my butt as he lifts me off the tailgate.

There are only ten minutes to go until he's scheduled to be on stage, so we race back to Honky Tonk Central. Savannah and Tori both raise a curious, teasing eyebrow as I return to the table, and Blake pulls out the stool for me. He tucks my hair behind my ear and leans in close, his breath tickling my neck.

"I better make my final guitar checks," he murmurs, and I nod. I don't need to wish him luck as he walks away – honestly, he is so talented that he doesn't need it.

"Well, that was kind of hot," Tori says with a dreamy

sigh. "Whispering in your ear like that. You guys are very ... touchy-feely."

"Yeah," Savannah agrees, watching me inquisitively. "Way more so than usual. What happened when you slept over at Blake's on Saturday, Mila? Care to share?"

I nearly choke on my own saliva. Embarrassed, I grab my soda and start sipping at my straw, drinking for so long that it answers the question without the need for words. Savannah exchanges a giddy look of surprise with Tori, and I know Savannah is going to ask a thousand questions while Tori makes teasing comments, so I cut them off before they can even begin.

"We better move up front!" I say, finishing off my drink and jumping to my feet. Blake wants me to be front and center, cheering the loudest, so that's exactly where I'll be and what I'll do. The dance floor is already busy, so we better stake out our position.

"That, Savannah, is called tactical avoidance," Tori mutters in Savannah's ear, both their eyes following me, and I laugh, unabashed, and blow them a kiss. I do not want to discuss the events of Saturday night, especially not with Savannah, Blake's *cousin*.

I move freely through the bar area as the two of them follow close on my heels, edging our way around the bodies on the dance floor toward the small stage. The current performer is wrapping up her set, and we find ourselves a nice spot just in front of the stage, right next to the amps, so I prepare myself for the ringing in my ears I'll probably suffer for the next two days.

"Blake's voice is so dreamy, isn't it?" a voice to my right gushes. "He's going to be amazing."

I crane my neck, ready to agree, but then my cheerful mood instantly plummets, replaced by a dark rumble of jealousy. I see that Lacey is by my side, swaying rhythmically along to the music, a drink in her hand. I'm not naive – I knew she would be here, because *all* of Blake's friends are, but *why* does she have to be up front? Sometimes I wish Cindy would stop sneaking off with Myles every chance the two of them gets, because then maybe she would keep Lacey company. It seems to me that when Lacey is a free agent, she gravitates toward Blake the way a moth is drawn to light.

I seal my lips shut, channel my inner Zen, then face back to the stage without entertaining her deliberate attempts to get under my skin. On the other side of me, Tori nudges me and offers a pointed nod at Lacey, and it makes me feel much better that other people can see how obviously scheming this girl is.

The woman closes out her set with a dramatic bow and sweeps off the stage as a guy, maybe the owner, takes over the mic instead. "Let's hear it one more time for Janet Bee. That girl is fire!" he says with a whoop and a grand gesture, as he runs his eyes over those of us on the dance floor, the packed tables and the crowded bar. "I hope all you folks in here tonight are ready for our next musician. Making his Honky Tonk Central debut, give it up for Blake Avery!"

We erupt into whistles and cheers, and I make sure I create the most noise. I'm applauding, my hands are in the air, I'm whooping and whistling. Most of Blake's friends are all on the dance floor, with the rest of the bar packed by tourists and locals, who just so happen to have dropped in for a drink or a bite to eat. They are in the right place at the right time. I was worried beforehand that Honky Tonk Central would be quiet on a Monday evening, but I've been proven wrong.

Blake swaggers onto the stage, his Gibson Hummingbird already slung across his body, and he hooks it up to the amp with the same rock-star charisma his dad had in Memphis. He squints and cups a hand over his eyes, shielding them from the blinding spotlights as he gazes out over the joint. "Hey, y'all," he says, adjusting the mic stand into position. "I'm Blake Avery, born and bred in Fairview, and this is my first live show ever, so enjoy – but please take it easy on me, huh?" He cracks a charming smile and then backs up from the mic, testing out a few strings and making a few strums one final time, before moving forward again. He looks down at me standing exactly where he hoped I'd be, and winks.

A shiver runs down my spine and goosebumps prickle all over my skin the moment he begins. The twang of Blake's guitar is so magical to me, but even more so this time as it reverberates from the speakers all around the bustling bar, dancing in my ears. He opens with the song he planned to, the one he rehearsed so many times in his backyard over the weekend, so I recognize it by now. It's a cover of "Home Sweet" by some guy called Russell Dickerson, and it's fast-paced with a dramatic climb to its hook. Blake's voice sounds even stronger than usual, fueled by passion and a genuine love of performing.

I dance on the spot, rocking my head from side to side, swaying and jumping whenever he hits choruses. He moves through his set list with ease, each transition smooth, and his presence becomes more and more seductive with each song he nails. It's so mesmerizing seeing him lose himself, breaking away from the mic and utilizing the stage whenever there's a guitar solo. Four songs in, he's sweating beneath the burning lights, his confidence growing as his level of expertise doesn't falter.

I'm mid head-banging to his cover of that same Luke Bryan song his dad sang in Memphis when an elbow digs into my ribs. I write it off as an ordinary dance-floor peril until it happens again as Lacey shoves me out of the way in her attempt to press closer to the stage.

"You sure you have enough space there, Lacey?" I ask sarcastically.

Lacey flicks me a look of contempt over her shoulder. "Not with you taking over the dance floor."

"Excuse me?"

"I've supported his music way longer than you have," she hisses, turning her back on the stage to lock eyes with me. Over the sound of Blake's performance thundering around us, she glowers at me with the disdain she's had for me all this time, but has never publicly displayed until now. "It's pathetic, you jumping around like that as though you're his number-one fan. So attention-seeking. You didn't even know Blake existed until two seconds ago."

"But I know him well enough now," I respond with a laugh as I flippantly wave my hand at her. "Get out of my face."

"Don't worry, I will," she says, while in fact moving threateningly closer. "Oh, and I heard you're leaving tomorrow, Mila, so I trust you have a safe flight home." Then with a smirk, she murmurs, "I'm sure there's plenty girls around here who'll take care of Blake for you."

Rage. Pure, blinding rage – that's what ignites inside of me. I lose my cool entirely as I shove Lacey away and she falls back into the stage. She gasps at me as though I've just assaulted her unprovoked, pulling off the perfect weepy expression of innocence as she glances up at the stage to see if Blake has noticed. He has. Of course.

This is so not a good look.

The song comes to an end, and Blake leans down to grab a bottle of water from the stage floor, lowering himself nearer to Lacey. "What the hell are you doing?" he discreetly hisses.

"Blake—" I try, but Lacey beats me to the punch, whining, "Can you ask Mila to stop pushing everyone around?"

"Will you cut it out? It's embarrassing," he snaps, and I recoil with shock when I realize his words are directed at only me, then – as Lacey flashes me the most triumphant, patronizing smirk *ever* – he lines himself back up with the mic as he attempts to regain his momentum as though his focus hasn't been broken by two girls squabbling over him. My heart sinks in shame.

"How many folks in here love some Taylor Swift?" he asks the room, upbeat and charming.

But only a few people reply. Instead, a wave of hushed voices moves around the bar, and I look behind me to see what's going on now. Everyone's attention has shifted to the opposite corner of Honky Tonk Central, to where a bubble of people surrounds one person as he enters the bar.

"O.M.G." Savannah emits an excited squeak. "Mila – it's him, isn't it?" I can only shrug, all thoughts of Lacey forgotten, as she exclaims, "What is your *dad* doing here?"

The hushed voices are punctuated with the odd callout. Dad tries to edge deeper into the bar, but he can't move far thanks to a handful of strangers approaching him. I throw my hand up in the air and attempt to wave him over, but as I watch, heads turn at the bar and customers quit stuffing tacos into their mouths. My heart sinks further and further. All attention is on the celebrity who has just waltzed through the door, half the crowd starstruck and rooted to the spot, the other half clambering toward Dad. The music has died, leaving Honky Tonk Central without a heartbeat. Blake has stopped performing.

"I invited him," I whisper, but I don't think Savannah hears me.

She takes off with Tori across the dance floor, and even Lacey has disappeared, and as Dad gets picked apart like a carcass thrown to crows, I stand alone and paralyzed at the front of the dance floor. This wasn't supposed to happen.

Before Blake picked me up earlier, I invited Dad to the gig. He likes watching people chase their dreams, after all, and he seems to like Blake. It's our final night in Tennessee, the paps are no longer stalking his every move, and I thought that if he came …if people heard Everett Harding was at Honky Tonk Central on a Monday evening …that it would help draw in a crowd. More people for Blake to perform in front of. More people to fall in love with his talent.

But I didn't realize I had nothing to worry about in the first place. Honky Tony Central was already packed; packed with music lovers who are now no longer caring about some teenager's honky tonk debut, who are now overcome with the thrill of having a celebrity in their midst. My blood curdles cold inside me as I realize that with all the excitement of seeing Blake on stage, it totally slipped my mind that Dad *did* say he might swing by.

Horrified, I turn to the stage. Blake stands there alone with his guitar in his hands, wounded and abandoned, his gig at a standstill. The owner rushes onto the stage, stepping in front of him and taking over the mic, a born ringmaster.

"It looks like we have a very special guest here tonight! Everett Harding, welcome to Honky Tonk Central!" he cheers to a far bigger round of applause than the one Blake's entrance received, and I can physically *feel* my heart breaking apart as Blake's face falls. "Everyone, please calm down! I'm sure Everett will be more than happy to sign autographs and take pictures, so there's no need for quite such a frenzy." He laughs, awkwardly, then instructs, "Please return to your tables, order yourselves another beer. Listen to some great live music. Oh, and Everett, your drinks are on the house!"

Much to my horror, as everyone hollers in appreciation of Dad's presence, Blake tears his guitar strap from his shoulder and strides across the stage, holding his guitar by the fretboard, his fist clenched tight around it. He doesn't stand a chance of stealing the limelight back from Dad. His set is suddenly, agonizingly over, and his heartache is veiled by fury. His dream crushed right in front of me.

"Blake, wait!" I yell, jumping onto the stage to try to catch up to him.

He storms down the wooden side steps as though he is about to walk straight out of this place, but then in a split second, he decides he needs an explanation. As he twists sharply on his heels to face me, I bump into him and flinch at the thunderous look in his eyes.

"What the hell is your dad doing here, Mila?"

The guilt of knowing I've put a stop to Blake's performance gnaws at my insides and my throat tightens, restricting my airways. "I ... I asked him to come. I didn't think this would happen," I admit as my lower lip quivers. Am I going to throw up? I think I might.

"He's a movie star!" Blake yells in my face. "What did you think was going to happen?"

"Blake, listen!" I beg, grabbing onto his shirt as he walks away from me. I pull him back, and we are against the empty bar, where even the bartenders have abandoned their positions. "I was trying to help! I invited him because I thought it would help you get a full house!"

Blake clenches his jaw. "You thought I wasn't good enough to draw in a crowd off my own back?"

"No!" I gasp, shaking my head fast as I squeeze my eyes shut, realizing how this seems. I was so happy ten minutes ago, dancing to the sound of Blake's melodic voice, but now tears press at the corners of my eyes. "I just wanted more people to see how talented you are!"

"Well, congratulations," Blake spits, "because now *no one* is listening." He violently dumps his guitar on the bar as though his love for it has diminished. "What a great debut gig this is. Truly memorable. My dad isn't here. And then, even before *your* megastar dad showed up, you were trashing it, Mila. Why the hell did you shove Lacey?"

"Because she wants you! The moment I board that flight home tomorrow, she's going to be all over you!" I stammer in exasperation, a million different emotions pumping through my veins. Fear that Lacey will make moves on my boyfriend once I'm gone, guilt and horror over inviting Dad here to ruin Blake's first gig, and the mounting panic that Blake and I won't survive as a couple when we're two thousand miles apart. "You dated before and I'm sure she's hoping history will repeat itself!"

"I don't care about Lacey!" he snaps, his voice low but as sharp and terrifying as I've ever heard it. He's never displayed anger like this before, but he's probably never felt disappointment like this. He pulls at the ends of his hair, throwing his head back to the ceiling as he groans. Eyes pooling with questions and his voice softening only very slightly, he looks at me. "You're going home tomorrow?"

*Oh no.* That wasn't how I meant to break the news.

"I was going to tell you," I blurt, covering my face in my hands.

"When? After you'd already left?" he growls, and I can hear furious betrayal woven through his voice. He slams his fist down on the bar next to his guitar, only just missing it. "What the hell, Mila? What is it with your family and weird secrets?"

"It's not a secret. I just didn't want to ruin our last few days together! I didn't want to give you any distractions before tonight!" I desperately try to explain, but my tears have broken free, and I doubt he can make sense of what I'm saying between my muffled, messy sobs. I didn't mean to shove Lacey, I didn't mean to stop his gig, I didn't mean to keep anything from him. "I thought if you knew, we'd have just spent the past few days feeling on edge about it!"

"Do you know how long I have waited for this chance?" He's nearly snarling at me, his face distorted, and I take a step away. "And you ruined it, Mila. You fucking ruined it," he adds venomously, shaking his head as though he's fighting back his own tears. I pathetically grab onto his shirt again, trying to hold onto him so that he can't walk away, but he removes my hand and there's not a scrap of love or tenderness in the gesture. "You don't have to wonder what will happen to us when you go home *tomorrow*," he says, drawing his dark, tortured eyes level with mine, "because, Mila, we're already done."

My heart splices. Blake grabs his guitar and turns away from me, his body as much of a barrier as a closed door.

Tears streaming down my cheeks and my breaths shallow, I force myself to look across the bar as my world unravels around me in slow motion.

Dad at a table, just like all the other customers were only a few minutes ago, his Hollywood smile dazzling. The bodies pressing around him from every angle, the raised voices, the poised cellphones, the pens and napkins being thrust through the air. I watch in horror as more people stream in from the street outside as word spreads down Broadway. It is complete pandemonium, and everyone is rammed at his side of the bar, leaving this half of Honky Tonk Central empty.

Shrugging his guitar onto his shoulder as he walks away, Blake heads for the fire exit at the back of the bar, his pace determined and resolute.

"Blake, please wait!" I cry, but either he doesn't hear me, or he really has decided I'm not worth waiting for.

He kicks open the fire door, setting off a shrilling alarm. I almost lose my balance in despair, so I sink to my knees, oblivious to the floor sticky with spilled beer, and shake my head over and over and over again. This can't be happening. Blake can't end things between us, not when I have to board a flight first thing in the morning, not when there is no time left to fix this complete mess I've created. As the alarm rings in my ears and my eyes sting with tears, I lift my hair from my face to find Blake one last time through the blur. With his head bowed, he walks straight out the door, his silhouette disappearing into the Nashville night. Just a boy and his guitar.

I watch until he's gone, until I have to give up hope that he might turn back to me, make things better with his easy smile inviting me to draw in close.

And I don't know it then, but it will be the last time I see Blake Avery for the next two years.

# Playlist

Check out the music that kept me inspired while working on *Trusting Blake*.

| | |
|---|---|
| Speakers | *Sam Hunt* |
| She's With Me | *High Valley* |
| Dance | *Rascal Flatts* |
| Our Song | *Taylor Swift* |
| Move | *Luke Bryan* |
| Somebody Like You | *Keith Urban* |
| To Us It Did | *Mitchell Tenpenny* |
| I Want Crazy | *Hunter Hayes* |
| Home Sweet | *Russell Dickerson* |
| Stuck | *Redferrin* |

# Thank You

Thank you a million times over to my readers for being such amazing champions of Mila and Blake even before ever reading their story, and for supporting every step forward I take in my writing journey.

Thank you so, so, so much to all of the team at Black & White Publishing for being the greatest publishing team I could ever wish to have behind me since the very beginning. Thank you to my editors, Emma Hargrave and Janne Moller, for your guidance and expertise. Special thanks to Campbell Brown and Alison McBride for continuing to make possible my dream of having my name on bookshelves.

So much love for my closest friends for keeping me sane. Rachael Lamb, Heather Allen, Rhea Forman and Bethany Stapley: thanks for the road trips for ice cream, endless cups of tea, and true friendships that I cherish.

But most importantly, thank you to those who make my world shine brighter:

My mum, Fenella, for all of the amazing memories we continue to make together.

My dad, Stuart, for always reminding me that I can achieve anything I set my mind to.

My sidekick, Bear, for filling me with joy whenever you look at me with your little puppy eyes.

My best friend, Rachael, for being the person I laugh the hardest with.

My granda, George, for being equally as stubborn as me, but who I wouldn't change for the world.

My grandma, Fenella, for always being so full of warmth and love.

My sister, Sherilyn, for being the strongest person I've ever known.

And my nephew, Anders, for always being the shining light at the end of every tunnel.

## JUST DON'T MENTION IT

The one all DIMILY readers have been shouting for ... Tyler's story!

As irresistible and dazzling as its Californian backdrop, here is Tyler's story – his heart-stopping tale of past hurt, finding hope and figuring out who the hell he wants to be.

## DARE TO FALL

A new take on teen romance that explores how loss affects young lives and relationships.

In Windsor, Colorado, two teenagers experience bereavement much too young. It's left MacKenzie terrified, but Jaden refuses to dwell on the past. Will MacKenzie dare to fall for the person she's most afraid of growing close to?

## THE WRONG SIDE OF KAI

A story of broken hearts, forgiveness, vulnerability – and the exhilaration of falling in love.

Vanessa doesn't believe in serious relationships. In fact, she doesn't believe in any kind of relationship. But when her casual fling with Harrison ends in the ultimate betrayal, she's out for revenge. Enter Kai.

## THE JOURNEY STARTS HERE

@inkroadbooks